THE GOOD AMERICAN

The Good American

A Novel
Based on True Events

Ursula Maria Mandel

Writers Club Press
San Jose New York Lincoln Shanghai

The Good American
A Novel Based on True Events

Writers Club Press
an imprint of iUniverse.com, Inc.

For information address:
iUniverse.com, Inc.
5220 S 16th, Ste. 200
Lincoln, NE 68512
www.iuniverse.com

ISBN: 0-595-16032-8

Printed in the United States of America

To Husbandlein

Epigraph

"But the effect of her being on those around her was incalculably diffusive: for the growing good of the world is partly dependent on unhistoric acts; and that things are not so ill with you and me as they might have been, is half owing to the number who lived faithfully a hidden life, and rest in unvisited tombs."

George Eliot, *Middlemarch*

Prologue to *The Good American*, a novel by Penelope Karstens:
Sometimes, after some insanity, after war, murder, mayhem, some ordinary woman or some ordinary man set out to put the pieces of civilization back together again. They ask neither for fame nor for glory nor for gratitude. To do what they feel is right, because they are human beings is, it seems, quite enough for them. Ruth Karstens and Ted Whitman were such people. This is their story, and though Ruth's story, because of the nature of her journey, takes up a larger part of this narrative, hers would not have been possible without his. Nor mine, nor Alex's journey to me.

Contents

Acknowledgements

Thanks to my friends Cathy Pleska, Nicole Hayes, and Monika Hoffahrt-Zelloe whose feedback was invaluable and who encouraged me to send the book out into the world. Cathy read the manuscript and helped me get the bugs out. Nicole and Monika helped with the final touches. I could not have finished the book without their critique, their love, and their support. Very special thanks to my son Steve who encouraged me to write and who gave me a marvelous computer to accomplish the task.

1

Politics: A Fragment

On a summer day in 1948, Ruth Karstens, a young widow, and Pauli, her five–year–old niece, made their way gingerly down a densely forested mountain somewhere in eastern Germany. Both were hot, muddy, and exhausted. Pauli, holding on to Ruth's hand, lagged behind more and more, and so it looked as if Ruth were dragging the child down the mountain. A fresh breeze that had stayed behind after a thunderstorm parted the leaves of the trees now and then and gave Ruth a view over the vast, green pastures and barren fields toward where she was headed: a round village at the far horizon out of which stuck a church steeple. In the haze of that humid summer day, the hamlet looked more like a mirage than an actual village, but the image was enough to inspire Ruth to keep going.

In the same dense and silent forest, near the foot of the same mountain, a Russian soldier sat on the ground. He guarded a wide, muddy strip of land, a kind of road that hugged the foot of the mountain. His task was to make sure that no one would cross it.

The strip was about fifty yards wide and had been thoroughly cleared of trees and underbrush and, particularly, of the network of brambles of the wild blackberries that used to grow there. The children of the village used to come in the summer to collect the berries in tins and baskets, and their mothers used to make the most delicious jams out of them. But the children did not come that summer. In fact, no one went near the mountain for fear they would be shot.

That day in 1948, the raped tract of land, now looking sad and desolate, didn't have the least scent of the brutal notoriety that would define it for the next fifty years when it would be called 'The Iron Curtain.' By dividing the world into East and West, it would have more power than any other piece of real estate ever. That afternoon, it looked innocent enough. Not far from the soldier, in the part that was called 'The West' and that was occupied by the American Armed Forces, a young farmer tilled a field with an ox. Ruth could see him as she came down the mountain. She had the distinct sense that, once she crossed what appeared to her a muddy creek and made it to that farmer, she would be home free.

The soldier, a gun in his lap, fished a cigarette out of a crumpled pack and struck a match. But before the match could make its way to the tip of the cigarette, a twig snapped brightly in the silence of the forest. The soldier froze, holding the lit match between his fingers. All his senses strained as the small sound of leaves crushed by soft steps came haltingly closer from somewhere above him. Without making the least sound, he blew out the match, lifted his gun, and rolled behind a tree. Ruth and the child walked directly and unsuspectingly toward him....

2

A History of Sorts

In the end, it was loneliness, I think, that made me, finally, write to Penelope Karstens. Not my father's last wish or a sense of urgency but because the house grew too quiet that night in the summer of '92 as I sat reading. I had picked up Tolstoy's *War and Peace*, trying to conquer the tome for the second time. The book had made no sense to me when I read it the first time years ago for some college English project that I failed. All those Russian names were an enigma to me, and I couldn't keep the characters apart to save my life, except for Pierre Besuchov whose name wasn't quite as foreign. For a reason I can't define, I had felt a connection to the man. Maybe because he always seemed strangely out of place.

I had put on a tape of Mozart's clarinet concerto when I began reading, but that had sounded out long ago, and I looked up. There was no sound at all. I thought I had gone deaf. Outside my dark window, a void. The traffic in the street, never heavy, had ceased altogether. There was no wind, no bird. The children that had played in the yards earlier had long gone home. I listened, motionless, taking on the silence like a challenge. If I sat listening, if I absorbed it like a sponge, letting it seep deep into my body and from there into my mind, what would happen? What angelic vision or what monstrous conception would rise from my unconscious and obliterate me? I could hear my heart beating in my ears, a steady, rhythmic thump like the hollow sound of time.

A car droned by the house, and I shook myself and jumped up and put the book down. I walked into the kitchen though I had no idea why I went there. Had I meant to get coffee? I looked at the closed laptop that kept a smooth and slate gray company with the stack of bills I had paid earlier, and the coffee mug. And beside that, the picture of Ruth Karstens and the children. I should write to Penelope, I thought. I have been putting it off for far too long already. I should have done it immediately, as soon as she was found.

I entirely forgot, that moment, that I had had no desire to get to know her or to make friends with her. I couldn't imagine a more awkward scene than to meet with the daughter of my father's mistress, though it was cheap to call Ruth Karstens my father's mistress. It smacked of the infantile rage of an eleven–year–old boy who wanted to degrade her to punish him.

I opened the laptop. For all I knew, Penelope was a mousy little creature with stringy hair and bad teeth. And then again, maybe she was like her mother, tall and proud. She lived in the country, about a two–hour drive from D.C. where I lived at the time. Once, having nothing better to do, I traced my way to her on the Virginia map and my finger came to rest on a smudge of green without a name. The spot conjured up images of trailers and sheds with stovepipes sticking out and rusted cars all over the place.

I poured a glass of wine and searched for the pack of cigarettes that I knew was somewhere in the kitchen cabinet.

I had come back, that morning, from a flight to Frankfurt, and I felt as I did most always when I closed the door to my house behind me. I shut out the droning of the airplane engines, and the voices of two hundred people, and I shed the cloak of responsibility and conscientiousness and amiability. As most always, I just went to bed and slept till early afternoon when I showered and made coffee and checked the mail that had piled up, and I paid bills. Waking into the quiet house, I listened, as I had so often, for the sounds from the kitchen where Alice would be making dinner, or for the scraps of music, mostly rock, that fell out of Charlie's room. And then I remembered. Alice was happy in her new house, and Charlie was away at college.

I didn't know I was lonely. Few men would admit to that, and I didn't either. It began Christmas, I think, but I didn't recognize it.

I got back from a flight to London late afternoon on Christmas Day, and when Janie Black, my co-pilot, and I left the cockpit, I said, "Merry Christmas!" which came out far more cynical than I had intended. She looked up, concerned.

"Any plans?"

"Charlie's home. And after that, there's a stack of books I've wanted to read since last Christmas." This sounded almost bitter which made no sense. I had been waiting for years to read a book without interruptions.

"Come to dinner tonight, the both of you," she said. "I mean it. Ken and Annie are coming. Mike. Peter. Lucas. Gwen. Mike said he'd cook." She smirked, because Mike is about the worst cook that ever took a spoon to a pot. But he loves it and none of us would ever tell him. We always made sure to encourage him, no matter how sick we felt, hoping that, given moral support, he would improve in time. Only I wasn't in the mood after that trip—the weather rough over the Atlantic and would we be able to land before the nor'easter hit with a blizzard—for peanut butter and cheese sauce on broccoli.

"Not this time," I laughed. "Maybe when I have one of my masochistic days, or when I'm really depressed and need something explosive to jolt me out of it. Besides, it's Charlie's first Christmas home."

Since I don't cook, I was going to take her out to a fancy restaurant—tuxedo and ball gown required—for a party with dance and food and drink. She said, "Hey, cool, Dad," pondering whether her prom dress would be appropriate but then decided to hit her mother up for something more sophisticated. Her prom dress had already been more than sophisticated for my taste, cut way too low, and I wasn't ready yet for her to be a woman. But I had never interfered in my daughter's attires and left it up to the women to make such choices. If I was lucky, some young guy would be smitten by her—she's a knock-out—and dance with her all night so I could just sit and sip my drinks and think my own thoughts.

And, hopefully, she had decorated the tree. It had been standing, forlorn and pitiful, in the corner of the living room since the very afternoon she walked in the door. Her first act had been to go to the attic and drag every Christmas ornament down her mother had left behind. But all sorts of things distracted her. Phone calls. Going shopping with her mother. Meeting old friends. Going to this Christmas show and that. And so the tree, half decorated and looking lost, protected half unpacked boxes of ornaments with its wide, fake branches, and tissue paper lay scattered around it for an added festive touch.

I was all right when Janie and I said good-bye and I began the long trek to my car. The terminal was deserted. After all, it was Christmas Day, and maybe it was the steady, rhythmic beat of my heels on the endless linoleum that echoed from the arched walls and made me aware of my solitary stroll. I saw myself as if from a distance, on a dull film, a tall, lanky guy in a uniform, carrying a briefcase and a winter coat, sauntering down these empty halls with an air of authority, confidence, and preoccupation, the expected stereotypical demeanor of pilots. And this guy smiled amiably and condescendingly at a group of teenage girls who happened by and stared at him, awed, then giggled, at once proud and embarrassed, when he was passed.

I shook myself walking out into the cold. It had begun to snow, but the fat, droopy snowflakes melted in the empty parking lot. Briefly I considered putting on my coat but I decided against it. It wasn't that far to the car and a big, strong, youthful pilot shouldn't be so squeamish about a little snow. I got into the old Mercedes and shut the door. Alice had been after me for years to trade it in for something "more presentable", but I was used to the old jalopy. I knew all her tricks and quirks, and she knew mine, and she had never given me any serious trouble. I took good care of her, and my body fitted comfortably and familiar into the old seat. I loathed getting something that would feel new and uncomfortable and needed to be broken in. I pulled out into the countryside, Dulles Airport being a ways away from the city, not seeing much aside from the road, the sky hanging low and dreary. I was beat and I knew it. I needed some sleep.

The traffic was scant, which was unusual and great, and my mind began to wander. I hoped I would be able to give Charlie a good time, though I would never be able to make the place as festive as Alice could. Even so, Charlie had decided to spend Christmas with me and New Years with her mother. Alice had her two sisters in and their brood and her parents, and I was not welcome, of course. We were going through a divorce, after all, but that was not the true reason, I suspect. Things were a little uncomfortable all around and everyone was tight and no one really knew just how to act or what to do around a couple that was about to divorce. Should they sit us together or apart? Should whoever was there refer to old stories in which the both of us appeared? Should they say, remember when Alex did such 'n such and then Alice, and then they'd have to stop as if caught in some impropriety that might be unpleasant to either her or me.

Personally, I saw no reason why we couldn't all be friends. I didn't hate her and as far as I knew, she didn't hate me. She had been exasperated with me for a long time. I had begun to hate going to auction parties and dinner parties, and hated coming home to yet another house full of people when she would want to show me off and I just felt like going to bed, and sometimes I did. We'd been married twenty-seven years and just grew apart, I guess. She liked antiques, I liked flying, and we didn't share much in between though I like to think that we always respected each other.

I got to the city, and I saw myself, as if from a distance, a guy alone in a car, driving slowly through streets dizzy with Christmas decorations and pulling up to a large, dark house. It's a kind of blessing of nature that something automatic takes over when you drive and your thoughts are elsewhere, and somehow you manage to get to where you're going without having a wreck. It startled me when I pulled up to my house and had no recollection of getting there, driving through the old familiar streets and stopping at the stop sign up the road, wholly unaware of the traffic, sailing through it all unscathed. Scary.

I fished the mail out of the mailbox and wondered where Charlie was. The first thing she headed for each morning, for a reason I could never figure, was the mailbox. The only correspondence I'd ever seen her engage in was the phone, considering the size of the bill I paid each month when she was still living at home.

I opened the door and flicked on the light in the foyer which opens into the living room and that looked like a disaster area. I put down my briefcase and hung up my coat, took off the jacket, loosened the tie and stood awhile, surveying the mess with some amusement. Definitely the tell tale signs of a young woman—jeans over the couch, clothes on chairs, stockings dangling from a lampshade, shoes scattered. Her mother would've never permitted her to make mincemeat out of her elegant home. But Charlie figured, I guess, that I was an easygoing guy. And maybe a little rebellion was mixed in there too, because her mother had kept a nearly compulsive order in the house that tended to look, when there wasn't any company, like a Victorian museum complete with lace doilies, silk scarves, and golden tassels. My taste is more modern, but I never had a say, or dared a say, in the furnishings of the house.

I carried the mail to my chair, a Victorian affair, very comfortable, that Alice had given me some Christmas before. She liked to see me in it, sort of like a Victorian husband/father/master of the house figure, relaxing sternly with a book in his hands after a long day's work. Though I think she got that scene out of a stage production for Ibsen's A Doll's House. She once suggested that I take up smoking a pipe and get off of cigarettes that I smoke when the mood strikes me, but I resisted that Victorian image adamantly. I'm a pretty modern guy. Antiquated patriarchal images have never appealed to me. I like technology, fast planes, computers. Though, oddly, nineteenth century literature, particularly the Russians.

I fell into the chair, turned on the table lamp, and pushed the button on the answering machine. While it rewound, I flicked through the mail. An official looking envelope caught my eye. The return address said 'Circuit Court' and made me curious. The machine clicked just as I opened the envelope and then Charlie's voice sang young and unencumbered into the room.

"Hi, Dad. I've gone to stay with mom for awhile. I think she needs me more than you do. Sorry about the mess. Shove it under the couch if it bothers you. Will come tomorrow'n get my stuff. Love you. A lot."

I gave the machine a disbelieving look and pulled the document out of the envelope. The words 'Decree of Divorce' were prominently printed on top and startled me. They could have waited for the good news until after Christmas, I thought, and I understood now Charlie's cryptic message. Alice probably got the news at the same time I did. And women stick together in these things, which is, I guess, as it should be.

I studied the somber words. Decree of Divorce. I thought them over and somehow they didn't make sense. What did they mean? That we both had suddenly disintegrated? I put the papers back into the envelope without reading them. She had told me that she would file under irreconcilable differences. Which was fine with me. Anything, actually, except infidelity. I was a bit touchy on the subject.

The answering machine clicked again and rewound. I sat, staring at the clutter before me, suddenly weary. What now? My marriage was over, it was final, and there was nothing I could do, and maybe I should have done more. But I didn't have the slightest idea just what I could have, should have, done differently if I wanted to save it. And maybe I knew long ago that I didn't want to save it. So I sabotaged it. Unconsciously. It was possible.

The phone rang and jolted me out of my thoughts. I let it ring, waiting for the machine to pick up.

"Alex? Forster. If you're home, pick up." The jovial voice of my father's lawyer boomed into the room. He could, by that voice alone, keep anybody awake in a courtroom. And what was he doing working Christmas day?

I picked up.

"Hey, Glenn. How's Colorado?"

"Hey, Alex. Fine, fine. Listen, my source just called me. He found one of the daughters. Let me know what you want me to do. No rush. She so happens to live, of all places, in Virginia."

"How far?"

"Shenandoah Valley, about two hours from where you are. Or so he tells me. Why? You want to meet her?"

"I don't know. Do I want to pry into my dad's secrets or don't I? I don't know. It may be a can of worms . . ."

"True, true," he interrupted, always in a hurry, a running meter attached to his words. "It's up to you. You've got five months or so if you want to tell her yourself. If you don't, I'm required by law to notify her of the inheritance sometime thereabouts. I mean, I have to notify her in either case, but I can give you a head start."

"Good." I paused. Frankly, I didn't know just what to do and so I asked: "Tell me, brutally honest, should I contact her or not?"

"If I were you, which I'm not, I would want to know what this is all about. But then, I'm a lawyer. It's my business to know stuff so I would want to know. Then again, you may be right about the can of worms, who knows. By the way, I'm sending you a box with personal stuff. Pictures, papers, mementos, a small, locked box. I didn't pry."

I had turned everything over to Glenn after my father's funeral in early November. I was not familiar with my father's house. I'd visit him, dutifully, once in the summer and once at Christmas while I was still in school and, later, in college. I didn't really care to know my father's house. I liked to hang out at the hanger of the flight school he had built and always had a great time with the guys there, and even with my dad, so long as we were not alone together and I could sense him watching me, trying to figure me out.

We'd go skiing in the winter, and in the summers, he taught me to fly. Sometimes, we flew to California to hang out on the beach for a couple of days. We had nothing much to say to each other except for the flying. Sometimes, he'd try to sound me out—what I liked, what I hated, what made me happy, what made me sad, what I liked to read, what girls I liked. Mostly, I shrugged. I didn't want him to know anything about me. It was not until long after I was married and Charlie was born that I took a good, hard look at myself, realizing how ridiculous my behavior toward my father was, always sullen and grouchy and unwilling, and I tried to do better, for Charlie's sake. And so I said to Glenn, "Thanks. Send me her address. Just in case."

"Will do. Talk to you in a coupla days. Take care."

"You too."

I hung up and surveyed the mess before me once again. It was so consistent with the way I felt. Should I or should I not contact the daughter of my father's mistress? I got up and got a bottle of whiskey out of the house bar and poured myself a good one. It went down my throat like turpentine and burned in my innards and drowned out the grief over my father's death that came on suddenly and without warning, surging up like a bright flame. I shook myself. What now?

I guess the date with my daughter was off. I looked around the disheveled living room. I could go to Janie Black's for Christmas, or I could stay here. Or I could get drunk and sleep for two days. I wouldn't have to fly again until the twenty-eighth. Instead, I got the laundry basket and began collecting Charlie's things one by one and dropped them into the basket, her stockings and magazines and shoes and scarves, and took them up to her room. Then I finished decorating the tree. It was Christmas, after all.

Alice had moved out in June, though she came near every day for awhile to take more stuff out of the house. She had bought another, a Victorian mansion outside the city that was more suitable for all her antiques. Her actual leaving was a gradual process, and we were always pleasant to each other. Sometimes, we even joked and I helped her take things out to the car. The movers came and picked up the furniture she wanted and left me with the most rudimentary stuff, couch, armchair, stereo, coffee table, bed, dresser. She took the whole of the dining room, something Victorian she had bought in England. I guess I thought that the gradual disappearance of my previous life was a kind of dress rehearsal toward something that would go on indefinitely, and the finality of divorce swam in some future distance that would never materialize. Since I did get to see her often, it didn't really hit me until I held the decree in my hands that we were now truly separate, and that I was now alone in this house.

Although, in a way, I was glad when the furniture gradually disappeared, and when I came home to an empty house after a flight. I could read, finally, which is a passion of mine, and I could write when I felt like it. Not any fiction. Just a journal that I began when I first began flying. Maybe it grew out of having to keep a log and, sometimes, that didn't seem sufficient. Besides, all these foreign places I eventually flew into intrigued me, and the people who are so remarkably the same all over the world. I told myself that, when I was gone to the hereafter, Charlie might get a kick out of her ol' dad's journal. But writing it became a kind of habit, and I thought, after awhile, that not all of it would be fit for Charlie's eyes.

Or rather, I wouldn't want her to know, for instance, that in all the twenty-seven years Alice and I were married, I never once saw her without make-up. Not even at night. She once confessed that she waited until I was asleep before she slipped back out of bed to take off her make-up and to do whatever maintenance she felt her face required. And she always made sure to be up before I was. It had been difficult to exuberantly throw my arms around her, because I forever mussed her hair, or her dress, or smeared her lipstick. When I was young and enthusiastic and passionate, I ignored her little cries for caution, thinking that she must want what I want. But in time, it became more difficult to hug a woman who, ever so slightly, shrank away from my embrace or my kiss for fear I ruined her looks. I gave it up, finally.

Sometimes, at night, she would reach for me as if she felt guilty that we had not made love in months. Had I withdrawn, she would have felt even guiltier, and I certainly didn't want to punish her. And so we'd make love. But it was not what I had imagined it to be when I began dreaming of women.

3

A Picture Worth A Thousand Words

As the laptop fizzled, hummed, and sang itself together, I picked up the picture of Ruth Karstens and the children, studying little Penelope, five years old then and now a woman. What should I say? Dear Ms. Karstens, You are now a quarter of a million dollars richer, that is, you and your sister Eva. My father, Col. Thaddeus David Whitman has...what?

I slid the picture, face down, under the stack of bills. It clouded my judgment and made me less certain that my writing to Penelope was a good idea. I had found the picture in my father's trunk in the attic when I was eleven. I'd gone there with my friend Emily, also eleven, and I can't remember why we went there, maybe to play or to find something. I saw my father's trunk that had been sitting there since he came back from the war and I opened it. His uniform lay neatly folded on top, all the medals still shiny. I took it out and put it on. It was much too long for me, but I felt proud just the same because he was a flying ace during the war, a hero, and I loved him more than anyone else in the world. Just what made me put my hand into the inside pocket, I don't know, but it came out with that picture in it.

And there we were, head to head, staring at it, Emily and I, and Emily, much wiser in the ways of the world and in that which goes on between a man and a woman, looked at me, and I knew because she knew: he was having an affair. We looked at each other as if *we* were the ones who had committed the crime and not he, because the sudden confrontation of a secret, this secret, such a secret, scared the hell out of us.

That's when I saw Penelope Karstens for the first time. Of course, I didn't know who she was, but there she stood, cute as a button, her dark hair done up in a kind of hummingbird-size bird's nest on top of her head and her dark eyes smiling and happy, and her round face dimpled. She held on to some woman's hand, coming down a path in some forest. They came so happily and triumphantly toward me, in black and white, so in my face, I hated them instantly: this tall, slender woman in her flowery dress, a beautiful woman I had to admit, and that other tiny little girl on her left, her blond hair in pigtails, wearing a little jumper. God, I thought, these people are so in your face, or rather, so in my father's face because, no doubt, my father had that camera plastered on his face and that's who they were walking toward in all their happy-smiley exuberance.

I felt grim and I must've looked grim when I looked at Emily and ripped that picture straight in two and stuffed it back into that cursed pocket. I tore the jacket off and stuffed it back into the trunk and slammed the lid down. Then I climbed on top of it and stomped on it and stomped on it as if I could stomp out the vile knowledge in my head. My father, flying ace, war hero, dad on the pedestal, loved more than anyone in the world, by me, had done something abominable and vile. He was nothing. A betrayer. A liar. No good.

'Alex?' my mother's voice came from the bottom of the attic stairs. 'What are you two doing up there?'

'Nothing,' I hollered back. 'Just playing.'

'You keep that up, the ceiling's gonna cave in.'

'We can play something else.'

'I'd appreciate it, angel.'

Angel. As if I were a baby. Made me cringe every time, but when she said it this moment, with Emily there, I hardly heard it. I would have to protect my mother from that vile secret.

'Don't you dare,' I said to Emily, 'don't you dare tell anyone about this. Do you hear me? You tell anybody, 'n I kill you!'

Boy, did I feel tough. But that moment, I think I was fully capable of killing her if she breathed a word of this.

'I won't,' Emily said though she couldn't help but plunge that brutal dagger a little deeper into my young heart and twist it because she whispered, mournfully and significantly: 'He must love her more than his life. Look how the picture was in that pocket. The face is turned right to his heart. You take it out and you don't even have to turn it over.'

In hindsight, I can see how incomparably romantic this must have been to her who had already begun to look at boys with emotions she did not yet understand herself.

Though she had promised to keep quiet about this, I lived in constant fear that her mother with whom my mother played Bridge would walk in one day and say to her: Emily told me a really weird thing.

But Emily kept her mouth shut, because her mother acted as she had before. And so did mine though I watched her like a hawk for any sign of change or depression or of being sad or down. Of course, it's possible that Emily's silence had more to do with her mother than with her promise. Her mother was a very prudish woman. She had once slapped Emily when Emily and I did homework together at their dining room table. We must have been nine then, and I made a wholly innocent remark:

'Mrs. Siegel sure has gotten fat,' I said. I don't remember what sparked that brilliant declaration because, at the age of nine, I was neither interested in the shape of women nor in their looks.

But Emily, wise beyond years, said: 'She's fat because she's pregnant.'

Her mother came in just then and, faster than a viper, slapped her so hard, it was like an explosion. I couldn't fathom what the slap was for.

Emily, her hand on her cheek that had turned bright red, didn't even cry. I suppose she knew her mother better than I, and she knew that her mother would consider such an innocent remark very naughty.

Emily and I still talk, sometimes. She's in Texas now, doing something with computers. She doesn't have any children. She doesn't want any. She's afraid that she might do to her child what her mother did to her, and she sees no sense in the perpetuation of emotional abuse. We never talked about the picture again. She never brought it up, and I certainly had no desire to talk about it.

Only, the cursed picture appeared once again, on the day after my father's funeral. I had met with Glenn Forster who had flown with my father at the beginning of the war when they dropped bombs in the Pacific. Glenn's plane was shot down. He survived, badly burned, and lost a leg, all of which did not deter him to go to law school as soon as he looked well enough to face other people. When the war was over and the rest of the guys came home, he made sure that he helped them with all their legal needs. Not being able to fight with them, he fought for them in other ways from then on.

Glenn had handled all my father's legal and business affairs, and I had a hunch that he knew more than he told me. I was convinced that he knew who the people in the picture were, but he would never say. Certainly not if my father swore him to secrecy.

The picture came with a letter my father had written to me, and Glenn gave it to me before he gave me the will, as per my father's instructions. Then he left the office to give me time to read it.

I opened the envelope slowly. For some reason, I had the same sinking feeling that comes when you sense that something is wrong with your plane, and you have two hundred people on board, and you pray to make it down before the problem blossoms into a catastrophe. The picture, lovingly taped, lay in the folds of the letter. And so it is possible that I remember Penelope so distinctly only because I saw her once again, and I was about to find out who she was, or at least, what her name was.

"Dear Alex," he wrote, "I know that what I am about to ask you will be difficult for you. I have divided my assets between you and Penelope and Eva Karstens. Penelope is the dark haired little girl and closest to you in age. She would be a woman now, and so will Eva, of course. It is my most ardent wish that you will find them and tell them of my wishes yourself.

Sorry the picture is torn. I don't know how it happened. I don't want to accuse your mother because we have always respected each other's privacy, but I can't imagine who else might have been angry enough to tear it. You certainly wouldn't have had any interest in it. And, remembering the inquisitive little boy you were, I'm convinced you would have asked me who these people were. I taped the picture as best I could, and I hope it will be of some help in locating Ruth and the children. Glenn has all the details—of where they last lived and such. He will help you find them.

There's also a letter to Ruth, and I hope you can deliver it to her personally.

I wished we had been closer, you and I. It seemed to me sometimes that you held a grudge against me for some reason that I could never discover. I can only assume that the reason for it was my being away, in the Pacific and in Europe, when you were very small. There is this new-fangled word now, 'bonding'. Maybe we never truly bonded because I was gone so much when you were little. But I don't know. It seems we got along fine once you became a pilot, and it made me happy that we could share this, at least. There didn't seem to be that wall between us when we talked about flying.

I have always loved you, as you must know. And I want you to know this also: once you meet Ruth and the children who aren't children anymore, and once you hear our story, I want you to remember this about me: I was a parent, but I was also a human being with feelings and desires and faults and dreams. Take good care of yourself and of those you love.

Love, Dad"

I dropped the letter into my lap and looked up and at the wall behind Glenn's desk. A poster of Justice with her scales looked down at me, blind. "Damn! Damn! Damn!" I said to that poster, my eyes burning.

"Damn," I said again. All I could do was shake my head. There is no word as devastating as 'never' and I could not stop thinking it. Never again would I have a chance to tell my father that it was I who did this stupid, dumb, infantile thing. Never would I be able to tell him that I loved him. Never would I be able to talk things out with him, set things right, tell him that his betraying my mother and me, because I thought he was perfect, was more than I could handle when I was eleven. Never would I be able to explain why I had built a wall between us that permitted nothing but amiable respect. No real warmth. No expression of affection. And how he must have craved that at times. As did I, but I couldn't jump over that shadow. As the years went on, that shadow became faint, but I could never quite wipe out that pale stain on my father's character.

I folded the letter softly, tucked the picture back into it, and put both gently back into the envelope. A voice in my head said: But you were only eleven. And another: That's no excuse. And the first again: For all you knew, the people in the picture were a threat. You were too young and too dumb to understand. And the second again: All you had to do was to ask one small question, Dad, who were the people in the picture?

I didn't.

Sometimes, he sat, wrapped in his thoughts, smoking silently, his gaze far away at something I couldn't even fathom. Sometimes, he smiled as if he remembered something that made him happy. Sometimes then, he glanced at me to see if I had seen that smile as if he felt caught, and I always pretended that I had not even looked at him. In hindsight, it was as if we had played a kind of cat and mouse game, both of us decent people and intelligent, both of us having the gift of speech and neither one of us said a word. I may have been able to forgive the picture and concocted some innocent story around it eventually to pacify myself. But my father left us a few months after I found the picture. I had recovered from polio the year before, and my father had come home to help take care of me. The way my parents hovered over me made me believe that they were exceptionally close, for as much as I could gauge these things as a child. When he left and moved to Colorado, he only confirmed for me what I already knew: that he loved this other woman and her two children more than he did us. And so the betrayal and his leaving became a double-edged sword that cut into every positive emotion that wanted to well up within me.

As I sat, hunched over in my chair in Glenn's office, I studied the straight letters of my name in my father's handwriting. But no salvation came from them. For some reason, I thought of Parzival and of his search for the Holy Grail. There it was, all the while, in the very castle that Parzival came to and where, so indifferently, he failed to do a very simple thing: to ask a question. And then I broke down.

4

Procrastinations

In the five months I debated whether or not I should write to Penelope Karstens—I could, after all, leave the whole unpleasant business to Glenn—the house grew quieter each time I came back from a trip.

Charlie came at Easter, but she stayed only two days and then went off to go shopping with her mother, and then on to some shindig in Florida. And now that I had the time to read between flights, I tired of it quickly and often just sat in my chair, the book in my lap, staring at some middle distance without thinking anything at all. I guess I didn't mind being alone, but I suppose loneliness is something entirely different.

My friends looked out for me. There must have been something in my aura that told them that I was lonely. I didn't think I was. Janie and Mike had me over for dinner now and then and did me the favor of not inviting some woman, hoping we would hit it off.

I flew to Houston twice to see my mother who had settled there once I went off to college. Though she asked me how my father's estate and the inheritance were coming along, I didn't mention Penelope or my father's wishes. As far as I knew, my mother didn't know of Ruth Karstens, and I wasn't about to tell her, and if she had somehow found out, it happened so many years ago, there wasn't any point in opening up old wounds.

And so, until the night I wrote to Penelope, life went on as routinely as always. I did my rounds of flying, to London, to Rome, to Paris, conscientious as always. When home, I did the ordinary things that needed doing. I paid Emma, the woman who cleaned my house once every two weeks though there was hardly anything in it, and I wasn't home a good deal of the time. But the wood floors gleamed when I walked into the house, and I could have easily given a ball in the empty dining room. The kitchen never stopped shining since I kept to TV dinners when I was home and, mostly, I ate out. I paid the yardman who kept the shrubs controlled, and the lawn cut. Somehow he managed to keep the flowers alive that, before I hired him, looked sad, neglected, and hungry. Now and then, I talked to Charlie on the phone. Mostly, when I called her in Vermont, she was out. Now and then, I met the guys I fly with at some pub to have a beer. There were days when I thought neither of my father nor of Penelope.

The box came with the 'mementos' as Glenn had called them. In it were my father's medals and his war time papers and some other personal things, pictures, model airplanes he had built, and a small, smooth box made of dark wood. It contained a bundle of love letters from my father to Ruth Karstens, the envelopes looking as fresh as if he had addressed them the day before. Some were sealed, some not, but I did not pry. I would give them to her as he had asked me to. I put them, for now, on a shelf in the bedroom closet, a strange, new item on the shelf where my shirts lay, neatly folded and banded, as they came from the cleaners. The box startled me anew each time I opened the closet, a strange, mysterious item that had a kind of uncomfortable history attached to it. Finally, I put it into the bottom drawer of my dresser where I keep old pants and shirts that I had used when I still took care of the yard.

The letter to Penelope gave me heaps of trouble. I fired three pieces of unsuccessful eloquence toward the cabinet door by the sink where the trashcan was. I needed something to lighten me up. I put on

Gershwin's *An American in Paris,* and maybe it was the soulful rhythm of the music, but the fourth beginning made more sense to me than the others.

"Dear Ms. Karstens,

My father, Col. Thaddeus David Whitman, died last November. Among his papers, I found a bundle of love letters. Forty, to be exact. They were neatly tied with a ribbon, properly addressed to your mother, and never sent..."

I gave her my address. I told her that my father wanted her to have some personal items, among them a letter that had come with the will that was also addressed to her mother and which he had asked me to give to her personally. I asked her to call me or to write to me. I did not mention the inheritance which I thought was best done face to face. Besides, no matter how emotional the whole business, I felt I should also be prudent. After all, I did not know her or her family, and if she knew that my father had left her a sizeable fortune, she might not be willing to tell me the story that had led to the inheritance. I mailed the masterpiece on my way to a flight to Paris. She called me ten days later.

I tried to imagine her as she talked. Was she short and heavy? Tall? Slender? Attractive? Ugly? Did she talk on a wall phone in the kitchen while looking out the window or while stirring something in a pot on the stove? Her voice, warm, quiet, measured, did not give her away, though she sounded pleasant enough. She spoke English perfectly, only a few of her words revealed that English was not her mother tongue. I puzzled a little over her British accent and asked her. I could feel the smile coming over the phone line, or maybe it was just attached to words.

"They teach Oxford English in European schools," she said. So much for American preeminence.

When I asked about her mother—Did she live in the States or in Europe?—she seemed cautious and answered me haltingly, as if she suspected a telemarketer's scheme—Would it be possible to discuss this when I came to see her? She was quite polite and nothing in her voice made me think that my visit to her would be anything but an amiable encounter between two strangers that fate had, for some reason, briefly thrown together.

5

Penelope

I went to see her at the beginning of July. In the days that preceded the trip, I came to think of it as a kind of necessary journey, full steam ahead, into the past. A kind of facing the music. Which had invited other thoughts, thoughts of a philosophical nature, as I puttered around the house, paid bills, got my laundry together to take to the cleaners, made a shopping list. Was it better to leave the past behind and move on? Or was it better to face the past, work your way through it, and then move on? Or was it, as Santayana said, imperative to remember the past for fear we'd have to repeat it? Interesting questions that contained such dichotomous wisdoms, no wonder I was unable to decide whether or not I should have any dealings at all with Penelope. If I let it ride, I might regret it. If I didn't let it ride, I might regret it just the same. After all, I didn't know this woman and my letter could well have arrived in a hornet's nest of greediness and indifference. The ridiculous self-righteousness I had kept alive toward my father all these years seemed to thrive best when I imagined mother and daughters in the most negative light.

Though I must admit that, on the night I wrote to Penelope, the picture of her beautiful mother had nibbled away at the edges of my imagination, and the idle image of Penelope as an attractive woman did flutter through my mind occasionally like an illusive butterfly.

The days prior to my visit were hot and humid. Coming back from a flight to Rome, I walked out of the airport and into the eastern summer sauna that hits you like a wall of steam. For an instant, your lungs grope for oxygen and your mind gets fogged until you realize that you can, actually, breathe and might make it to your car that would be hot as an oven because it's been sitting in the sun for three days. The short sprint through the boiling hot parking lot made me crave the arctic Freon that would penetrate every cell of my body once I got the car going.

The next day, thunderstorms moved in and blessed cooling rains came down in torrents and hail iced the steaming pavements. The morning I drove out to the Shenandoah Valley was pleasant enough. A calm haze hovered over the lush, green meadows and fields, and the deep forests and the mountains I soon drove toward were misty like a dreamscape. I had not been to the country in a long time and seeing all this pastoral splendor was a kind of revelation. This country, no matter what its problems, is one hell of a beautiful place. I thought that I should do what I had done in college, take Kerouac's *On the Road,* and travel west and east again, taking my time. The thought appealed to me. I was free now. I could do as I pleased. Alice was not there to remind me that we had, actually, planned a cruise with the Soandsos to Key West or to some other tropical wherever. Strange how I could, after not quite a year without her, no longer remember the names of all 'our' friends.

I had no trouble finding Penelope's address, though she did send me down some winding bucolic roads that seemingly led to nowhere. And Glenn was right, it did take two hours to get there. Her driveway curled away from the road and ran up a hill to a good-size A-frame, a very modern affair with a glass front. The house was shadowed on both sides by trees and looked as if the architects had sought to celebrate the hill with something akin to the top of a church steeple. The rest was open grassland, fenced by a ranch fence. One wouldn't expect, sitting at the mouth of the driveway, that a couple of hundred yards would take one to the top of the world. Or so it seemed to me, because the views were unobstructed and spectacular over rolling terrain of pastures, farmland, and forests, running up and down low hills to the horizons miles away.

To the left of the house, a good sized pile of wood sat neatly stacked. The garage door was open and packing boxes spilled out of it which confused me. I couldn't tell whether she was moving in or out. She had not mentioned either on the phone.

The Mercedes died with the few, soft rumbles it always rumbles, as if it were about to die on me for good, while I stared into the gaping mouth of the garage which held no car. Amazing how, in moments of great import, the most idle and trivial thoughts flit through your mind. I wondered how she got up to this place if there was no car. I came to the logical and bright conclusion that, of course, it would be parked someplace else, behind the house, or beside it if she had a garage full of boxes. And also, since this was a two car garage, who owned the other car, if there was one? I got a hold of myself. I mean, who cared where her car was or who owned a companion car.

I opened the door to get out, and there she stood, like a sudden apparition, having come around the house with an armful of flower-pots. She startled me as much as the Mercedes startled her. She had obviously not heard me come up. And since I had envisioned, worst case scenario, a gray-haired farmwife of ample size wearing an apron, my mind galloped around wildly before it finally locked into what was actually before me: a tall and slender woman, forty-ish, thereabouts, with an armful of empty flowerpots and wild dark hair that she had tied back but that had come loose as she worked. She wore a plaid shirt, sleeves rolled up, and jeans, and she was barefoot. She stopped dead in her tracks.

I sat in the car, door open, one leg out, one in, staring at her like an idiot while she just stood, staring at me, surprise and flight in her eyes, and since I couldn't sit there forever, I finally got out, and she met me halfway.

"Penelope?" I asked, cautiously, just to make sure. Maybe I did drive up the wrong driveway which would have been extremely disappointing. My mind was already concocting the sad, nay, tragic scenario of my having to drive back down, saying 'Damn, damn, damn', all the way down. And she would stand, with those flowerpots, looking after me, and I wouldn't be able to think of a single excuse that would permit me to go back up that driveway to find out who she was.

"Is it one already?" she said, looking flustered. Her eyes searched my face as if, if I said no, she could relax because this meant that it wasn't me. Maybe her vision of me had been as distorted as mine had been of her. She glanced at her wrist that didn't have a watch and then looked around as if here, on top of this hill, clocks were to be found in abundance. But then she put the flowerpots down, held out her right hand and withdrew it to wipe it clean on her jeans. She laughed, holding her hand out once again.

"Hi," she said, her dark eyes warm and a little apprehensive. What kind of a guy would I turn out to be? She had freckles on her nose and beneath her eyes. And suddenly, a wholly insane notion came over me, because I felt like taking that whole flustered, apprehensive creature into my arms and dancing her around on the blacktop. I haven't a clue where that notion came from because I am a pretty undemonstrative guy, but for just an instant, such a crazy image did come to me. I didn't do anything of the kind, of course, but shook her slender, firm, and dirty hand and said:

"Are you moving in or out?"

"Out."

"Out?"

She nodded mournfully. "The owners called last week. They want to sell the house." She shrugged. "So. I have to move. I don't want to wait until somebody actually buys it and wants me out in a week."

"Where are you going?"

"Don't know. For now, I'll be staying with friends up the road." I looked in the direction of her pointing arm, but I saw no dwelling in the spectacular geography that surrounded us.

"Beautiful, isn't it?" she said.

"Phenomenal! And you don't want to buy the house?"

"I could never afford it."

If I had known her longer than just a few minutes, the timing would have been perfect for me to spring the inheritance on her. But this was not the time and I hung on to my secret.

I pointed to the boxes, changing the subject. "You hadn't mentioned the move on the phone," I said.

I hadn't meant for my remark to sound like a reprimand, but she blushed, said "I..." and burst into tears.

"You didn't have to mention it," I said, jokingly. But my words didn't even elicit a smile.

"I know," she sobbed. I was totally lost as to what to do. I reached into the car window to get the box of Kleenex, ever practical Alex.

I ripped out tissue after tissue, standing helplessly with them in my hand, not knowing what to do. She reached for one of them which seemed to make her cry even harder. Finally, I had no other recourse before all that misery but to be a big brother or maybe a dad. I put my arms around her as I had often done with Charlie when she came home broken up over something and offered her my shoulder to cry out whatever distress had suddenly befallen her. Maybe someone dear to her died just before I arrived.

Having broken down myself some months ago in Glenn's office, it seemed to me that the agony she cried out at my shoulder came from someplace deep inside and could be stopped only by letting it run its course. And maybe my gesture was inappropriate. After all, I didn't know this woman, but then, as they say, unusual circumstances require unusual methods.

"There, there," I said. Her hair smelled like freshly cut grass or maybe like forest leaves. Aside from my pitiful 'there', I didn't know what to do or say except to study those windblown curls in which there was, here and there, a bit of gray. I don't know why this made me smile.

She calmed down, finally, and moved away from me. "I'm sorry," she said, "Thanks," taking the tissues I had held so chivalrous all this time. She blew her nose, looking down at her feet. But when she looked up, there was a spark of a smile. Embarrassed, no doubt, but at least I didn't have to deal with a death.

"It's just that," she stuttered, "ever since…ever since your letter came, I've been a wreck. All my past came back to me, and I began packing. Trying to calm myself down." I tried hard to remain serious. A quick, puzzled frown came over her face. "I didn't mean that I packed to get away from my past…oh, well…I really wanted to be a little more presentable than this." She waved her hand over her shirt and jeans. "I didn't know I was going to lose it."

"Don't mention it."

"Wanna start over?"

I grinned. "Let's."

"Hi," she said with great formality though there was a clown in her eyes. "Good to meet you, finally."

"Good to meet you too. Finally."

"Was it difficult to find my house?"

"Not at all. You give excellent directions."

"I'm so glad."

And there we were, Ms. Penelope Karstens, whom I had dreaded to meet, and I, on top of a hill, as if we were the only people on this earth, and I would have been a liar if I didn't admit that I liked her immensely.

We didn't know what else to say after that formal, social overture and waited for the other to begin again.

"Maybe we need a glass of wine?" she said.

"I'll take the bottle," I said. She motioned formally to the porch that, with its white wicker furniture and colorful pillows, looked inviting and comfortable. In front of the porch, a small garden bed spilled over with flowers and yellow roses climbed from there up the porch columns. I had, no doubt, come to a fairytale cottage.

"Make yourself at home," she said. "I'll just go in and clean up a little."

"Do you need help?" I asked. She had turned toward the door already and turned back, shooting me a puzzled look, and I realized what I had asked.

"I meant getting the wine, *etcetera*."

"No, thanks, that's okay. I've got everything ready. I won't be long. I could bring you the paper to keep you company?"

I shook my head. "No thanks. I think I'll just sit here and get over my shock." She smiled at that, not understanding the remark, and wandered into the house. I made myself comfortable in a wicker rocker.

So this was Ms. Penelope Karstens. And what on earth had made me wait so long to meet her? If her mother had been only half as attractive and confused, no wonder my father fell in love with her. But I didn't know the story yet and, for the moment, I was content not knowing it but to sit in the shade of the porch, doing nothing at all except to look out over the countryside and to wait for Ms. Penelope Karstens to come back. I had not asked Glenn whether or not she was married. It had not occurred to me, though it would have been somewhat awkward if, as she lay in my arms, her burly husband walked out the door.

I didn't have the map of these parts of the country distinctly in mind, but I figured that I looked out over the Blue Ridge Mountains that I had crossed on my way here and which were now east of me. I settled back and gave myself over to the stillness and beauty of the place. Aside from the trill of an occasional bird and the humming of bees, it was intoxicatingly quiet. Now and then, a soft breeze carried fragments from a Rossini overture out the window to me on the porch. It must have been the tranquility that made me slip a little deeper into my chair, wondering whether she'd mind if I kicked off my shoes. And then it hit me like a ten-ton brick, and I sat straight up: What if she was my sister?

In all the years I had known of her, it had never once occurred to me. Not once. Oh, for God's sake! How dense could I be? What was I thinking? Of course! The chill of it made me get up and walk off the porch and into the sun. She could easily, logically, be my sister. I remembered what my father had said in the letter, "She is closest to you in age." Damn. And here I was about to waltz her around on the tarmac by some incomprehensible urge! Damn! I slapped my forehead. How could I have been so utterly dense? My mind raced to reconstruct the years when he was in the service. I couldn't even count, the shock was too violent. I came back to the porch and sat back down, trying to think clearly. When did he enter the service?

She must have seen the horror on my face when she came out of the house with a tray and put it down between us on the table.

"What happened?" she asked.

"Nothing," I said. "I think I forgot to unplug the coffee pot."

"Oh," she said. "Can you call your wife?"

"My wife?"

"Isn't she home?"

I shook my head and came to my senses.

"She left a year ago."

"She did?"

This was getting ridiculous. I decided to be honest. I mean, what was I trying to do here? So what she was my sister? I best do an about-turn and let my emotions run into the proper track if she was.

"Tell me this," I asked, "are you my sister?" My voice was hoarse. I hoped she didn't notice.

She sat down and stared at me, wholly mystified. "Your sister? Whatever gave you that idea?"

I fell back in my chair, laughing. Good God! What in the hell was the matter with me? I'm a levelheaded, even-tempered guy, mellow, steadfast, confident, reasonably intelligent. These last five months must have done a real number on me.

"I'm sorry," I said, because she sat scrutinizing me, wondering whether or not I was sane.

"Sorry," I said again, "but it had never occurred to me until just now. I mean, it would've been possible."

"I suppose." She thought it over. "Actually, it would've been nice."

I didn't inquire why for fear of saying something as intelligent as what I had just asked and took up the wine bottle instead to open it.

She had taken a shower. Her hair was wet and fell in ringlets to her shoulders. She wore a long dress, a kind of flowery print, and was still barefoot. She had applied a little lipstick and maybe even a little perfume that made me want to get closer and put my face in her hair. She had brought a plate with finger sandwiches along with the wine.

"I thought you might be hungry," she said.

"Thanks," I said. I was starved. I had had breakfast and bought a cup of coffee on the way, but now it was near two. She was wholly composed now and seemed more reserved and formal than before. I guess we both had dropped our social masks in the confusion of our first encounter, and she seemed to find it appropriate now to put a little of that mask back on.

"I also made lunch," she said, taking the wineglasses, small plates, and the finger sandwiches off the tray, "but I thought we'd have that a little later." She stopped. "Unless, of course, you're absolutely starved?"

"Not at all," I lied, working the bottle, the cork having a mind of its own.

"It's dry," she said. "I hope you like dry wine. I guess I should have asked you."

"No, great!" I said, hoping that this formality wouldn't suddenly grow into an invisible wall between us through which we would, for the rest of the afternoon, exchange polite and empty pleasantries. Ceremoniously, she lifted her glass. "To your dad! To my mother!"

We sipped our wine, scrutinizing each other over the rim of the glasses, both of us, suddenly wistful. She took the second rocking chair and put her feet up on an ottoman and reached for a cigarette. I relaxed. She had not changed. She wasn't uncomfortable with me in the least. Her feet were brown and pretty, no polish on the nails. I jumped up to light her cigarette.

"Thank you." She sat, smoking, shaking her head. "This is absolutely surreal. Unreal. Not true. Can't happen. Wouldn't happen in a million years." She stopped, shaking her head some more and turned to me.

"What's surreal?" I asked.

"You sitting here."

"Why?"

"Because I wrote their story down two years ago. I don't know why. Therapy, I guess. And then I put it in a box and into a drawer. I didn't know what to do with it. Sometimes, I take it out and work on it really hard for a couple of days, and then I put it back in the drawer. When I came out of the house just a minute ago, I was convinced you were gone, because I can't kick the feeling that you came straight out of my novel instead of my past."

"How did you know about me when I didn't know about you?" I asked and stopped. "Actually, I did know about you. I saw you in a picture once, but I didn't have a clue who you were."

"You saw me in a picture? What picture?"

"You were walking with your mother and your sister down some path in a forest."

She smiled as if I had handed her a present. "Oh, I love this picture. It's sitting on my desk, actually. I guess you know that your father took it?"

"I didn't know. But I assumed. We never talked about it." I looked away from her which gave me away. I could sense her studying me, could feel the puzzled line between her brows.

"You don't have to tell me," she said, softly, after awhile. "I mean, why should you. But I sensed that his letters were not the only reason you came to see me."

"How did you know?"

"I didn't know. But it's never the big things that tell you about people. It's always the small, infinitesimally small things that give them away. You wrote that you had some letters and personal things he wanted us to have. But when you got out of the car, you didn't reach for them to give to me. And you haven't mentioned them. It made me think that, maybe, you didn't come for that reason."

I leaned back in the chair, rocking silently for awhile. What would I forfeit if I told her? How much did she know about my father? She obviously knew about me. But this was not the time to play games. I had traveled back to the past for the truth, no matter how condemning it could be to me.

"We were not," I said, "very close. And then he died, and then there was nothing I could do to make it up to him. That's it. In a nutshell."

She waited. Gradually, I told her the rest of it. The picture. My suspicion. My sullen behavior toward my father. My ridiculous self-righteousness. "So, I don't really know why I came. A connection, I guess. To him. I don't know. Because you knew him, I guess." I thought it over. "Redemption, I guess. Something like redemption."

It is possible that I would not have been able to open up to her if she did not have the most expressive dark eyes. She seemed to listen with her eyes, the way I had seen children do. It unnerved me a little, the way she looked at me, as if she were looking right inside me at the place where my thoughts formed themselves into words. And even the intonations of regret or laughter or sadness in my voice were almost instantly reflected in her eyes. I had never met anyone who listened so closely, and I was sure that, if I had lied or colored the truth, she would have sensed it in a heartbeat.

When I was done, we were both silent for some time, looking out from the top of the world toward the hazy mountains far away. Fat, dark bumblebees buzzed into and out of yellow rose buds. Rossini had stopped orchestrating out the window long ago, and the air was still. The sky was nearly steel blue, and now and then, gauzy streaks of clouds wandered into it and dissolved.

"You may have done him an injustice," she said quietly into the silence.

"I was afraid of that." It's why I had waited so long to write to her. I knew that now. A shadow had fallen on this lovely porch, but I knew that I had to go through it if I wanted to live with myself. I think she knew when I first called her.

She began softly, almost haltingly, "When I was a child in postwar Germany, a place bombed beyond recognition, and living on CARE packages and hand-outs from the local relief center, a man named Ted Whitman came into my life and started a kind of hunger in my soul."

Briefly, she turned to me and smiled at the mention of my father's name as if making the connection to me were just as pleasing to me as it was to her.

"I was only six when he stood in the door for the first time, and I didn't know then that you could change someone's life just by smiling. No one I knew ever smiled. Life was grim and the grimness was written on the faces of the people. My mother and my Aunt Hannah were the only two people I knew who would, at the drop of a hat, burst out laughing over some private joke whose humor we children could never discover. Which didn't mean that they smiled at us. Their lives too were grim. They had trekked across country from east to west with us after the war, having lost everything, their families, their friends, their homes, their furnishings, their gardens, hoping for a better life for themselves and for us. Instead, they ended up in another bombed place."

She talked to the mountains rather than to me, turning her wineglass in her hands round and round. Her words were without emotion as if she were telling someone else's story, repeating something she had read somewhere. I had reclined comfortably in my rocker, wholly open to anything she might tell me, and so the words 'grim' and 'bombed' and 'only six', caught me off guard. I leaned forward, toward her, as if to hear better, because the words had fallen so unexpectedly into my complacent world. They didn't fit the smiling child that had skipped beside her mother in that fateful picture and nothing in the face of that child would have made me think that words like 'grim' and 'bombed' were connected to her. I didn't know just what to feel. Disbelief, I guess, a kind of sad wonder.

She shot me a quick smile. "Don't you feel sorry for me. There were a million children just like me."

As if this were consoling. I settled back and let her continue.

"This grimness that comes after some disaster," she said, studying the wineglass, "translated itself to us so that we didn't dare laugh or smile, except when we played with other children. And even then we knew instinctively to hold it down. Not that anyone ever asked the question, but it permeated the air. How dare we laugh when there was nothing to eat? When everything was bombed? When everyone was poorer than a church mouse and life hardly bearable?"

She looked at me and smiled. "But this man smiled. Open and friendly and a little embarrassed. When he saw us children, his eyebrows raised a little as if he were surprised, and his smile was on us for awhile as if he wanted to make us feel comfortable. Or maybe even as if he were our ally and we didn't have to be afraid. I didn't know that this smile buried itself into my soul, like the mere whisper of a recognition, not yet a recognition, but the mere whisper of something that was possible. What that was, I didn't understand. It was like a seed that fell into my being, and there it lay, dormant, for many years without my being in the least aware."

She stopped again, the memory of my father's smile lingering on her face and in her eyes.

"I know it doesn't make sense to you. Yet. But I wanted you to know what your father meant to me. And when you're only six, you sense things, feel things more than you can say them. Besides, the moment he stood in the door, I was far more interested in the huge cast on his left foot. It was covered with scribbled writings, and in his arms, the man carried a large brown paper bag out of which billowed a cloud of flowers. He left some months later. When I came to the States as an exchange student, I searched for him, occasionally. But I could never find him. There were far too many Whitman's, and I didn't even know which place he came from or went back to."

She stopped again, pondering something, frowning.

"Do you believe in fate? In destiny?"

I shook my head. "I mean, of course, there is a certain biological pre-determination, looks, personality, things that are passed on to us by our parents. But beyond that, I don't think so. Why?"

"I never did, but when I look back over my life there is a definite pattern that I don't quite understand. And maybe it was merely I who decided to take a certain course, but your father standing in the door that day had, most definitely, something to do with that pattern." She shot me a quick smile. "All so cryptic, I know, and you didn't come here to hear my story but theirs, but I am, of course, in the story."

She put the glass down and ran her fingers through her hair and fanned it out as if to dry it, but she was thinking of how to continue. She was wholly unpretentious, and I had a sudden, distinct sense of dread. Once she told me the story, I would have to leave, and I might never see her again.

"My Aunt Hannah held the door open and stared at him. She was petrified. He wore a uniform and was obviously an American. He had come to see my mother, and the moment couldn't have been more awkward, because my mother caught, just minutes before, a tango on the old radio. She grabbed my Aunt Hannah, and they danced the most perfect tango right there in front of Eva and me, and we applauded like crazy. My Aunt Hannah, who had escaped from a prison camp, was petrified of everyone wearing a uniform, though this man looked quite friendly and didn't seem threatening in the least. Except that his coming to see us was a very rude awakening. For me."

"What did he do?" I asked.

She repeated the question thoughtfully, studying a fat, black bumblebee searching the roses. "What did he do?" The question made her smile. "He brought food, along with the flowers. And a catalog. Sears, I think, but I can't remember. I didn't know that such food existed. Or such things as were in that catalog. Dolls and clothes and toys and furniture. It was unreal. A fairy tale from a fairyland. I knew that these things did not really exist because I had never seen them, and at the same time, I knew that they did exist. In a land so far away, I would never, ever get there, never be there, never see it."

When she mentioned the Sears catalog, I almost laughed because it seemed funny that he had brought something so pedestrian. But the words following, 'I didn't know that such food existed', or 'such things as were in that catalog' moved me deeply. I could only feebly imagine what such a catalog would mean to such a child. And since she had said that I should not feel sorry for her, I did not reach out to touch her, and if only her hand, to let her know how deeply her desire for the things in that catalog had touched me.

She got up and stretched. "Let me make us some coffee," she said. "This wine is making me ridiculously sentimental." She walked to the porch railing and put her hands on it, looking out toward the mountains. "Isn't this the most beautiful place you have ever seen?"

"Spectacular!" I said because it was.

She looked up at the sky that was getting hazy now and said: "My mother was a storyteller. She was excellent. I appreciate this only now because I teach literature. I'm not even half as good. I wish I had been able to tape her stories. That is, I wish so now. By the time I left home, or even maybe a little before then, I couldn't have cared less, and now I can remember only fragments. The rest is gone. We never understood each other, and in the atmosphere of not understanding one another, we clashed constantly. We were both headstrong and passionate. But while I was a dreamer, she had both feet firmly planted in reality. Except for her stories. I left home when I was eighteen and didn't turn back." She shot me an impish glance over her shoulder. "Actually, I headed toward your father's smile."

She turned abruptly and went into the house. Seconds later, Gershwin's *An American in Paris* orchestrated out the windows behind me. Her words had left me thoughtful, but at the sound of the music, I half turned toward the window, amused. How could she have known that this music had accompanied my writing to her? She couldn't, of course, but the coincidence of our liking the same music was nice. Still, I felt pensive. I couldn't even imagine what life was like for a six-year-old child in a place decimated by war. My mind filled with the images I had seen on television. But for as sorry as I felt for the children, I had no connection to them. Mostly, I just changed the channel, because there was nothing I could do to help them. Except to send money. But even that I had left up to Alice. I vowed to do better. It was, that moment, the best I could do. The resolve lessened my dismay a little, but not much. What if Charlie had grown up in such a place and under such circumstance?

"Good God, no," I said out loud. She had been such a perfect angel, and I tried to imagine her looking up at some man in a uniform carrying a bag full of food. The picture distressed me enough, I got up out of my chair and walked off the porch, looking up at the gauzy clouds in the sky. A hell of a world, sometimes. So ugly and so beautiful.

But before I got wholly sentimental, Penelope came back out of the house.

"What are you doing?" she called to me.

"Just felt like stretching my legs," I said as cheerfully as I could and returned to the porch. She had turned the music down.

"I thought," she laughed, "I'd put on some rhythm to get us out of that mood. I didn't mean for us to sit here all somber and depressed. But it was a bit loud. It's perking," she said of the coffee, holding a manuscript box out to me.

"I thought that, in a few minutes, we should go inside and have lunch. And afterwards, if you want, I shall let you read the manuscript. It needs work, I'm sure, but you'll just have to overlook the bad places. I'm a much better writer than a storyteller. And I'll just sit with you and you can ask me questions of what you don't understand. I've worked on it so much, I think I've memorized the whole thing word for word."

I took the box, holding it stiffly in both hands, a quick rush of alarm welling up in me as if danger lurked somewhere in that box. She misunderstood the gesture of my holding the box as if it were a bomb.

"You don't have to read it if you don't want to. It's just that I don't think I could tell it as well as I wrote it."

I looked at her. I didn't know what to say, because in this slender box lay all the apprehension I had felt since my father died, and everything I didn't understand, and possibly, my own condemnation.

I shook my head. "I wouldn't leave this house until I've read every word," I said. "You couldn't throw me out. I'd refuse to leave." And then I reached out and touched her hair and wrapped one of those wild curls around my finger. I didn't know I was going to do it until I did. Somehow, she had gotten inside of me, her moving little stories, her tanned feet, her fairytale Sears catalog. Or maybe it was I who was in need of a consoling touch and so I reached out to her.

She unwound the curl off my finger and put my hand back on the box, feigning a frown.

"Lunch," she said. I followed her into the house, still holding the box away from me.

6

An Attic of a Different Kind

We walked into a large, bright open room with a cathedral ceiling and a massive stone fireplace that stood, floor to ceiling, square in the middle of it. Two oversized armchairs stood in front of it, and it didn't take much imagination to picture yourself curled up in one of those in front of a fire with a book, and you wouldn't ever want to leave. By the east window, a couch-loveseat-armchair arrangement with bright pillows looked out over the Blue Ridge Mountains. Oriental and hand-woven rugs lay on the floor or hung on the walls. The colors of the room were soothing and quiet, soft browns and rusts and muted yellows and reds. Earth colors that she had brought in from what she saw outside.

Halfway up the legs of the A-frame was the span of a loft. Through the railing, I could see built-in shelves with books and an overstuffed chair and an ottoman and part of a desk and a bed. Since the west side of the house was made of glass as well, she would have a view over the Appalachians as she sat reading or writing. It was probably as near to heaven a place for a writer as I could imagine.

"Reminds me of a ski chalet," I said. "I'd hate to leave."

"I don't even want to think about it."

She took the box out of my hands and put it on the coffee table by the couch arrangement. The space beyond the fireplace to the west served as the dining room where she had already set things up for lunch.

"Cold meat and cheese and a salad," she said. "Is that all right?"

"Perfect," I said.

And while our parents had taken up the first part of our getting to know one another, this part dealt with a lighter fare, our children and us.

"I didn't go to college until after it was absolutely clear to me that my marriage was over," she said. "And I regret the lost years. Having such a late start. But I thought I was doing what I was supposed to do, marry, have kids, be a better cook and bottle washer, just like most women my age. Which was completely unrewarding, aside from raising my son."

I looked around. Nothing in the house indicated a male presence.

"Where is he?"

"Trekking through South America with a friend. He's a psychology major. He starts graduate school in the fall."

"Where?"

"Yale," she said.

"Wow!"

She shrugged. "He worked for it. He deserves it." She shot me a bright smile. "Am I proud or what?"

I told her about Charlie who had no idea what she wanted to study but was bent on having a good time and making it through her semester with, at least, a C.

"She'll find herself," Penelope said, consolingly, though I wasn't worried. So long as Charlie didn't get married too soon. Not anyway until she knew who she was.

I told her a little of myself, what I did, the places I flew into. That I loved Rome and Paris which she had also seen and wanted to go back to.

"Remember the Tuileries?" she asked. "I sat on a bench once, beneath these lovely old trees, watching the children launch toy boats in the pond by the fountain, and the most heavenly music rained down on me suddenly. Beethoven's Fifth. It came straight from the trees. I thought I had gone blissfully mad. I sat and listened to all of it, but then I couldn't help but get up and search for the source of that music, and here they had put speakers into the trees. It was wonderful."

The pleasure of the encounter was written on her face, and my mind conjured up images of my taking her to Paris. Walking with her, I'd probably see twice as much as ordinary mortals but I did not, of course, make any such offer. I didn't even know whether or not she was free to accept such an offer as flying to Paris with me, and would she even want to.

We discovered that we shared a love for Russian writers, Dostoevsky, Chekov, Bely. We both stopped halfway through a discussion of Bely's *Petersburg* as if we sensed, both at the same time, that we could talk about books till evening, but there were other and more important matters to be discussed.

"Let's have coffee over there," she said, getting up, pointing to the cozy couch corner with the colorful pillows. I helped her clear the table, taking things to the kitchen while she put everything away there.

"Go," she said. "Sit down. I'll bring the rest," and I settled, obediently, in the armchair and watched as she brought cups and saucers and sugar and cream and, finally, the coffee, which she poured, and a plate of cookies.

"Store-bought," she smirked before I could even ask whether she had actually gone through the trouble of baking cookies. Ceremoniously, she lit a fat yellow candle on the table and, finally, sat down on the couch and curled her legs under.

"Don't you want to take off your shoes and put your feet up here on this ottoman?" she asked. "You'd be so much more comfortable."

I smirked and took my shoes off. No holes in my socks, and so, my legs comfortably stretched out, my feet on an ottoman, I said: "I think you have just acquired a permanent houseguest."

"You hope."

She opened the manuscript box and took out a neat stack of pages, leafing through them aimlessly as if she were not yet ready to give them to me.

"I should, probably, give you a little background so it all will make more sense to you, because the story of my mother and your father begins on the night my Aunt Hannah fell in the door. "

"Hannah?"

"My mother's sister. Two years older. Anyway, that was in the spring of 1948, and we, that is my mother and my sister Eva, lived in an attic room that my father had somehow organized. Most everything in Germany was bombed, of course, and people lived wherever they could find a hole with a bit of a roof over it. My mother was a refugee from a village at the border between Germany and Poland. When soldiers marched into her village after the war, driving everyone of German descent out and herding them west, she grabbed us, that is, my sister Eva, who was a baby, seven months, I think, and me, and, yes, her silverware." She stopped. "I don't want to get into the politics of it all. Besides, you probably know the history as well as I do."

I didn't, though I had a vague memory of millions of refugees over-running the scarce resources of Western Europe after the war. But where that bit of history came from, I couldn't remember. And so I just nodded and she continued.

"Mercifully, I was barely out of diapers and remember little. But she told me that we walked most of the way. Sometimes, a farmer gave us a ride. Sometimes, we were able to catch one of the few trains that still ran and that took us along for a short distance. I remember that we hid in barns, deep in the hay. Sometimes, a kind farmer's wife would bring us something warm to drink. I will never know just how she got us through. My father was in a prison camp. Somewhere in France, I think, and so she came west alone, with us children and the clothes on her back. And her silverware."

She held the manuscript out to me with something like a determined resolve and I reached for it. I realized that her previous hesitation had more to do with her having written it than with the contents of the story.

"You are sure about this?" I therefore asked.

She nodded eagerly, forcing the stack into my hands.

"Only one more thing. I began writing it as a memoir. Of course. But somehow it didn't work and for the longest time, I couldn't figure out why. I finally realized that I kept writing the story from my point of view, and all my judgments against her kept creeping in which was wrong. And so I began writing it as a novel, in the third person, calling her by name, Ruth. Because it's neither my mother's story, nor your father's. It's the story of a man and a woman. If I had told it as if she were my mother, I could not have done it. She wouldn't be a woman then, but my mother. It would have been an entirely different story."

"I don't see the difference," I said.

"The difference is that I saw my mother only in relation to myself. Of course. She was my mother. It had simply never occurred to me, until I began writing, that she was a human being in her own right with all her dreams and failures and emotions and her laughter and her losses. She didn't live only in relation to me."

I remembered my father's words, 'I am a parent. But I am also a human being with feelings and desires and faults and dreams.' I wanted to get up and get the letter that I had left in the car. But I decided against it for now. Though the coincidence in what she tried to do and what he expressed was uncanny.

"I thought that, as you read, you could hand me the pages and I'll just sit here quietly and edit with my pencil here," she said. "This wouldn't bother you, would it, while you read?"

I shook my head and turned my attention to the manuscript. The title page said *The Good American*. I shot her a comical smile, took a deep breath, and turned the page.

7

The Sanctuary

In April of 1948, in a dim and Spartan attic room in Wiesbaden, Germany, Ruth Karstens, a young woman of twenty-six, mended a dress. It was the only dress she owned, a wildflower print on a pale yellow background, and it was not the first time she needed to mend it. This time, she had ripped it when she went to a job interview at a small, newly re-opened grocery shop. Walking in the door, she had caught the dress on a nail that ripped a perfectly triangular tear into a cluster of poppies and daisies and summer vines that congregated on the dress. She tried hard to work the stitches in such a way that they would follow the outlines of the flowers and vines. The tear, she figured, would be less obvious that way.

She worked beneath the light of a tall, elegant lamp that was wholly out of place in the room and did nothing to soften its appalling poverty. Its meager furnishings consisted of a table and four chairs that didn't match, a cot, an elaborately wrought but slightly rusted iron bedstead, some boxes, lined up where the slanted roof of the room met the floor, and an old radio.

The cot was neatly made up with a blanket that had woven in its margins the letters 'US ARMY'. Beyond the sphere of the lamplight, in the soft shadows, two small children slept in the bed. The small skylight above the bed was like an afterthought in the slanted wall that made up the roof of the nineteenth-century Victorian apartment building where

Ruth lived. The skylight was propped open to a mild evening sky filled with stars.

As she sewed, Ruth looked, now and then, at a glass filled with grape hyacinths, wild daffodils, and anemones. She had gone for a walk earlier that day with the children. They had left the city and had walked through a park that, before the war, had been a calm and tranquil refuge from city life with neatly trimmed lawns and benches and quiet paths beneath high old trees. But now the lawns had gone wild and the paths were overgrown with weeds. Not that it mattered to Ruth or to them. They had collected wildflowers and scouted out the places at the edge of the woods for blackberry vines that had just begun to bloom and would yield a wealth of berries later in the summer.

Ruth made a mental note of just where the blackberries were, because they were food and they were free, and if she could hoard sugar, which might be impossible but she could try, she could make jam.

The battered radio on the floor beside her chair played a lively waltz that was barely audible. Now and then, Ruth hummed softly along with the music without making the least sound and tapped her foot to its rhythm as she sewed. At times, the radio sputtered, which she registered with a frown and fixed by tapping it sharply with her foot.

The sudden, jarring ring of a doorbell beyond the room so startled her that, with an unconscious gesture, she put her hand to her heart. With an intuitive gesture born of fear, she turned the radio off and waited, sitting stiffly, straining to hear the least sound. The bell rang again, loud and insistent. Again there was silence. Finally, a door creaked open somewhere and slow footsteps shuffled along a corridor. Muffled voices came through the door as another closed beyond with a thump, and someone knocked. Ruth put down her sewing. The children lifted their tousled heads.

Ruth turned to them who, rosy-cheeked and sleepy, sat up now. She put her finger to her lips. The children slipped under the cover so only their eyes showed, fearful and curious, as Ruth cautiously opened the door.

In the dim light of the hallway stood her landlady, Mrs. Garske, wearing a housecoat and curlers—she had obviously been startled out of deep sleep—, grimly holding on to an emaciated, desperately filthy, and utterly exhausted young woman. "Hannah!" Ruth cried out and ripped the door open wide. It slammed against the wall with a bang just as Hannah collapsed at the threshold.

8

A Wonderful Place

I put the pages down. "And you were one of the children sleeping in that bed?"

"Of course."

"But what did this do to you?"

"It gave me a good night's sleep," Penelope said, feigning ignorance.

"All right, Miss Smart Aleck!"

She grew serious. "I know what you're asking. But if you expect me to feel sorry for myself, you've come to the wrong person."

"I didn't mean that. I meant, it must have left…" I didn't know what to say. Wounds? Scars? Depression? Anger? What? A very deep and negative impression, to say the least, I would think. ·

"Actually," she said, "we were very lucky. Millions of people slept on the floor. Or dug out some kind of shelter in the rubble of bombed houses or office buildings. And we had furniture, even if we dug most of it out of the bombed house next door. And the cot came from the relief center. So." She shrugged. "It wasn't all bad. At least not then. I mean, what does a child want? To be loved and to feel safe. I felt loved and I felt safe."

"I suppose," I said, hesitating. I didn't believe her.

Painfully slow, as if it were an object that could break just by touching it, she took a cigarette out of the pack on the table.

"The wonderful thing about kids is that they are quite happy if they don't know any better. And, I didn't know any better. I thought that's the way people all over the world lived. Of course! This was my world. I didn't know any other. I mean, if you're born into a bombed world, that's your world. And if you're born into a world with little food and few clothes and shoes, you take that for granted. Going to the relief center was a way of life. I didn't know that there were stores where you could buy clothes. I mean, there weren't any. They were bombed. I won't ever forget the day when lollipops first appeared in the grocery store across the street. Of course, lollipops had existed before the war. But I did not know that, or I was too small and had forgotten. I didn't know what they were, but they looked so cheerful and yummy, I admired them for weeks. Once, when my mother sent me to the store for our weekly ration of milk—a quart, I think—I bought one of these delicacies, and then I lied about the amount of change I returned to her. Of course, she knew I was lying. And she was relentless and I had to confess, finally. She let me keep the lollipop. But that was after she spanked me, for lying and stealing."

The small, dull pain in my chest was my heart that ripped just a little. In my mind's eye I saw the pint-size girl in the picture with her hummingbird size bird's nest on top of her head, the dimples in her cheeks and the desire in her eyes for something so ordinary as a lollipop. They used to hand them out free in the drugstore where I shopped with my mother. Strange thing is that I used to think that I didn't have a heart. Good, ol' Alex whose eyes would glide so casually over the homeless sitting on the benches or piling up their boxes in the alleys. But that's not true. It wasn't even casual. I did not see them. And when I did, I gave them no thought at all. Theirs was a way of life. Something one could not change. Pointless, even, to try.

I could not look at her after she told me the story of the lollipop. I pretended to be in dire need of some coffee. Was I going to look at her and have her read what I felt that moment? Not on your life.

But she didn't look at me anyway. She smiled out the window at the memory of that delicious lollipop.

"And you mustn't forget," she said, turning to me, "that everyone I knew lived just that way."

I looked up then, and she must have read the misery in my eyes.

"Hey," she said. "I've had a hundred lollipops since."

I couldn't help but shake my head.

"And that bombed house was a wonderful place for us kids. Of course, under penalty of death, we were not to play there."

"A wonderful place?" I said, dumbly, leaning forward to study her face. Surely, she was kidding.

"Oh, it was Heaven!" she said, dreamily. "We found the whitest chalk there. And books that had refused to burn. And cut crystals from the chandeliers that had crashed…"

I must have looked utterly dumbfounded, because she laughed.

"And sometimes even canned food. I thought it was all perfectly normal. Until your dad came along. And what he brought, shook me to the bone."

"I can't even imagine what such a playground was like."

"Yes, you can. You've been to a construction site, haven't you? I mean, you were a boy. Did that not fascinate you? Or when they demolished a building, didn't you ever want to go in there and see what was left behind?"

"True," I said.

She got up. "Stop reading for a minute," she said, "until I come back."

She disappeared into a side room and came back with her purse, rummaging inside.

"Do you know Voltaire's *Candide*?" she asked.

"Vaguely."

She held out something to me in a fist.

"When Candide and Cacambo came to El Dorado," she said, "they found these funny shining pebbles in the streets. The kids were playing with them and threw them away when the schoolmaster called them. Do you remember?"

I shook my head. Our hands touched, and I wrapped mine around her fist. I don't know why I did that, but it was as if I were charged inside with an emotional tension so high, it could only be discharged by touching her. As if, by touching her, I could let go of the tightness in my heart so it could beat normally again. And it did, that moment. But she seemed not aware of a thing, did not withdraw her fist as if it were the most natural gesture, me holding on to it as she spoke.

"Candide and Cacambo saw plainly that these pebbles were the most precious gems. They scooped them up and, reverently, offered them to the schoolmaster…" She laughed. "…who threw them down in disgust. In El Dorado, gold and gems were nothing. Worthless rubbish. Pebbles. Rocks. Nothing. So, you see, it's all relative."

I took my hand off her fist and held it out to her. She put a tear-shaped crystal into it.

"Hold it up against the light," she said. I did and the crystal did what crystals do: it broke into fire and spread rainbow colors. Something so ordinary, in a way, and so special to her and, now, to me. I could not look at her but turned the darn thing in my hand over and over.

"Compared to you," I said, "I was born with a silver spoon rammed into my mouth." Briefly, I put my hand on hers. "Does this make you sad?"

She shook her head. "Not sad. Just angry. Which I didn't know for years. That I was angry. Because she made very sure that we were not spoiled and sometimes it would had been heaven to be spoiled." She sighed. "Heaven!"

I closed my hand around the crystal and continued reading.

9

The Attic Room, Improved

A month after Hannah fell in the door, the attic room seemed even smaller and more cramped. They had added a rickety shelf unit of bricks and boards that held meager household goods and the radio. A second cot leaned, folded, against the wall. It was late May now and quite warm. The open skylight did little to cool the place.

Hannah sat, tailor-fashion, on the bed, reading a letter. She wore reading glasses that had been fixed at the hinges with a bit of thread. Most everyone in their family had a tendency to farsightedness, and if she had held the letter far enough away from her eyes, she could have read quite well. But it was a strain, and they had considered themselves lucky when Ruth was given a broken pair of reading glasses at the relief center.

Hannah had recovered well and, that day, had gathered all her blond hair on top of her head in a sort of bun that kept coming loose and looked more like a disheveled crown. She sat on the bed so that Ruth, on her hands and knees, could scrub the floor.

It was Sunday which was usually the day they cleaned house because it was the only day they did not work at whatever work they could get, mostly cleaning the rubble of bombed houses or doing other cleaning work. They preferred food for payment, or ration coupons, but sometimes, they accepted money even though one could barely buy anything at all. And if something was to be had, it was frightfully expensive.

Hannah had heard of a job in a bakery that paid little but would mean steady income if either one of them could get it. They decided that *she* should apply rather than Ruth who had the children to look after and taking them along while cleaning rubble, she could watch them. Hannah had come back from the interview at the bakery excited. The baker had decided to give her a try.

As she rubbed and scrubbed, Ruth sang and hummed along with an unknown soprano an aria from an opera. Ruth had a lovely voice, and she got into the song with gusto, mimicking the soprano's emotions as if she were herself on stage. They had sent the children outside to play and over the music came, at times, the voices of a horde of children playing in the street five floors below.

The more Hannah read, the more troubled she looked.

"She wrote that she can't possibly come," she said, finally. "She broke her ankle." She took off her reading glasses, and the hand that held the letter fell dejected into her lap.

Ruth stopped singing and mimicking. Wiping her hands on her apron, she reached up to turn down the radio, frowning.

"Let me see!"

Hannah handed her the letter and the glasses, studying her sister's face not to miss the minutest of Ruth's reactions. Ruth looked up, exasperated.

"That bitch!"

"Ruth!"

"What's next? Cancer? That woman has no intention of bringing that child here. That's clear!"

"She wouldn't do that!"

"Oh, for God's sake, Hannah! She is going to wait until the Russians blockade Berlin. Then she can't get out, and we can't get in, and she'll have Pauli all to herself."

Hannah took the letter and glasses back. Her eyes filled with tears.

"So you don't think she broke…"

"Oh, for God's sake, Hannah! You are the most gullible…"

Ruth ripped the letter out of Hannah's hand, began reading again, realized that she couldn't see clearly and reached for the glasses. She put them on, began reading, and took them off again. Slyly, she said:

"Can you read with these, sister, dear?"

Teary-eyed, Hannah looked at her, surprised.

"Oh, I can read wonderfully well with them."

"You can, can you?"

Slowly, Ruth lifted a corner of her apron. With deliberate slowness and smirking all the while, she gave the glasses a thorough polish. Hannah burst out laughing, and Ruth joined in and both of them laughed until one was doubled up on the bed, the other on the cot.

Their laughter mingled with the laughter of the children playing in the rubble of the bombed building next door which was a treasure trove. The elegant lamp had come from there, somehow all right although a little tattered, and the shelves and the bricks and the radio had also been found there. Of course, the children were not supposed to go into the ruin, but the rubble spilled all the way out into the street and the boundary of where the house once began and where it had ended up was blurred. As the children dug and searched, they shouted and laughed whenever they found some small treasure. Penelope held a tear-shaped crystal up to the open sky that was framed by the skeletal remains of what were once walls, windows, and doors.

"Oh, look! Look! Come here!" she shouted to the other children. "Look what I found! I found a diamond. A real diamond!"

Ceremoniously, she held the diamond up against the sky.

"Oh!" she said. "Oh!" when it began to sparkle in all the colors of the rainbow. Had adults been present, they would have told her in a minute that the diamond was but the cut crystal of a long gone chandelier that had crashed when the bomb hit. But no adult was present, and in a flash, fifteen children began digging in the rubble to find diamonds as lovely as the one Penelope had found.

10

Determination

That afternoon, done with the chores of cleaning, Ruth opened the door to the attic room carrying a small, steaming pot. Hannah jumped up and put a piece of cardboard on the table as a kind of trivet.

Ruth put the steaming pot on it while Hannah got two cups from the rickety shelves.

Ruth laughed. "If it looks like coffee and smells like coffee, it must be coffee."

Hannah smirked. "Well?"

"Roasted barley and chicory. Yum. That's all I could get at the relief center."

Hannah laughed as Ruth uncovered the pot and inhaled deeply.

"But let's be thankful," she said. "If Mrs. Garske didn't let us use the kitchen, we couldn't cook at all." She shrugged. "Not that we have anything to cook, but…"

"Can we afford to splurge and spruce this 'coffee' up a little?" Hannah asked. "The baker promised me a pound of sugar a month. If I work hard."

Ruth thought it over.

"Oh, why not. Let's splurge. We can mix the Cornflakes with dried carrots for the kids. Just this once. That would make them sweet, wouldn't it?"

Hannah dug deep in the shelves and came back with a small jar half filled with sugar. If they didn't hide the sugar, the children would eat it, because there were no sweets of any kind to be found anywhere. And what little sugar there was, Ruth had gotten on her ration card weeks ago. She used it mainly to sweeten the dreadful dried flaked corn that the children ate in the morning.

Hannah put the jar on the table as carefully as if it were a treasure.

"He said I could have the old bread. A loaf a week, at least. Maybe even rolls," she said.

"Heaven! The kids will go crazy." Carefully, Ruth measured a half a teaspoon of sugar into the 'coffee' and stirred thoughtfully. Hannah also measured a little sugar into her cup. She took a sip, frowned, and shuddered as if she had just tasted poison.

"I'd give both my arms for a good cup of coffee!" she sighed.

Ruth turned her eyes heavenward in imagined bliss.

"If there's any old cake, I can have that too," Hannah said.

Ruth stared at her, faking shock.

"Cake?"

Hannah nodded emphatically.

"Stop making me drool," Ruth said and sat up straight. "Anyway. I've been thinking."

"About what?"

"Pauli. I've decided to go to Berlin and get her."

Hannah was so shocked, she upset the cup, spilling the 'coffee' all over the table which she barely noticed.

"Are you crazy?"

"No. But I have a passport and you don't."

"Never!" Hannah said. She jumped up and angrily began cleaning the spill.

"Do you want your child or don't you?"

"Do I want my child or do I want my sister dead or in Siberia? A hell of a choice! Of course, I want my child! But do I want you in Siberia? No!"

"Why should they send me to Siberia?"

"They'll always find a reason. You know those bastards. I mean, I was on my way home from work and they got me."

"You didn't have papers. I do. Besides, my mind is made up. I'm going."

11

Bureaucracy

I stopped reading. "Hannah didn't have a passport...couldn't she get one?"

"Actually, she didn't have any papers at all, and everyone in Germany is required by law to carry at least an ID. Generally, that's a simple ID card, like a driver's license, and she was, of course, not the only one who had no identification papers. Millions of people lost their papers, birth certificates, ID's, passports, baptismal certificates, driver's licenses, whatever, in the bombings. My mother, who had lived in England for awhile, had a passport. But what she meant was that she could, therefore, get a transit visa. After the war, Germany was divided into Allied sectors, as you know, of course. French, British, American, and Russian. You couldn't travel from one sector to the other without a transit visa. So my mother was the only logical choice for getting such a visa if she wanted to leave the American sector where we lived to go to Berlin which was in the Russian sector."

"What happened to the rest of their family?"

"My grandparents and aunts and uncles had been driven out also, of course, but they got only as far as Dresden where they were herded into a holding camp. I guess the masses of humanity streaming west was simply too much for the British and American governments to handle. I mean, we're talking hundreds of thousands of men, women, and children. Young people, old people, sick people. But after some political calm had arrived, my grandfather decided to take the rest of the family back home. He couldn't bear the thought of living any-where else. A great mistake, of course, for all those who went back, because they were stuck behind the Iron Curtain for good once that became a permanent border."

"A sobering thought to imagine that, if your mother had not decided to head west, you would have ended up there as well."

She nodded thoughtfully. "Frightening, actually. But we made it, somehow." She paused, thinking. "And I don't know how. I can't even imagine though I was there. Just too small to remember much of it. Many women made that trek, actually. So she was not alone in making this dreadful journey." She laughed. "It's not funny, but her fear of the Russians was greater than trudging through snow and ice, I guess."

I tried to imagine the pint-size creature trudging alongside her mother, trying to keep pace.

"Weren't you terrified?"

"Not really, or rather, I can't remember. I mean, what did I know? Did I know about geography? About distances? About politics? I mean, I was what? Three years old? Something like that. I don't know. Besides, what's so wonderful about children is that they live so completely in the present. And going on a hike was fun. I mean, what did I know about soldiers and dangers."

My heart went out to her, but I had no words to let her know how deeply the image of her trudging alongside her mother moved me. I thought of Charlie when she was three or four, and how proud she seemed walking with me, and how proud I was walking with her, her face always happy and sunny and unafraid.

"I can't even fathom what this hike was like. Seems to me you went through hell."

For just an instant, she gave me a quizzical, almost helpless stare as if I had touched on a dark door that led to an even darker place. But she caught herself and looked away from me, out the window where immense thunderheads stood snow white and blinding in the east, forecasting a storm. She did not answer me. I sensed that, if she had ever explored that dark place, she did not want to do so now. And if she had not explored it, she was not ready to do so now. When she turned back to me, her lips smiled but her eyes were serious.

"As I said, I'm in the story, of course, but it's not my story. Though I've begun to write this as well, but it will take me a long time. From what I've written so far, it's been excellent therapy." Her smile got deeper and in the end her eyes smiled as well. "Just look at this." Her arm swept the dayroom and everything beyond the windows. "Is this beautiful or what? Who would have thought that I could ever leave that attic room? But I did. As I said, through all the tough times, there was always your father's smile, and I kept walking toward it. But you had asked about my mother and the passport. So. Without that important document, she would never have met your father."

With just these few words she skillfully changed the subject. Which didn't mean that I didn't want to know more about her, and how she had dealt with it all, and how she managed to escape it all. But this was not the time to push that dark door open. Besides, I had only just gotten to know her, and it was preposterous of me to think that she would open up to me. Why should she? Though it occurred to me, as I studied her, the lively dark eyes, the sunfreckles, the thin lines that went from her nose to her mouth, the thin line between her brows, that the tears she cried when we first met had something to do with that dark door.

"So, in order to get to Berlin," she continued, determined to keep herself out of the limelight of the story, "she needed a transit visa for which she had to apply to the Allied authorities, in this case the Americans. They had a base in the middle of Wiesbaden which was the city where we lived. I think the base was called Lindsey Air Station. So she went and filled out an application and gave her reasons for going and marked it 'Emergency.' Your father had been temporarily grounded with a complex fracture in his left foot and ankle. She told me that he had tried to make an elegant exit off a plane, jumping, I guess, to impress some girls. He was sent to the hospital in Wiesbaden, and since he couldn't fly for awhile and spoke a little German, they had assigned him to the transit visa office. In any case, a few days after she had put in for a visa, she went back, hoping that it had been granted. After all, she didn't have a phone." She pointed to the manuscript. "The story picks up there."

"All right," I said, smiling at her dumbly, I guess. I had been staring at her, trying to read just what went on inside of her, wanting to explore the dark places and the light but, dutifully, I returned to the pages in my lap.

12

Hunger

Ruth waited in the long hallway of a military barracks among civilians of all walks of life who were largely malnourished, despondent, and hopeless. Wearing the pretty dress she had been mending, Ruth was decked out in a hat, earrings, and a necklace. She looked refreshingly like an accidental flower in all that misery, and more than casual glances fell on her from the military personnel happening by.

She struck up a conversation with a young woman who, poorly dressed and looking weary, held a tired little boy who was not very clean and looked ill.

"Is he sick?"

"No. Just hungry. They ran out of food at the relief center just as we got there."

Ruth rummaged through her bag and pulled out something wrapped in newspaper and held it out to the young woman.

"Here. Take this! My sister works in a bakery now. It's a little old but it's still quite good." The little boy perked up and looked hopefully at his mother who hesitated. Resolutely, Ruth pushed the packet into her hand. "Here, take it! Margarine with a little sugar on top. But it'll hold you."

The woman took the gift with a despondent little smile, acknowledging at one and the same time that she was grateful but unhappy for taking the lunch Ruth so obviously needed herself.

"Thank you very much."

"Where are you headed?" Ruth asked, looking at the packet as the woman made no motion to open it.

"Up north. Into the British Sector. My brother is there somewhere."

Pleadingly, the little boy held out his hand, staring at his mother's eyes. Almost reverently, she peeled the newspaper off the sandwich and gave him half of the bread, wrapping up the rest.

"You better eat something yourself," Ruth said.

"I can wait. You know how it is. He needs it more than I do. Where are you going?"

"Berlin."

The young woman stared at her horrified.

"We came from Dresden yesterday. The Soviets have started making that border permanent. Believe me! Started chopping down everything that's in the way. Forests. Villages…"

A sergeant came out of one of the offices.

"Mrs. Karstens?"

"Here!" Ruth said.

He looked for the voice as Ruth gave the young woman a hug, stroked the boy's hair, and got up. "Good luck!" she said, kindly.

The sergeant looked immensely pleased as Ruth walked toward him, graceful and pretty.

13

The Supplicant and the Victor

She waited calmly just inside the door of a room crammed with file cabinets. The young officer at the desk was busy writing and did not look up as if the never-ending stream of supplicants entering his office were not worthy of the most meager civility. The sign on his desk read Major Thaddeus D. Whitman.

Ruth studied him for a moment. His dark hair was wavy and neatly combed. It seemed to her that he had sunfreckles on and around his nose, but she could not be sure, standing twelve feet away. She could not discern much else about him aside from that he wore a uniform and that his hands were long and slender. Between his brows were two deep furrows as if what he wrote required much concentration or was unpleasant.

Ruth permitted herself a quick look around the room. On the wall behind the officer hung a large map of the divided Germany, the various Allied sectors clearly outlined. She studied the map for a moment, then grew impatient.

"Excuse me!" she said. He looked up crossly. For an instant, he stared at her, vacant and distant. But, as if confronted with an apparition, his expression changed to one of being utterly dumbfounded. He smiled, a little forlorn, and awkwardly got up.

"I'm sorry," he said, and she saw that he was tall and slender and quite handsome. His eyes were blue, which she had not expected. Not that she had consciously thought of the color of his eyes, but the color of the hair had, somehow, suggested, dark eyes.

Slowly, he came around the desk and hobbled toward her. His left foot was huge with a cast. He held out his hand, which she took gingerly, his injured foot having sparked an unconscious tenderness in her.

"Major Whitman," he said, smiling, studying her, in his eyes the pleasure of seeing her fresh and pretty face.

"Pleased to meet you," Ruth said, forgetting for an instant why she had come, feeling, for just an instant, the rush and excitement of the pleasure in his eyes.

He was about to release her hand but held on to it instead and leaned closer as if he hadn't heard right.

"You speak English?"

"A little."

Major Whitman was more than a little pleased. He pointed to a chair. "Please. Have a seat. May I offer you some coffee?"

Ruth looked up at him blankly.

"You mean real…"

She caught herself and sat up a little straighter. He turned to a percolator not far from his desk on a narrow table.

"It's probably old," he said as he began pouring. "I should ask Sarge to make a new pot…" His voice trailed. But then he added. "No, it looks all right, I guess."

He brought the cups and held one out to her. She reached for it and he couldn't help but notice her hands. She had taken great care to scrub them clean, but they looked as if she had hauled bricks with them. Aware of his look, she curled her fingers tightly around the handle of the cup and hid the other, in a fist, in her lap. Whitman sadly raised his eyebrows and returned to his chair.

Ruth, with her eyes closed, inhaled the scent of the coffee deeply and took a first cautious, blissful sip. Whitman studied her, smiling. He picked up a folder and turned his attention to the documents it contained.

Turning a page, he had a faintly visible shock. He looked up and at Ruth who, just that moment, took a sip of coffee, unaware that something was amiss. He turned back to the page. A black stamp ran diagonally the length of Ruth's visa application. The letters spelled a very definite 'DENIED.' He turned the page and looked up once again. His face revealed nothing of what he knew.

"And why doesn't your sister go herself?" he asked, casually.

"Because she has no papers."

"Lost in the bombings, I assume?"

"No. Her husband burned them."

"Burned them?"

"So she couldn't leave Berlin."

"And why is the child not with her mother?"

"Because Hannah was arrested during a document check in the Russian sector of Berlin. She'd gone to the country to barter some jewelry for food, and she didn't look all too clean on the way home. They put her in a prison camp because she couldn't identify herself. If you didn't have any identification papers, you were assumed to be a vagrant. And vagrancy was a crime for which the Russians sent people to Siberia. Still do, I guess. Of course, her husband or Martha could have vouched for her, but they never came forward even though Hannah was able to smuggle out a note telling them where she was."

Agitated, Ruth got up and started walking up and down the room holding her coffee cup. Whitman couldn't keep his eyes from wandering over her face, her body, her hands, and back to her face. When she suddenly turned and looked at him, she caught him off guard. He cleared his throat, picked up her application, and attempted a businesslike demeanor that wasn't quite successful.

Ruth pretended that she hadn't noticed. Besides, the fate of her sister's child was more important that instant than an embarrassed American officer.

"You see," she said, "Hannah escaped from that Russian camp and came west. She had no choice. Had she gone back to get the child, they would have arrested her again. Martha—that's Hannah's mother-in-law—would have seen to that. She's always wanted Pauli. She's obsessed with her. And Pauli doesn't even like her. Major Whitman, Hannah needs her child, and it's such a small thing for me to do. A truly small thing. It's only six hours by train. I can be back the next day," she said, imploringly. Whitman, smiling, shook his head.

Ruth sat back down.

"Mrs. Karstens, you should know that we deny all applications at this time. Aside from dire emergencies. I'm sure you know that Russia has threatened to blockade Berlin. Again. They did so in March, as you know, for ten days. Though they did permit train travel then, even if they did search everybody and everything before the trains entered Berlin. But now, with the German currency reform threatening them, they will blockade all modes of transportation. There's no doubt in our minds. And when that happens, they will also close the east-west border, and, we assume, for good. This will not be just a ten day baby blockade, as we called it back in March. You and the child may be trapped there…for good…."

His voice trailed. He studied the papers, turning the pages, but he thought hard about something else.

"How can I get in touch with you? Can I reach you by phone?"

Ruth looked at him as if he were mad.

"Phone? Major Whitman, I don't know if you noticed, but Germany is a little bit in ruins?"

"Sorry. I wasn't thinking. Can you come back, then? Say…in a week?"

"A week? Major Whitman, I need to go now. If I don't, I might never get her out. Hannah needs her."

Whitman got up and limped around the desk to get another cup of coffee. He reached for hers, but she shook her head and smiled.

"I would. If I could take it to Hannah."

He returned her smile and, coming back with his cup, made himself comfortable at the corner of his desk.

"Tell you what—and I can't promise—but maybe we can say the child is ill." He thought this over. "I'll do my best." He looked at the papers. "I guess my driver can find the street where you live—that is, if I can get you the visa. If I can, I'll bring it."

Surprised, Ruth stared at him, but his eyes were bright and innocent. She blushed, lowered her eyes, and looked straight at his cast. She looked up again.

"But I live on the fifth floor."

"I'll manage."

Ruth looked at him with more admiration than the good major was used to. Whitman cleared his throat and straightened his tie.

Ruth got up and held out her hand. Whitman's eyes were soft.

"Thank you very, very much."

She was about to walk out with Whitman looking after her, when he remembered something.

"Wait."

Ruth turned as he pulled open a drawer at his desk and came back with a handful of chocolate bars. He seemed a little embarrassed.

"For the children."

Ruth looked at the chocolates, then at him. The warmth in her eyes made Major Whitman melt. She took the chocolates and held them in both hands as if they were a treasure. He closed the door behind her and stared at it, smiling.

Ruth walked down the long hallway, holding the chocolates in her cupped hands, her eyes full of tears. She walked as if she were alone in the world. She did not see the envious looks of the people on the benches or the astonished ones of the military personnel that happened by. No one had been kind to her in a very long time, and it nearly broke her.

14

The Many Uses of Silver

Four days later, Ruth and Hannah sat around the battered table beneath the elegant lamp and mended children's clothes. A hem had come loose on a little skirt. A sock had a hole in it. A blouse had lost a button. Once a month, they went to the relief center where used clothing was passed out to the refugees. They had gone there that afternoon, and although Ruth tried hard to choose things that, if not awfully attractive, were at least in good shape. But there always seemed something wrong with the clothes and so they went through the batch they had been permitted to take and mended what could be mended.

The children slept peacefully in the bedstead, their heads close together, one dark haired, the other blond. The radio, playing Mozart, was turned low, and the women talked in hushed voices.

Ever since Ruth had decided to go to Berlin, Hannah had been troubled. She knew Ruth well. Once Ruth made up her mind to do something, she usually did it. But if they closed the Iron Curtain before Ruth got out with the child, she might be stuck there forever. Hannah agonized over the sacrifice her sister was about to make, just as she agonized over never seeing Pauli again if Ruth didn't make that sacrifice.

"You can't go anyway," she said suddenly with a satisfied sigh, pushing an old light bulb through a sock in preparation for darning a small hole in it, "we don't have any money."

This pacifying thought had just come to her and it would solve everything. Ruth couldn't go, and she, Hannah, would find a way, some-how, to get Pauli. No government could be so heartless as to permit the separation of a mother and her child.

But she had underestimated Ruth who put down her sewing, got up, rummaged through one of the boxes way beneath the slanted roof, and came back to the table with a bundle.

"Never! Absolutely never!" Hannah cried out in a hushed cry. The children stirred but did not wake up. The bundle turned out to be a pair of slacks wrapped around a set of silverware. Ruth, unwrapping it, fingered the cloth.

"Wool, you see. The silver hasn't tarnished hardly at all." She studied the set wistfully as Hannah began to cry.

"Ridiculous, when you think about it," Ruth said. "Here the Russian Army descends on me, and what do I think of saving? My kids and my silverware." She laughed. "It's hilarious, really. But it doesn't do us any good sitting in a box."

"I'm not going to let you do it," Hannah sobbed.

"You don't have to," Ruth said. "I'm going to do it all by myself. Hey! Stop that!" She pulled a handkerchief out of her apron pocket and handed it to Hannah. "We've been to hell and back, and here you cry over a little silver. Cut it out!"

"What if you can't sell it?" Hannah sobbed in a vain attempt to hold off the inevitable.

"Who said I was going to sell it? I'm going to pawn it. And when we're rich, I'm going to get it back. It's really very simple."

Proudly, she laid the twelve-piece set out on the table where it gleamed in the lamplight.

15

A Shopping Trip

Two nights later, Major Whitman hobbled out of his barracks. A sign lit by a dim bulb above the door read 'BOQ.' It was raining as he climbed cumbersomely into a Jeep and tried out the gears which was no picnic with his clump foot. He finally got it started but trying to drive it was a different story. He cut the engine off several times before he got it going, though once he did, the Jeep proceeded jerkily down the road until he got the hang of maneuvering the gears.

Slowly, he drove to another barracks that said 'Base Exchange' where he got out and went on a shopping spree. He put a can of coffee into a cart, some candy, a carton of cigarettes, some chocolates and some canned goods like beans and soup. Some canned meat. Sausage. At the checkout counter, a bucket with flowers stared at him brightly. He took two bunches. On the way out the door, a stack of Sears catalogues attracted his attention. At the spur of the moment, he took one, wheeled everything out to the Jeep, and took off into town.

16

A Different Kind of Shopping Trip

Earlier that day, Ruth had walked down a street lined with elaborate villas on her quest to sell the silver. The pawnbroker had been a cutthroat. He named a sum so low, she said, just to make sure:

"For one piece, right?"

"The set, lady," he said. "The set. This is a business, not a charitable institution."

The realization that he had just dashed her dream of having a good sum of money to go to Berlin with sank in only slowly as she stared at him with utter disbelief. But he gave her no further thought, turning to another desperate customer instead. Ruth packed up the silver, wholly at a loss as to where to turn next. Undecided, she stood outside the shop, thinking.

"You should go to the Americans with this," a man said. She turned and recognized the man who had stood behind her in line. "I couldn't help but see what you have there. I knew he wouldn't give you nothing. But the Americans have money. They buy lots of stuff."

"And where are they?"

The man explained, and Ruth set out determinedly. But once she came to the part of town the man had pointed out, she lost heart. The neighborhood, elegant and quiet, lay serenely in the summer sun, and she drew in her breath with the pain of it. The villas, of nineteenth-century splendor, expansively laid out, their masonry elaborately embellished, were lined with ornate cast iron fences and gardens filled with flowers. High old trees and ancient shrubs hid one neighbor from the other and the immense silence made her wonder whether anyone lived there. But there were cars parked along the road and she thought she heard children laughing somewhere.

"Rich folk lived there once," the man had said. "Now the Americans have confiscated the whole neighborhood and put their officers in there."

"I don't mind," Ruth had said. She was rarely intimidated. Only, she had not counted on the beauty and the serenity and the grandeur. None of the people who opened their doors to her would know that she, too, had once had a home and a garden filled with flowers, and the distance from these villas to the attic room seemed, suddenly, insurmountable. She would appear, to these people, as she never had wanted to appear to anyone: poor and destitute.

She stood by a gate and looked toward the first villa she came to. A prince could have easily lived there, it seemed so rich and flamboyant. An American flag whipped gaily on a pole extending from a window. She squared her shoulders, opened the gate, walked up the path, and determinedly rang the doorbell. A young woman, about her age, opened the door. She carried a crying toddler and was casually dressed in slacks and a blouse. She had a ready smile, but when Ruth unwrapped the silver, she shook her head at which the toddler screamed even harder which, in turn, made both women smile with the kind of commiseration known only to mothers.

As she walked back toward the street, the small scene stayed in her mind and pushed the insurmountable economic distances and the quirks of fate into the background. She had come to sell her silver so she could get her sister's child out of Berlin before the Russians closed the border. And, for all she knew, if she worked hard, she may, one day, have a house of her own again and a garden. It was not impossible.

She was about to open the next gate when a sudden gust of wind carried the voices and the laughter of children to her from somewhere further down the street. She looked up at the sky where huge thunderheads had gathered portending a summer thunderstorm. At the spur of the moment, she left the gate and turned toward the loud and cheerful shouts. Shrubs and the low hanging branches of the trees obscured her view, but when she rounded a hedge, she stood at a fenced yard where a birthday party was going on. The yard was decorated with colorful streamers and balloons and a young and perfectly coiffured woman in a pink dress cut a birthday cake at a shaded picnic table. A horde of children crowded excitedly around her, holding bright yellow plates out to her.

Ruth smiled at the brightness and happiness of the scene, but the sadness in her eyes was profound. She scanned the yard that was full of toys, carelessly scattered everywhere. A particularly beautiful doll in a turquoise dress caught her eye and, for just an instant, she wondered what the children, back at the attic room, would do if she took that doll home to them. It was a good thing she had not brought the children with her. They would see, in a second, what they did not have compared to these children and it would break their hearts. She turned to leave and looked up just as the young woman did. They looked at one another for a moment and smiled at the same time. The woman raised her hand for Ruth to wait. She cut a piece of cake, put it on a plate, walked toward the fence and, smiling, held the cake out to her.

Ruth looked at the cake and back at the woman with a thankful smile and shook her head. She couldn't speak, suddenly, and lowered her eyes. For lack of anything to say, she unwrapped the silver and held it out. The woman studied it and nodded. Ruth couldn't help but see the pity in her eyes.

"How much?"

Ruth shrugged. She could not, for the world of her, say a word. The woman waited.

"I don't know," Ruth brought out, finally.

"Wait here," the woman said and went into the house. The children, busy with their cakes and laughing, paid no attention to them, and Ruth, watching them, wished she were far away. The young woman came back, handing Ruth some bills.

"You speak English. Obviously." She smiled. "I know a little about silver. I don't think I cheated you." Ruth handed the silver over, not bothering to count the money.

"I know you didn't. Thank you. Good bye." Ruth turned to leave and turned back. Maybe, if the children did not want it, she could buy the doll. Maybe not for Penelope and Eva, but for Pauli. It would be a bribe, maybe. To be used as a bribe, maybe. For all that she and Hannah knew, Martha may have brainwashed the child and a doll as pretty and elegant as this may make all the difference. She pointed to the doll in the turquoise dress and held out some of the money.

"I wonder if you would let me have this doll." She laughed. "I have some money now."

The woman regretfully shook her head.

"It belongs to my daughter," she said.

"I understand," Ruth said, looking at the doll one more time. It had been so carelessly flung and obviously meant little to the child it belonged to. Once again, she turned to leave.

"Wait," the woman said.

"Amy?" she called out to the children and a little girl came running. As the woman explained, the child studied Ruth out of serious eyes. When her mother was done explaining, the child looked at the doll, then back at Ruth, and again at the doll. With slow, dignified steps, she walked to the doll, picked it up, brushed it off, and handed it to Ruth. Ruth held the money out to her, but she shook her head with a quick, determined shake.

Ruth stood by the fence, with the money in one hand and the doll in the other, devastated. Her eyes filled with tears, but the child had already taken her mother's hand and pulled her away from the fence. Ruth turned away and walked slowly down the street, sobbing uncontrollably.

17

Bananas, A Doll, and A Visitor

That evening, at about the same time Major Whitman went shopping at the Base Exchange, Hannah, looking troubled, sat at the table in the attic room, trying to repair a shoe with glue. Rain pelted the skylight. The children, on the bed, leafed through a tattered picture book and talked in small voices. The old radio played piano music that ended abruptly just as Ruth, wearing a raincoat and a kerchief, tore the door open and excitedly whirled in.

The children jumped off the bed.

"Shh!" Hannah said, loud and urgent, leaning toward the radio, turning it up.

The children froze. Ruth closed the door softly and just as softly put a bulging cloth bag on a chair.

"The breakdown of negotiations between Soviet and Allied delegations," the radio said, "makes a total blockade of all routes of transportation to and from Berlin imminent..."

Hannah turned the radio down as the children rushed toward Ruth.

"You're not going!" Hannah said.

Ruth took off her wet kerchief and coat, shook them out, and hung both on a nail at the door.

"I'm going!"

She bent down to hug and kiss the children.

"Hello, my sweet things. Were you good for your Aunt Hannah?"

The children threw their arms around her.

"What's in the bag?" Eva yelled. "What's in there? Something for us?"

"Shh!" Ruth said as she lifted the bag onto the table. "Yes, I brought you something. But you wait just a minute, just a tiny little minute. First, there's something for your Aunt Hannah!" She put her hand into the bag. "Well, dearest sister, I brought you a present."

Hannah looked up, surprised, her thumbs and fingers clamped around the shoe to set the glue. The children could hardly contain their excitement. Their small hands fidgeted, ready to delve into the bag the moment they were given permission.

"Don't you dare touch that! First Aunt Hannah has to guess."

The children jumped up and down with excitement. Hannah laughed.

"Bread!"

Ruth frowned.

"Would I bring you bread when you work in a bakery?"

"Chocolate."

"Chocolate?"

"Meat."

"For Heaven's sake, Hannah! Where would I get meat?"

Ruth reached into the bag and pulled out a small brown paper package. Smiling with anticipation, she handed it to Hannah. Hannah smelled the package and jumped up to hug Ruth.

"Oh, my God! Coffee! Wherever did you get coffee?"

"Black Market, of course," Ruth said.

The children, now very impatient, tugged at Ruth and Hannah.

"And what's for us? What's in there? Let us see, please, please, please."

Ruth pulled out something wrapped in newspaper that fell away, revealing two bananas. The children were severely disappointed.

"What are they?"

"Bananas."

"What's a banana?" Eva asked.

"You eat them." Eva was about to bite into hers.

Ruth shot a profoundly sad look at Hannah who took the bananas out of the children's hands, peeled them, and handed them back, smiling.

Ruth, with tears in her eyes, meticulously folded the newspaper.

"You go on now," Hannah said to the children who had taken small bites of the bananas and now looked at each other as they had seen adults do, their eyebrow drawn up and nodding approval.

"Up on the bed with you," Hannah said, turning them around and giving them a playful push toward the bed. Then she pulled out a handkerchief and dabbed at Ruth's eyes.

"Let me make us a good cup of coffee, yes?" she said kindly as the children, chattering and studying their treasure, trundled toward the bed and climbed onto it.

"They don't even know what a banana is," Ruth sobbed quietly. "Can you imagine? Before the war, we used to eat them by the crates...."

She stopped right there, swallowed, shook her head, took the handkerchief out of Hannah's hands and wiped her eyes.

"Enough. Enough of this. You can make coffee in a minute. First, there's something else." She gave Hannah a big, fake smile, brushed her hair back with her hands and picked up the bag.

"Sit down."

Hannah sat down expectantly, glancing at the children who were busy with their curious delicacy.

"I have something for Pauli," Ruth whispered. "In case I have to bribe her."

"That pawnbroker must have been very kind," Hannah said, studying her sister's eyes as if she could discern some kind of confirmation in them.

Ruth, clutching the bag, changed chairs so she sat with her back to the children.

"I sold the silver."

Hannah looked at her, aghast. Ruth shrugged.

"God, Hannah, these American children have everything. Turquoise dresses even. Imagine."

She opened the bag and let Hannah peek inside. The eyes of the doll, blue with thick, black lashes, looked up at Hannah cheerfully. As the bag moved, the lovely lashes opened and closed dreamily. Hannah covered her mouth to keep from crying out. Quickly, she glanced at the children on the bed who, giggling, were almost done with the bananas, taking but smidgens of bites now to make the delicacy last.

"Are you crazy?" she whispered. "That doll must have cost a fortune."

"Well, sort of, it didn't."

"What do you mean by sort of?"

But Ruth looked away from Hannah and toward the radio, puzzled. Then she jumped up and turned up the volume.

"Quick! A tango! Let's go!"

With lightning speed, they moved chairs and table out of the way, then danced as perfect a Tango as they could in that small space. The children laughed and clapped happily, jumping off the bed trying to get in on the dance. When the music ended, Ruth and Hannah formally bowed to their small audience. Laughing, they put chairs and table back when an assertive knock on the door gave them all a start.

"Oh, oh!" Ruth whispered, giving Hannah a smirking sideways glance.

"Sorry, Mrs. Garske," she hollered through the door. "We won't do it again."

But there was a second knock. This time louder. After an instant of rueful silence, Hannah walked to the door and opened it. An American officer in uniform took off his cap. Hannah was about to have a heart attack. Quickly, she gauged the distance between him and the bag with the doll, but it was too late to hide it. Besides, the officer carried a bag out of which billowed a small cloud of flowers which made him seem less threatening. He also had a book tucked under his arm, and his left foot was huge with a cast. He managed a bright smile, and a brighter one even when he saw the children who, instinctively, sought refuge at their mother's side.

"Hello!" he said. He was a little embarrassed and a little shocked. Mrs. Garske, in the background, closed the front door to the apartment with deliberate slowness to glean what she could of the scene. Ruth, in the attic room, stood like a statue.

"May I come in?" Whitman asked.

"Ruth?" Hannah snapped sharply.

Ruth finally came alive and began stuttering: "Oh…Yes. Oh, dear. Please."

Hannah looked from one to the other. Something was going on here she knew nothing about. Whitman limped in, and Hannah closed the door. He put the bag and the book on the table and took out the flowers, formally handing one bunch to Ruth, the other to Hannah, and now everyone felt just a little embarrassed. He pointed to the bag.

"And a little something for the children," he said. "I hope you don't mind."

Hannah pulled out a chair for him as Ruth did not seem to be able to get out of her paralysis. She just stood dumbly, holding the flowers. Whitman lifted the bag off the table onto the floor, and the children dug into it. Soon the table was covered with food. Whitman watched the children with great interest to prevent him from having to look at the women. He felt a little awkward as Good Samaritan.

Ruth and Hannah looked at one another. They had a hard time holding back their tears. They hadn't seen such food in years. Whitman looked up. He wanted to say something but hesitated. He watched the children a moment longer then looked up again.

"I came to say…regret to say…that your second request for a visa was denied. I'm truly sorry."

Ruth and Hannah stared at him blankly. When they comprehended what he had said, both sat down. The flowers clutched to their chests, they stared at him in utter despair.

18

Date with a Twist

He stayed but half an hour. Ruth introduced everyone and briefly filled Hannah in on her acquaintance with him. Whitman tried hard to keep his eyes on the women or the children and not let them wander over the room that told him more of the circumstances of these two women than anything Ruth had said. He tried to keep the conversation centered on the visa and explained the difficulty of obtaining one at this time. Unless travel was urgent because it involved the impending death of a family member, all visas were denied. And maybe even for good. The women were not quite with him, both of them struggling with the agonizing thought that, if Ruth could not go to Berlin, Pauli might be lost to Hannah forever.

The children, having heaped the food on the table, began smelling each of the packages as they had seen Hannah do earlier with the coffee package. In spite of their serious conversation, Whitman couldn't help but smile at the children's curious behavior. Finally, they discovered the chocolate and crowded in on their mother, whispering, pleading. Ruth nodded absentmindedly, and Whitman got up.

"I'm sorry," he said. "I tried my best. I said that the child was seriously ill. But they wanted proof. A doctor's written testimony. And I knew we couldn't provide that."

"I understand," Hannah said, at once teary-eyed and relieved. It meant that Ruth wouldn't be able to go. Fate had made the decision for her. "But thank you for all you've done."

"I'll have to take you downstairs," Ruth said. "They lock the door after nine."

She walked ahead of him down the long stairs, deeply in thought, a large key in her hand. He hobbled laboriously and crestfallen behind. When they arrived at the entrance, she was about to put the key into the lock to let him out, but he touched her arm. Vacantly, she looked at him.

"There is nothing we can do," he said.

"I understand."

He took her hand that held the key.

"Sometimes, this world can get awfully screwed up."

"I know."

"Would you consider going out with me tomorrow night?"

Ruth was momentarily startled at the abrupt request, but she smiled. After a moment's hesitation, she shook her head.

"It's a nice club," he said. "The food is excellent. There's dancing…"

"I don't have a dress."

Whitman smiled.

"Seems to me you wore a dress in my office."

"It's been mended too many times. And the jewelry and the hat…I borrowed that from my landlady."

"I think the dress will do fine," he said, kindly. "And you don't need any jewelry. None at all."

The compliment made her smile.

"I can't. I really can't." The desire to go was in her eyes as she hunted for an explanation for her refusal. "Hannah will be alone. And the children."

She put the key in the lock.

"Do you know what a doggy bag is?" he asked.

19

The Spoils of War

I put the pages down and sat straight up. "You mean he bribed her with a doggy bag?"

"Of course," Penelope said, not perturbed in the least.

"But that's abominable."

"What would you do if your children were hungry?"

I had already opened my mouth to protest to whatever she could possibly say in favor of the doggy bag bribe and shut it because I thought, Yes, just what would I do if my children were hungry? If Charlie had gone hungry?

"Near anything," I said. "Of course."

"Of course!" She mocked me though her smile lay between us and softened the reprimand. "But no, the promise of a doggy bag was not why she said yes. She knew about doggy bags, and she knew that he was joking, something like a pitiful and humorous last-ditch effort to get her to go out with him. She was aware just as he was that thousands of women slept with the soldiers or the officers in exchange for food, and for such ordinary things as clothes and underwear and nylons and baby powder. Or diapers. Or eggs. Has there ever been a war in which this kind of exploitation didn't go on? And yes, it is abominable. And it's so easy to judge these women whose hearts were bleeding as some man they hardly knew lay on top of them. But unless you have been in a place where there isn't even soap to wash with, you can't appreciate what these women went through, having to feed and clothe their children, and sometimes even elderly parents, and keeping disease away because there was little water and nothing to wash with. Which clothes were you going to change into if you had only what was on your back?"

I held up my hand to stop her from going on. "You know," I said, "I've always considered myself a fairly compassionate guy. Emphasis on fairly. Certainly not less compassionate than a good many other people. But the world you opened up to me is so mind boggling to me, I think I've lived on the moon all these years."

"Why should you have thought of it? You never went through a war. Or rather, nothing all too drastic changed in your life while the war was going on. So you mustn't be too hard on yourself. Besides, we were the enemy. We deserved it, I guess."

"Sure," I said, contemptuously. "A six-year old child with dimples in her cheeks is a real threat to the military might of the United States of America."

This made her laugh. "Let's not get into that," she said. "I could be a real terror if I wanted to when I was a child. I'm also very stubborn. But seriously now, let's face it. There have always been kind soldiers and deplorable soldiers, and some take royal advantage of a situation and others wouldn't dream of it. Your father wouldn't dream of it. Besides, he sensed that she was unbribable, if you will, if that's a word. She considered herself lucky. She had a roof over her head. She had running water, albeit cold, but it was there. She got food at the relief center. The Marshall Plan had seen to that. Though there was little meat and fewer vegetables, and certainly no fresh fruit, we were eating something. And now, with Hannah working in the bakery, we had old bread and sometimes even cake. No. She didn't need to be bribed with a doggy bag, though it was tempting, of course. His saying so made her laugh, because she realized that his interest in her was not purely sexual. Besides, he had trekked, on his cast, up the five flights of stairs to her attic room, and she felt ungrateful. But, ultimately, she was young and she loved to dance, and a date with him was so tempting. Life had been so miserable for so long, the mere prospect of being someplace that was civil and lovely and where there was music was irresistible."

She paused, studying her hands. "And that's just what I kept forgetting in my inner battles with her that went on long after I left home. That she was young. That she wanted to dance and laugh and be happy, just like everyone else. No. He was much too decent to take advantage of her."

"I know."

And I knew. Because he was. But did Ruth know, that moment at the door, that he had a wife in the States? A son? Something in me said, what the hell difference does that make? There had been a war. It changes people. And who was I to wave a moral flag? Still. The dull sense of betrayal didn't go away just by my mind telling me that it was not that big a deal.

I turned back to the pages, and we continued the ritual of my reading a page and handing it to her as she sat, tailor fashion, on the couch, making corrections in the manuscript now and then with a pencil.

20

A Mysterious Gift

The next day, a Saturday, Ruth and Hannah, together with a group of other women, worked side by side at the site of a bombed building, clearing away the rubble. The women, all poorly dressed and covered with dust, worked quickly, filling the rubble into buckets and passing them down a line to a waiting truck. In spite of the heat and the work, they talked and joked. The backbreaking task would be unbearable otherwise.

Nearby, a group of children, laughing and shouting, played hopscotch on what was left of a sidewalk. Little Eva, a thick piece of chalk in her small hand was busy decorating the outside of a hopscotch design with flowers. The chalk looked surprisingly like the piece of an ornate plaster cornice that had once decorated a room.

Hannah and Ruth talked without interrupting their work, though these conversations were more like verbal sparring, and they kept their eyes on the children at the same time. Ruth had just mused that, since she couldn't get the visa, she could take a train to the provisional border between the American and the Russian sectors and walk across, hitchhiking to Berlin.

"Absolutely not!" Hannah said.

Ruth looked up. "Where's Penelope?"

Hannah pointed to the bombed house beside the one they worked on where Penelope sat on a broken cement slab. A ray of sunlight fell on her and on a book she studied rapturously. She was dressed in clothes from the relief center that had been carefully mended. Her pigtails were tied with shoestring. The page-turner she couldn't put down was a catalog. Each page she turned revealed ever more colorful pictures of elaborately dressed dolls. Finally, she put the book down. Skinny elbows on skinny knees, she put her chin on her small fists and stared quizzically out at the sky through the ghostly frame of what was once a window.

"I wish," Ruth said, "he had not brought that catalog."

"Oh, let her," Hannah said. "Things will get better here. Besides, you're changing the subject, because you're not going to walk across that border! And that's final!"

"But you need Pauli! Besides, I'd love to give that old hag a piece of my mind."

"It's not worth it. You can't change people."

"But you can give them a piece of your mind."

"It's still not worth it. Besides, you're not going. There must be some justice somewhere. I will get Pauli one way or another. Even the bureaucracy can't be that heartless. Even the Russians have children."

But Ruth knew better. "There is no such thing as justice. Either I get her or you have to do without her."

An old, beat-up car that barely ran pulled up to the curb sputtering oil. An old man got out and studied the women, one by one.

"Any of you here a Ruth Karstens?"

Surprised, Ruth turned. "Who wants to know?" she asked combatively.

"I'm supposed to deliver something." The old man smiled. "He described her. Looks like it's you."

Ruth and Hannah looked at each other, puzzled. The old man opened the back door of the car and took out a flat box with a ribbon. The rest of the women had stopped working now and curiously observed what was going on. The old man handed the box to Ruth who stood open-mouthed as the women crowded around her.

21

Dubious Forgetfulness

That evening, Whitman, in civilian clothes, entered the long hallway where Ruth had previously waited for the transit visa. A soldier kept guard behind a brightly lit window. He saw Whitman and saluted.

"Hello, Kass," Whitman said, smiling. "Forgot something in my office. Won't be long."

Kass grinned.

"No problem, Sir."

Whitman hobbled down the hall and entered his office where he unlocked a cabinet and took out a document. He locked the cabinet, sat down at his desk, and filled it out. He left his office through a door that bore the sign: Col. Steven P. Brandon, Commanding Officer. He returned moments later with a small rack of stamps and a stamp pad, searched for the proper stamps and stamped the document and signed it. He returned the rack and pad to Col. Brandon's office and came back to his desk, waving the document in the air for a moment to dry the ink. Then he folded it carefully and put it in his breast pocket.

22

In the Eyes of the Beholder

While Whitman carried out the mysterious enterprise in his office, Ruth got ready for her date with him. She felt much calmer than Hannah who, after they were done with their day's work at the bombing site, told Ruth that she had to run an errand.

"What?" Ruth asked.

"The baker asked me to deliver a message," Hannah said, looking innocent. "And I almost forgot."

Ruth didn't believe her, but she asked no further questions and went on home with the children while Hannah walked on into town, stopping people on the way to ask where she could find some make-up. Someone directed her to an apartment where a young woman conducted a lively black market in American make-up. It would not have occurred to anyone to question how she got her hands on it. These were trying times and demanded innovation. Hannah found a lipstick there and some mascara, and she carried the trifles home like a treasure.

Half an hour before Whitman would arrive to pick her up, Ruth sat at the table, her long, dark hair still wet even though they had washed it an hour before. Calmly, she applied mascara to her lashes, her face all contorted in a small mirror propped against one of the cans of coffee Whitman had brought on his first visit. She had not applied make-up in so long, she kept moving away from the mirror and back toward it, trying to get it just right. All the while, Hannah tried to dry her hair by brushing it furiously whenever Ruth took a break from the mascara application. A hair dryer was nowhere to be found and brushing was the only way to get the hair dry.

"Personally," Ruth said, scrutinizing her face in the mirror, "I don't think I need that stuff."

"With your hazel eyes? Looks great. Really brings out your eyes. Truly."

The children sat cross-legged on the bed. Between them was a small heap of the cut crystals of a long gone chandelier. They amused themselves by holding the crystals toward the lamplight.

"Oh, oh, oh…green, blue," Eva said. "It's fire. Orange fire. Look. Look through this one, Pennelee."

Penelope took the crystal out of her hand and said: "It's a diamond." Looking through it, lost in its fire, she said:

"Say Penelope. Pe-ne-lo-pe. Say it!"

"Pen-ne-lee."

Hannah, brushing furiously, said: "It's still wet."

She looked around. Picking up a piece of cardboard, she waved it frantically around Ruth's head like a Chinese fan. Ruth burst out laughing.

"He'll just have to take me with wet hair. It'll dry on the way."

"And look like hell," Hannah said.

Ruth shrugged, got up, and took the lid off the box that the old man had delivered earlier that day. Almost reverently, she took out a lovely summer dress. It was red with small white flowers woven into it. It was cut low enough for her to show off a lovely piece of jewelry if she had had one, but she didn't. Hannah suggested that, instead, she wear one of the red dahlias that had come with Whitman's flower bouquet.

"Either right here, where the dress is lowest, like, between your breasts," Hannah suggested—Ruth frowned, "or in your hair."

"In my hair," Ruth said.

23

A Veritable Feast

As soon as they entered the club, Ruth felt at once exhilarated and intimidated. An elegant casino before the war, the Greek revival structure had been confiscated by the Americans as soon as the war was over and turned into a club. The gilded rooms that had once entertained German high society was now the playground of American officers and government officials. The marble foyer with its gilded mirrors was crammed with officers in uniform or suits or sports coats and even tuxedos, and the women, fashionably dressed, well coiffured and bejeweled, struck Ruth as magical. As if she had come upon a scene straight out of Cinderella's fairy tale, she stood in the door, the dazzle of voices, color, music, jewels, and perfume overwhelming her.

"I wish I had gloves," she said. It was the only clear thought in her mind, that her hands were rough and that she could never quite get them clean, no matter how hard she scrubbed and that none of these women would have such hands. And that, of course, the moment anyone looked at them, they would know that she was a refuge living in an attic room.

Though she made no motion to flee, Whitman sensed her apprehension and consolingly, he took her arm.

"You look stunning," he said.

She looked up at him. In her eyes lay all that she felt, gratitude and doubt, excitement and dismay, and she felt silly, suddenly, wearing a single dahlia in her hair when the women here were covered in gold and silver and gems.

They made their way through the crowd to the restaurant, and the cacophony of laughter and shouts and bits of conversation were intoxicating to her. She didn't want to stare, but her curiosity of how American women dressed and how they carried themselves got the better of her.

As they stood in line, waiting to be seated, she worked hard to let go of her intimidation and her apprehensions and to let the excitement of being in such a setting wash over her. Whitman studied her face, her hazel eyes bright. She hung on to his arm just a little tighter.

"That's better," he said. "You just don't know it, but you are the most beautiful woman here. Trust me."

They were led to a table not far from the dance floor. It was covered with starched linen and silver and flowers and a candle. Ruth sighed with pleasure when she sat down. A waiter appeared instantly, handing them menus, asking them if he could start them out with a drink.

"Wine?" Whitman asked. Ruth merely stared at him blankly. Wine? Of course, wine. Why not wine? When was the last time she had had wine? She shrugged, uncertainly.

"Wine." Whitman said to the waiter, and to Ruth, "Dry? Sweet?"

"Dry, if that's all right?" she asked cautiously.

"Perfect," he said, and the waiter went on his errand. Whitman looked at her who sat stiffly, holding the menu, not reading it.

"Well?" he asked. "Don't you want to pick out something?"

She nodded but made no motion of opening the menu.

"Is something wrong?" he asked.

She gave him a small, apprehensive smile, shook her head, and obediently opened the menu, pretending to study it. But the letters swam on the page and she could not read them. When the waiter put the wine and glasses with ice water on the table, she closed the menu, perfectly controlled.

"I'll have the soup," she said determinedly. "And a salad."

Whitman looked up, dumbfounded. He laughed.

"Strike that!" he said to the waiter. "Make that a T-bone, baked potato, green beans, carrots, corn, and salad. Make that two of everything. And a whole pie for dessert. With whip cream."

Ruth's eyes were huge as the waiter, with a straight face, wrote it all down.

"Butter and sour cream on the potatoes?" he asked.

"Of course!" Whitman said.

"And was that one pie each, or just one pie?"

Whitman looked at Ruth and grinned. Ruth, embarrassed, shook her head.

"One pie each," Whitman said, and the waiter, eyebrows raised, left them once again.

Whitman lifted his glass toward Ruth.

"To you," he said.

"To you and to all this," Ruth said, sweeping the room with her eyes. She took a cautious sip and then another. "I haven't had wine in so long, I'll be drunk before the night's over."

"Good," he said. "I think you need to get drunk. I'll get you home safely, don't you worry."

"I wish Hannah could see all this."

He reached out and lightly put his hand on hers. "Tonight is your night. No Hannah. No children. No attic room. No bombed houses. Just now. Think of now. One day soon, we will bring her and the children."

"Not the children," she said, alarmed.

"Why not the children?"

"Because...." She didn't know what to say. It had been a purely instinctual response. Not until days later did she know that she meant to say, 'Because it would break their hearts.'

The waiter came back with a tray and began loading the table. Ruth merely glanced at the food—the steaks as large as their dinner plates, and individual bowls, each containing a different vegetable, a bowl filled with salad, a bowl holding four large baked potatoes. The waiter put a sampling of each dish on her plate while she glanced around the club as if people watching were her most favorite occupation. When the waiter left, Whitman smiled at her whose look has returned to him, carefully avoiding the food.

"Dig in!"

Ruth, as if in a trance, picked up fork and knife and looked, for the first time and fully, at the steak. Gingerly, she took a green bean and, her hands visibly shaking, put it into her mouth. She chewed slowly, not looking at Whitman who beamed at all the good things on the table for her and observed her every move. He was proud like a father who was dealing with a finicky eater and the pride showed all over him. He was completely unprepared for her reaction. She swallowed and burst into tears. Whitman's smile changed into an expression of great concern and profound sorrow. He reached into his coat pocket for a handkerchief that he pressed into her hand. She dabbed at her eyes, but the tears would not stop falling. Never looking at him, she got up.

"Excuse me."

She dashed to the Ladies' Room, and, in a stall, shook with sobs.

When she calmed down, she came out and dabbed a little cold water around her eyes, hoping to eradicate their redness and puffiness. A woman who had walked in while Ruth sobbed in the stall watched her closely.

"If he makes you cry like that, honey, he's not worth it."

Ruth, drying her face, smiled.

"He didn't mean it."

"That's what they all say."

The woman, seeing that Ruth had no purse, handed her a brush and, after some reflection, a compact and a lip stick. Gratefully, Ruth applied a little powder.

"Thank you so much."

Whitman looked utterly crestfallen when Ruth returned to the table and sat down.

"I'm so sorry," she said. "You meant so well…but I can't eat…I just can't."

Whitman reached across the table and took her hand that he squeezed gently, holding on to it.

"I understand. But I wish you'd eat a little. You're skinny as a rail. Just a little. We'll have the rest packed up for Hannah and the kids. All right? Eat a little, at least."

Ruth nodded and bravely picked up fork and knife, but she couldn't look at the food. Whitman, as if he were about to speak intently to a child, leaned forward.

"If you eat even a little, I will give you a surprise."

Ruth's eyes lit up.

"What kind of a surprise?"

"Would it be a surprise if I told you?"

She laughed. "I guess not."

"So, do you want it or not?"

"I guess I do. If it's a nice surprise."

"The best."

"All right." And without further ado, she began eating, slowly and cautiously, at first, but then her young body that had craved good food for so long took over and she nearly finished the steak before she remembered that she had meant to take some back for Hannah and the children.

"Finish it," Whitman said as if he could read her mind. "We'll order another to take home."

"That would be too expensive," she said.

"You let me worry about that."

"Hey, Ted. Teddy! Thaddeus!" A male voice rang out over the clamor of the packed room, and a young man in a tuxedo pushed through to them.

"Hey, Buddy," Whitman yelled.

Buddy came up, and Whitman introduced him to Ruth. "We fly together," he explained. Buddy's eyes lit up when he looked at Ruth.

"Very pleased to meet you," he said.

"Thank you," Ruth said, and there came the terrible moment with the hands that she had dreaded because he held out his right hand. She squeezed it quickly and just as quickly pulled back. But he did not seem to notice, though he looked at her a moment longer, looked at Whitman and said:

"Wow!" which made her smile.

"Whatcha doing in the monkey suit?" Whitman said, laughing.

"Sheryl's birthday," Buddy said, looking around just as a very young and very blonde woman pushed through to them. Ruth understood finally what was meant by platinum blonde as the woman's hair fell in soft silver waves to her shoulders. She wore earrings of blue gems that sparkled when she moved and a necklace and bracelet to match. Her long evening dress—silk, no doubt, Ruth thought—was also blue. She looked altogether as if she had just stepped out of a movie. She seemed very composed, the push through the crowd had not put one hair out of place.

"Hey, Sheryl," Whitman said, getting up and putting his arms around her, never squeezing her as if she were a breakable porcelain doll that would crush if he touched her, kissing her with fake kisses about an inch away from her cheeks.

"Sheryl Hyde," he said, "Ruth Karstens."

"Pleased to meet you," they both said, and Ruth caught in the eyes of the woman the look she did not know she had feared—the look of genuinely faked pleasure with an edge of pity.

"I want you to join us," Buddy said. "Do. We're in the yellow ballroom."

He turned and pointed in the general direction of the room, but Whitman shook his head.

"First date, and we don't want you," he laughed.

"Oh, oh," Buddy said, winking at Whitman. Intuitively, Ruth understood just what Buddy and Sheryl thought that moment—that the food on the table was bait, that she was a one night stand, and that the payment for that night was this food.

"The food's good here, isn't it?" Sheryl said to Ruth.

"Yes, it's very good," Ruth said. "Excellent, in fact."

"You're not gonna finish?" Sheryl asked. "All that food?"

"I'm gonna take it back to the barracks with me," Whitman said, shooting a quick, good-natured glance at Ruth.

The waiter came up with a cart to bring the pies, put them on the table together with dessert plates, and began loading what was left over from the dinner.

"And pack another steak," Whitman said.

Sheryl stuck her finger into one of the pies and licked off the whip cream. Whitman shot a quick and concerned look at Ruth who could do nothing more civil than to ignore the trespass on the pie that was to go to Hannah and the children.

"I like your accent," Sheryl said. "Wherever did you pick up such good English?"

"In high school."

"They teach English here? Who would have thought? I have to tell you that it is utterly boring going into town. There is nothing there. You can't buy a thing. No restaurants. If it weren't for this club, I'd go absolutely bananas. Do you live in town?"

"Yes."

"With your family?"

"With my sister and my two daughters."

"*You* have children? How quaint! How old are they?"

"Five and three."

"Darling! Little ones. How quaint! Are you teaching them to speak English?"

Ruth studied her, puzzled. "English? Why would I want to teach them English?"

Only then did she become aware of the subtle insult. Sheryl took for granted that Ruth, in her mind one of those poverty-stricken German women, was hunting for a husband. But by this time, she had already answered Sheryl and could not grace her now with a more appropriate response. She could feel her cheeks burning with humiliation. But Sheryl rattled on.

"Oh, but you must. Life in the States will be so much more difficult for them if they can't speak English. We have a maid, up in Connecticut, where we live, that is, my parents and I, and she is German. I hope you are not offended, but it is absolutely maddening to ask her a question and you can't understand a word she says, her accent's so heavy. And she's been with us for years and years. She came long before the war even. Her husband is even worse, but he works the grounds, so I don't have to deal with him much, and coming here and no one speaks English…"

Ruth had enough. Coldly, she said: "Have you tried to learn German?"

"German?" Sheryl threw her head back and laughed a high and amused little laugh. "Why should I?"

"So you can order your maid around in German," Ruth said, smiling.

But Sheryl, skillfully, warded off the reprimand.

"You know," she said, "that's an excellent idea. But German is so frightfully difficult. I told my dad that I was going to sign up for a German course and he laughed and laughed, and you know what he said? He said, The whole world is going to be American soon anyway. Can you believe it? By the way, I love your dress. Wherever did you get it, considering that there is nothing to buy in town? And that flower in your hair! Simply stunning!"

The men had been talking of flying, but as Sheryl carried on, they fell silent and, silently, looked at each other. Whitman made an almost imperceptible motion with his head that meant for Buddy to get Sheryl out of there. Buddy winked in response and grabbed Sheryl's arm dragging her away just as Ruth blushed deeply at the latest insult.

"Let's go, let's go, honey," Buddy said. "They'll think we got lost, and it's your party, for God's sake. Let's leave those two love birds alone."

"God, I almost forgot!" Sheryl squealed. "Let's go, let's go," and now she, in turn, pulled him away. Buddy quickly reached for Ruth's hand, being pulled away, and, ceremoniously, kissed it.

"You sure are a hell of a beautiful woman. I don't know where this moron found you, but just in case he…Hope to see you again soon," he yelled as Sheryl tugged at him, blowing kisses at Whitman and Ruth, almost knocking down the waiter, who, with his full cart, was on the way to the kitchen to pack up the food.

As soon as the crowd had swallowed them, Whitman, who had been smiling after them, turned instantly serious when he looked at Ruth, who, crestfallen and seething, crumpled her napkin and would not look at him.

Sheryl's skill at being insulting had taken her wholly off guard. She had not expected such personal attacks from someone as stunning and seemingly gracious as that. Whitman put his hand on hers.

"Don't let Sheryl bother you. She's a knockout but she's an airhead. I don't know much about you, but from all that I do know, you are the bravest, most exceptional woman I know, and she couldn't tie your shoes. Honest."

"Thank you," Ruth whispered, looking up, her cheeks still flushed from Sheryl's insulting prattle. Having had to learn to survive in a world utterly broken, she had learned quickly that people were not kind and that she had to fight every step of the way just to stay alive. She was no stranger to insults or arguments and could hold her own in a crowd battling for food or clothing, but she had not expected such an attack on her in a setting as elegant and merry and seemingly civil as this.

"I'm so sorry," Whitman said into her thoughts. "You mustn't let someone like this make you feel bad. She's a spoiled brat who just rattles on and on, and I don't understand for the world of me why he would want to marry her." He laughed, suddenly. "Can you imagine living with her every day of your life?"

Ruth could only gradually let go of her thoughts, but the last question did penetrate her absorption, and she smiled.

"God, no," she said, and then, "Poor Buddy," and, finally, she laughed. She would have to forget about the affronts. She would have to let them go. She would have to try and get back to where she had been before that platinum beauty, so empty and thoughtless, had come to the table. This was her night, a special, wonderful night. She should be happy and laugh and enjoy it and remember every moment, because it might not come again.

Almost visibly, she shook away her dismay. She even brushed back her hair and sat up straighter as if to signal her mind that she was done with it. Her hand brushed against the dahlia.

"Do you think the dahlia looks silly?" she asked, suddenly self-conscious.

Whitman looked at her, deeply moved.

"You have no idea how beautiful you are. Here are all these women," he waved his hand as if to invite her to follow his look, "and they need all these baubles to make themselves look better. And here you are, so young and fresh and beautiful…" He did not finish, just looked at her as if he could not understand in the least how she could possibly ask such a question. The compliment made Ruth blush.

"I feel like Cinderella," she said. "Exactly like Cinderella. Come the stroke of midnight…" She didn't finish, but she smiled. It was all right. Everything was all right. At the stroke of midnight, she'd go back to the attic room. And that was all right.

"But for now, I will do what Cinderella did at the ball—I'll just be happy."

"Good for you," he said. "And since you are bent on being happy, I have something for you."

He reached into his coat pocket and leaned closer.

"I've been waiting for this all night." His face was bright with anticipation. "I will give you something. Something very important. But you may only briefly peek at it. Show no surprise. Just put it, as if it were nothing, into your purse. Can you do that?"

Ruth held his gaze and nodded. He took a folded piece of paper out of his coat pocket and handed it to her. She looked at him, puzzled. Carefully, she unfolded it, but not all the way. She peeked inside. The words 'Transit Visa' sprung out at her and the whole of her body jolted. When she looked at him, her eyes were bright with gratitude. Calmly, she slipped the visa into her dress and into her bra at which Whitman raised his eyebrows and grinned, making her laugh.

24

Revelation

After dinner, they retreated to a quiet lounge for a drink. Whitman put some coins into the jukebox and asked her to dance. Since his foot was in a cast, they were barely moving. But that did not matter to either one of them. The slower they moved, the closer he held her.

"Where you happily married?" he whispered into her ear. She shrugged.

"I think we were happy enough."

"Happy enough? Didn't you love him?"

"Of course, I loved him. Would I marry him if I didn't love him?"

"I wouldn't put it past you. If he needed you, you might. Sometimes, love and need are indistinguishable. I know all about that."

"You do?" she murmured, lulled by the food and the drink and the music, her face buried in his shoulder, taking full advantage of his warmth. She had needed just such a shoulder for a long time. And she had banned from her mind, just for this moment, all thoughts of Hannah and the children and the attic room and her abominable poverty of which there seemed no end.

For just this one evening, she would not think of troublesome things. For this one evening, she would simply be happy. He might never ask her out again. She might live in that attic room forever. Things might never get better. For breakfast, there would be shaved corn, and for lunch, stale bread with magarine and a little sugar on top. She might never have another dress and would be condemned to fill buckets with rubble to the end of her days because there seemed no end to bombed buildings. But for now, she had this shoulder and the attention of this very kind and very charming man, and she would just give herself over to the feeling. So what that the American women were more elegant than she was. So what that they looked down on her. She too used to be elegant. She used to make her own hats, the more outrageous and elegant they were, the better. She was tall and slender and beautiful, and men used to turn their heads in the streets and stare at her. She used to go dancing in Berlin, with all her girlfriends, fussing over her hair and her dress and her shoes like all young women did, and, most always, two or three men ran in her direction to ask her to dance.

Even as she sat with Whitman at the dinner table or danced with him in the lounge, men stared at her openly, and it felt good, being looked at. It was wonderful to see their pleasure over her and the smiles in their eyes. But more than these looks, it felt good to have Whitman hold her ever tighter, as if he were afraid that the lure of admiration might tempt her to leave him.

She drank in the boisterous gaiety of the club as if it were Nirvana itself. The longer the evening wore on, the more she felt at home in her new surroundings, and the less she wanted to think of what was outside the walls of this Eden. And so she hesitated when he asked her why she had married and whether or not she had loved her husband. That moment, she did not want to talk about her life, about the past. She just wanted to be held, to dance, to drink in the music, the atmosphere, the laughter, shutting out the images of years of deprivation, of bombed houses, of scrounging for food, of going through piles of old clothing. His questions reminded her of things she did not want to think about, as if, by not thinking of them, she could make them go away.

But then he said, "Love and need are most certainly cousins. I have asked myself a thousand times why I asked Lillian to marry me. I mean, we are about as unlike as an apple and a pear. But I needed her. I was being shipped to Hell, and not to have a connection to back home, leaving my youth behind, as it were, I could not bear that. I think that's what happened. I mean, the thought of marrying someone like Lillian had never even occurred to me before." He laughed. "So you see, I needed her. And it is absolutely beyond me why she said yes. And in this, we were very much alike, your husband and me. We were both being shipped off to Hell, whether we liked it or not."

"He didn't like it," she murmured. "He wanted to open a carpenter's shop."

"Let's sit down," he said.

She hesitated, not wanting to let go of him, not wanting to let go of his warmth, of the slow turning, the music, the having been lulled into a kind of sleepy, lazy happiness. But then she let go of him, and when she did, she felt cold, suddenly, away from his body, and the coldness was sobering.

He took her hand and, hobbling, led her back to their small table. The bartender came up and asked whether they wanted another drink. Ruth shook her head.

"A cup of coffee, maybe?" she asked Whitman.

"Make that two," Whitman said. The bartender took the empty glasses away and emptied the ashtray and wiped the table in a gesture that signaled to her that her journey to Eden was nearly over. She sat quietly, with her hands folded. Whitman studied her face that was, suddenly, sad.

"Did I say something wrong?" he asked.

She looked up, utter disbelief in her eyes.

"You? You could never say anything wrong. This has been so wonderful. So wonderful!" She shook her head as if she could not believe this evening had actually happened. "No. I was thinking of him. And my head's too cloudy to think it all through. Why did I marry him? Because that's what people do. They marry, and no one tells them that they should wait for the right person to come along. I mean, they say it, but they never tell you just how to recognize the right person when he—or she—comes along. And if you haven't ever been in love before, how would you know what that feels like? Besides, I wanted to be a travel writer. My mother said, don't be a fool. Here is this hard-working man who would walk on fire for you. What are you waiting for? Archangel Gabriel? But, I said to her, I don't think I love him. She said, love is a myth. And the closer it came to my wedding day, the worse I felt."

"And you couldn't just tell him that you wanted out?"

She shook her head. "Everyone had already conspired to see us married and everyone seemed so much wiser than I. Finally, I thought I was just scared. Of marriage."

"What was he like?"

"He was wonderfully skilled with his hands. He once made a swing for Penelope out of oak with wonderfully smooth braces and finials. No, he didn't like going to war. He hated it. He had dreamed of this shop since he was a little boy. And he was scared. But he was also patriotic, and the thought of not going never occurred to him. As it did not to you either."

She stopped when the bartender put the coffee cups on the table, neatly arranged the sugar dish and creamer, and left again. "He lived around the corner. So I knew him all my life. Like a brother. Besides, how do you say no to a man who's about to go off to war?"

"It's very simple," Whitman said, "you say, I don't want to marry you."

"I couldn't do that. I thought if he dies, at least he'll die happy."

"And? Did he die happy?"

Ruth sadly shook her head.

"He killed himself."

She had herself never seen the incident. The police officer who came to the attic room told her. But the scene became edged in her mind as if she had witnessed it, the picture of a train thundering into a station, and the dashing young officer who jumped toward it and disappeared beneath it.

Whitman stared at her, horrified. "But why?"

She shook her head. "I don't know."
"Let's get out of here," he said.

25

Heartaches, Great and Small

They drove down to the Rhine River and sat in a quiet meadow. The night was clear and warm, the sky full of stars. Silently, they sat arm in arm watching the moon rise from beyond the river, sculpting gradually, out of the darkness, the grotesquely broken city whose jagged shapes pierced the night sky.

"We were married," Whitman said, "two days before I shipped out. Nine months later, Alex came. I've seen him exactly six times. She is very good at writing and telling me what he's up to."

He was silent for a moment, looking up at the stars.

"But I know nothing about him. Nothing. The war has seen to that."

Ruth studied the moon.

"The war has seen to so many things."

"A little boy like this doesn't understand," Whitman said. "After my last leave home, I sat on the plane, replaying a scene over and over in my mind. A man in a uniform rings the doorbell to an elegant home. A little boy instantly opens it. The man squats down and puts his hands on the boy's shoulder. Hi, little guy, he says. He gives the boy a bear hug, and the child puts his arms around his neck. Hi, daddy, he says. But the sharing of affection is awkward for both of them, and the man's wife, who stands in the door now, in a business suit and heavily bejeweled, is aware of it. The man raises up and kisses her cheek, grinning. He's grown so much, he says. And she says, kids sort of do that."

As if to take the edge of the emotions that welled up in him, wanting to remind himself of the present, he turned to her and kissed her cheek. Lightly, Ruth stroked his arm to let him know that she understood.

"It's better that he knows you love him. The little he knows is still better than no love at all. He'll find a way to love you," Ruth said.

"God, Ruth," he said, "why is it that the world has a tendency to put all its energy behind a madman?"

She shrugged. "If I knew that, I'd be God."

They were silent for awhile. The river gurgled by just as silently and soothingly. In the peaceful night, it seemed absurd that there could've ever been madmen and war.

"When he found us," she said into the sky full of stars, "after the war, he said that he had received a groin injury. That's why we couldn't make love. Somewhere in that great war he had contracted some venereal disease that couldn't be cured."

"Whoa!" Whitman said. "Nice guy!"

"When they told me he had killed himself, I was furious. Not because of the women, but he had just deprived me and the children of his ration card. They don't issue ration cards to dead people. Eva didn't speak until she was three. The first word she said was 'Hungry.' And I hated him for that."

Whitman untangled his arm from hers and put it around her shoulder, holding her tight. And so they sat, looking out over the river and over the ruins of the city that were softened by the light of the moon and, now and then, they looked up and studied the cold stars.

"She was smarter than I," he said after awhile. "She knew we'd never make it. While I dropped bombs in the Pacific, she opened up a jewelry business, and as soon as the war was over, she put in for a divorce."

26

Enlightenment

I looked up, stunned. So it had not been my father who had initiated their break-up, but my mother. And if that was true, I had accused him of something he had not done. The light in the room had grown dim as I sat reading. Beyond the glass wall of the house, dark clouds had gathered in the sky, and it looked as if it might rain.

At some point, Penelope had turned on the lamp beside my chair. I nodded gratefully, not wanting to stop reading. She lit candles on the fireplace mantle and went outside. I heard an odd shuffling I didn't recognize and then the garage door closed with a rumble. I realized that she had moved the boxes inside the garage to protect them from the rain. I thought that I should have gone to help, but I could hear her in the kitchen then, the soft clinking of dishes coming from there as if she were straightening up after our lunch or maybe she was even cooking. I checked my watch. It was nearly five. I thought that I should not wear out my welcome. But I had no desire to go home.

As if she had sensed that I had put the pages down, she came out, wiping her hands on a tea towel. The light coming from the kitchen behind her gave her a kind of aura. There was something comforting and familiar about her. Maybe it was simply because she came out of the kitchen, such a familiar, nurturing place, wiping her hands on the tea towel as if she had been cooking. I smiled at her through my dull ache but my smile must have been crooked, because she asked.

"What?"

"Do you know when exactly my parents were divorced?"

She shook her head. "What I wrote is all I know. I've had to piece things together from the many fragments she told me during our good moments. But it's really all I know."

"So it is possible that they were no longer married when he finally came home?"

"It's possible. But wouldn't there be a divorce decree somewhere?"

I hadn't thought of that. Of course, there would be.

"Glenn Forster might know. He probably does know."

"And he is?"

"My father's lawyer. But if he knew, why didn't he tell me?"

"He probably thought you knew."

"That's true. But right now I don't feel too bright. You have no idea how many times I wanted to reach out to him, to hug him. I mean, somewhere inside I loved him. Or I wanted to love him. I wanted to jump over that shadow or whatever it was and just forget about it, let it go, throw it away, but I couldn't do it. And every time I had a chance to ask him, I decided against it. As if I didn't want to know. Which makes no sense."

"Yes, it does. You were only eleven, and it was all you knew. Like every child, you wanted perfect parents. What's wrong with that? I mean, when I realized that my mother was flawed—I mean, she was human—I took the responsibility on my own skinny little shoulders. I thought that if I had been a better child, she wouldn't hate me. Only it made no difference. I think it took me thirty years to finally admit that she was human and not some goddess on a pedestal. So, of course, you wanted him to be perfect. Who else would you look up to? To a hypocrite? Because that's who you thought he was."

"You are so wise," I said, because she was. "Is this what growing up in an attic room after a war does to someone?" I smiled at her. "Make you wise and insightful?"

She blushed. "I don't know about that. But I do know that it took me many years to cut through the guilt and the anger and the disappointments. It's the hardest thing I've ever done. Cutting through to what's true and what's not. I think I was a perfectly loveable child…"

"I can see that," I interjected, but she continued unperturbed, "…and her anger at me was unjust. Plain and simple. Sometimes, she just lost it, like we all do. Now whether or not I can forgive her for that, I don't know yet. I don't think I can. Because I don't think I deserved some of her words. But I'm working on it."

"It's a very odd and strangely moving experience," I said, leafing through the manuscript, "to have my father come alive to me in these pages. To see him when he was young. I never thought of him as young. In many ways, he's a complete stranger. And at the same time, the giving of the chocolates reminds me of that he was also very generous. With his time, with his knowledge, with money. There is so much I want to ask you and share with you about what you have written. But listen. Were you, maybe, cooking in there?" I nodded toward the kitchen.

She shook her head, smiling. "That's something I try to avoid at all cost. I've always hated to cook."

"How'd you manage when you were married?"

"It was one of the great sacrifices I made to the altar of marriage." She smirked. "Maybe that's why he left. He hated my cooking. And love, in a man, is supposed to go through the stomach, or?"

She had me laughing. "True," I said. "I mean, lunch was delicious, so you must've learned something. But I thought that I might keep you from further torture and take you out to dinner if you'd let me and if you don't have any other plans."

She raised her arms wide as a gesture of total freedom, and I said, "Good. Where can we go?" I motioned to the outside where there seemed nothing but hills, meadows, and farms.

"I know a lovely little place, actually. It's not far from here. Want to go around eight?"

"Great. Then I can keep on reading." I thought it over. "But this must be awfully boring for you, sitting here while I read."

"Actually, it's a test."

"A test?"

She nodded gravely. "Of my writing. No one's ever seen this before. I've worked on it for so long that I've lost all sense of whether or not it's any good. So I need to know whether or not it's good enough to send out into the world. And your reactions will tell me that. So, it's a test. A trade off. My story for your reactions."

"Really?"

"Really."

"I'm a guinea pig?"

She nodded. I could have gone on bantering with her for some time, but I said: "Off to the kitchen with you, woman." When she didn't move, I shot her a sidelong glance. "Well?"

I asked.

"I'm going to sit here and watch your face."

Just why I felt happy then, I couldn't say, but I turned my attention back to the manuscript, and she took up her pencil and her clip board and turned on the lamp beside her chair, and I fed her the pages I had read. And so we sat in perfect harmony, reading and correcting, as the sky outside grew darker, and the lamplight cozier and the candles flickered in the breeze that came through the open windows.

27

True Friends

Two days after Whitman had given her the visa, Ruth left for Berlin. Hannah had insisted on taking her to the station, but when they got up, at four, the children slept so sweetly and soundly, they did not have the heart to wake them, and Hannah stayed behind. Ruth liked this just fine. Not that she told Hannah, but what she did not want or need was for Hannah to cry and lament at the station. She just wanted to get to Berlin, get Pauli, and head back on the very next train. She did not think it was necessary to pack much but her raincoat and a fresh blouse, and, just in case she'd have to stay the night, a fresh pair of underwear. She'd wear slacks, and she packed a loaf of the bread Hannah had brought home.

Whitman had offered to make arrangements for her to use the American troop train that regularly ran between East and West, transporting American personnel. But she would have had to wait another day, and the news on the battered radio had become more and more urgent. The Russians were up to something. They were not happy with the currency reform the Allies had suggested to get the German economy back on its feet.

Ruth shared the compartment with two young American soldiers, Rob Wilson, a stout fellow, and John Stettman, a tall and wiry one. Specialists in airplane hydraulics, they had, only the night before, received orders to get to Berlin as soon as they could get there.

Happy over their pretty travel companion, who even spoke English, the soldiers offered Ruth chocolates, sodas, cigarettes, and soon the compartment reverberated with laughter as they shared stories of their childhood, determined to avoid, at all cost, things connected to war, destruction, and madmen. But their youthful enthusiasm grew quiet when the train rolled into Berlin.

Ruth's eyes filled with tears as the panorama of devastation moved by the train's window like a film.

"What a beautiful city this was," she said. "I used to take the train from my village—my friends and I, and we used to come up here to dance. An aunt of mine lived here, and an uncle, and we could stay there. We'd get all dressed up..."

The soldiers watched her with compassion. Stettman decided that logic was the only way to console someone so dreadfully sad.

"It was necessary!" he said softly. By which he meant the bombing of the city. Ruth couldn't help but smile at this brave, masculine attempt at nurture, and Wilson tried to lighten up the sudden change of mood even further.

"Don't worry," he said. "They'll build it up again in no time. You know those Germans. Work, work, work, and work. Like a beehive."

Ruth shot him a grateful smile but the sadness remained. When she was eighteen or nineteen, war and politics were as far from her mind as they were with most everyone of that age. She often thought that she should have been more vigilant, should have read the paper more, should have listened to the radio. Instead, she went shopping with her girlfriends and they'd eat out or went to the theater and to the movies. They studied the latest fashion in clothes and shoes and which hair-do was in and which was out. They laughed and gossiped and giggled, being young, and now she felt as if a whole lifetime had passed, and there was no way she could ever get back to where she once was. She remembered that she had been equally mindless as a young mother and a bride. One day she stood happily in her garden, taking the wash off the line, and the next moment, she heard the sirens and bombs started falling, and she ran to get the children and ran and ran to get away from the bombs.

The train discharged only a handful of travelers, among them Ruth and the soldiers. The terminal was crowded and filled with the urgent and agitated din of anxious voices. As Ruth and the soldiers made their way out of the terminal, a constant stream of anguished passengers hurried into it. Ruth, observing the onslaught of people, became apprehensive.

"I want to check on trains," she said to the soldiers. "I do need to get back home today."

She pointed to a sign that read "Tickets and Information," and they fought their way to it. Beneath the sign, a man in his thirties leaned against the wall. He supported himself on a pair of crutches that didn't match. One was metal, the other wood. He carried a backpack similar to Ruth's that he used to cushion his back against the wall.

Watching the crowd with melancholy detachment and a slight ironic smile, his resigned, wandering glance fell on Ruth's troubled face. A brief flicker of wonder came into his eyes as she came closer. She had her eyes on the sign and did not immediately see him. She was almost on top of him when, somewhat amused, he said:

"They closed it in wise foresight. They didn't want you to leave this paradise. And they certainly do not want to give you any information."

"What happened?"

"You are obviously not from Europe. We are going to have us a little blockade. More like blockheads, actually."

"Today? Already?"

"Tonight, I heard."

Ruth stared at him horrified. He shrugged and grinned as she kept staring at him, her mind racing.

"Do you know for sure?"

He shook his head.

"Rumors. That's all we have."

"But that would be awful."

"I know," he said, smiling broadly now.

On the way out, Ruth translated for the soldiers what the man had said, but Wilson and Stettman were just as much at a loss as to what was going on. All they knew was that they were to report to Templehof Airport on the double, and that usually meant that there were a bunch of planes to get ready to take off to someplace.

They said good-bye outside the station, and while Ruth headed toward a bus stop, having no idea if busses were even running, the soldiers headed toward a Jeep waiting for them at the curb. She had barely arrived at the bus stop when, inadvertently looking up, she caught Wilson, arms urgently flailing, running toward her.

"He said he'd take you," he said, smiling broadly, pointing at the Jeep's driver.

"Are you sure?"

"Yes, yes. We asked him, and he doesn't mind."

A little hesitant she followed Wilson to the Jeep. She had herself no idea just where Martha now lived, and Berlin was a big city. She shook hands with the driver who grinned from ear to ear.

"Jeff Carter," he said.

He was a little older than the others and seemed perennially unruffled and smiling.

"Hop in," he said.

Wilson and Stettman climbed into the back seat while Ruth pulled out an envelope with Martha's address and showed it to Carter. He grinned, shrugged, and patted the seat beside him for Ruth to get in. She did, and he took off, spinning his wheels to impress Ruth, and everybody else for that matter.

28

A Witch with A Broom

As they made their way through the bombed city, Carter stopped now and then and held the envelope out to passing pedestrians. Their first reaction was fear at the sudden appearance of a Jeep with soldiers in uniform. But realizing that they only wanted directions, the pedestrians couldn't do enough explaining, pointing, and being accommodating. Carter finally turned into a quiet residential street, nearly deserted, on the outskirts of town.

The street was wide and roomy and lined with high old trees. Elaborate villas, built at the turn of the century and exuding affluence, stood as proudly and serenely as if there had never been a war. The affluence was punctuated by the abundance of bright flowers spilling over ornate wrought iron fences. The street and the homes were not unlike those that had been confiscated by the Americans and that Ruth had walked through in her pursuit to sell the silverware. Only here, flags with the Soviet Red Star had been affixed to this or that door. Carter slowed down to a crawl so that Ruth could make out the house numbers, but looking down the street, she said: "There!" and pointed to a woman who was sweeping the sidewalk.

"The woman?" Carter asked.

"Yes."

The Jeep roared toward her and stopped with flair exactly parallel to the curb. The woman whirled around, saw three American soldiers in a

Jeep and was about to flee. But recognizing Ruth, her mouth dropped open, and she froze. The woman looked well fed though her face seemed perennially bitter and gray.

"Hello, Martha," Ruth said.

29

Pauli

On the front steps of the house, hidden from Ruth's view, sat Pauli, five years old. She was dressed in a bathing suit and tried her best to put a dress on a cat. At the sound of the Jeep's squealing brakes, she looked up, startled. The cat instantly sensed the opportunity, tore itself out of its torturer's arms, and raced for cover. Pauli stood up to get a better look over some tall shrubs, saw Ruth, jumped down the steps, and raced to the gate.

"Aunt Ruth! Aunt Ruth!"

Ruth, climbing out of the Jeep, turned toward the voice and burst into tears as the child came flying toward her. A joyous "Pauli!" escaped her as she scooped the little girl up in her arms and covered the little face and head with kisses. The soldiers, deeply moved, avoided looking at each other. Wordlessly, they collaborated instead to staring severely at Martha who, holding on to the broom, didn't dare move.

Pauli freed herself from Ruth's embrace and looked up and down the street.

"Where's Mommy?"

"She couldn't come, sweet thing! She sent me instead to take you home. Tell you what, let me introduce you to these nice gentlemen here, and then I'll explain everything."

Ruth took her to the Jeep, and proudly said:

"My niece, Pauli."

The soldiers smiled and extended their hands, which the little girl shook without the least self-consciousness. Ruth reached for her bag.

"Thank you. Thank you so very much."

Carter looked at her doubtfully. "I think we should wait right here and take you back to the station."

"No. You've done enough already." Ruth pointed to a bus stop a few yards away, but it was obvious that the soldiers didn't trust Martha who observed everything with utter distaste.

"We don't mind waiting," Stettman said. But Ruth shook her head.

"Meeting you was truly a gift. Truly. I never would've thought that getting here would be this easy. But you have done enough for me. I can manage from here."

Carter wrote something on a piece of paper and handed it to her.

"If there's trouble, call us. Tempelhof. Hydraulics' shop."

"I will. Thank you again."

Reluctantly, they took off as Ruth looked after them, smiling, waving. When they turned the corner, she turned to Martha who had regained her composure.

"What a pleasant surprise!" Martha said with a sour face.

"Pleasant, my foot! I'm the last person you wanted to see, Martha."

30

Inside the Witch's House

Ruth and Pauli had walked into a large and elegant foyer that opened into an immense living room, furnished exclusively in eighteenth century antiques. Ruth, impressed, let out an admiring whistle.

"Well, aren't we ever fancy?" she said.

Martha shrugged, trying to downplay the trimmings of wealth. "The Russians insist that we stay here. Karl is absolutely vital to them as an interpreter. Besides…"

But Ruth interrupted her. "Besides, he's probably joined the Communist Party as he joined the Nazi Party. We know all about Karl, don't we? Karl has always known on which side the bread is buttered."

"I forbid you to talk like this about my husband."

Pauli watched the exchange fearfully and finally reached for Ruth's hand trying to pull her toward a hallway.

"Let's get me dressed, Aunt Ruth! Come on, Aunt Ruth! This way. My room is this way."

Ruth squatted down.

"Can you get dressed by yourself, honey? I do need to talk to your Grammy for just a minute." But Pauli threw her arms around her and held on tight.

"What's wrong?" Ruth asked. "What's the matter?"

Pauli whispered loudly into her ear, "But then you'll leave without me."

"I would never do that."

But Pauli wouldn't budge.

"Mommy left without me, and Grammy says that she left because she didn't want me."

Ruth shot a contemptuous look at Martha.

"That's not true. She left because she was arrested and put in jail."

"Why?"

"Because she had no papers. But then she escaped and now she's free and she sent me to get you. Your Grammy just misunderstood. And I have no intention of leaving without you. So, how would you like to get dressed, and pack a few things you'd like to take, but not much, just what you can carry, and we'll be off. Oh, goodness!" she said, remembering the bribe which, it turned out, she didn't need after all, "I almost forgot! Your Mommy gave me a present for you."

Pauli's eyes were bright with anticipation as Ruth dug deep into the pack and pulled out the doll. Pauli screamed with delight as Martha, arms crossed, watched her exuberance with the greatest displeasure.

"For me?" Pauli screamed. "Just for me?"

"Of course, she's for you! Isn't she lovely? She's certainly not for your Grammy!"

Pauli smirked at that, and Martha had enough of all that coziness.

"Pauli," she said sharply, "go to your room and stay there until I call you."

Ruth shot Martha an incredulous look, while Pauli paid no attention to the woman whatsoever.

"She looks like a princess," the child tattled on. "I think I'll call her that. Princess. You think that's a pretty name?"

"It's perfect! Now how would you like to show Princess your room? Take my pack here with you. I can't leave without it, right?"

Pauli looked a little doubtful but nodded, finally. She let go of Ruth and tucked the doll under her arm. Reaching for one of the pack's straps, she dragged it, ever so slowly, toward a hallway and disappeared into a room.

Ruth looked after her, smiling. Martha, arms akimbo, could hardly contain her anger.

"You are not going to take that child anywhere!" she said, and before Ruth, still squatting down and looking after Pauli, could answer, Martha had resolutely walked away from her.

"Well, bitch," Ruth murmured, "I should've known this wouldn't be easy." Slowly, she got up and followed Martha.

31

True Caring

As the small scene unfolded in Martha's house, the Jeep with Carter, Wilson, and Stettman had gone around the block, heading toward their duty station. Suddenly, Carter stopped and turned to the others.

"You guys eager to check in?"

Wilson and Stettman shook their heads.

"I'm gonna head back," Carter said. "Circle a couple of times. I didn't like that bitch."

The two soldiers nodded vigorously, and Carter headed back to Martha's house.

32

Tales from the Past

Ruth walked into the kitchen just as Martha put something into a well-stocked icebox. She pointed to a glass on the table.

"For you," she said.

"You take a sip of it first," Ruth said.

"Don't be ridiculous!"

Ruth sat down at the table. As she drank, she scanned the kitchen that was roomy, well furnished, and immaculate. On the shelf of a cupboard was the picture of a stern looking, gray-haired man that Ruth studied contemptuously. Martha sat down as well, studied Ruth for a moment and, when Ruth's glance turned to her, said:

"I beg you, leave her here."

She spoke slowly and composed, but as the words came out, her eyes filled with tears. Ruth shook her head. But Martha was not deterred.

"Since Ralph's been arrested," she said, "I have no one."

Now her tears fell freely. "Karl's always gone, and I can give Pauli everything. Everything. Hannah can't. I know she can't …"

"Ralph shouldn't have beat the Russian officer to a pulp," Ruth said, contemptuously, wholly unmoved by Martha's tears. "Ten years in Siberia will do him a world of good. Maybe he'll remember what he did to Hannah."

"Oh, come on," Martha said. The tears now stopped flowing. "They were young. He didn't mean to hurt her. Come on! All young couples fight their way together, one way or another."

Ruth put her glass down hard.

"You mean getting a marriage license means that a husband may beat his wife black and blue every time he's drunk…or doesn't like the way she looks when she's pregnant?"

"My son…" Martha began, but Ruth interrupted her.

"Who cares about your son? Did any of you ever care about Hannah?"

Pauli, wearing shorts and a blouse, had made her way quietly along the wall of the hallway toward the kitchen. She held the doll, dragging Ruth's pack, which was quite bulky now, behind her. Waiting just out of sight, she hugged the doll tightly whenever the voices in the kitchen got loud.

In front of the house, the Jeep slowly passed Martha's house and turned at the next corner.

"Hannah is young," Martha said. "She can have more children. But I can't, and…"

"Martha, there are thousands of children who have no parents after this war. They have no home. There are no orphanages, and what there was has been bombed. They dig in the garbage for food. They go bare-foot because there are no shoes…" Agitated, Ruth got up. "If you want a child, there are thousands that need you."

"But I don't want a child like that," Martha said, belligerently. "I want Pauli. She is my own flesh and blood and…"

"Fine! It was just a suggestion. If you don't want one of these children, that's your privilege. But you can't have Pauli."

Martha jumped up, now desperate. "Listen! I have money! How much do you want? I know you guys are poor. You can buy things for your own kids. Why worry about Pauli? She has everything here. Worry about your own kids. I know what things are like in the West."

She ran over to a kitchen cabinet, knelt down, ripped the door open and rummaged inside, pulling out a large pot which she brought to the table. She opened the lid, startling Ruth. The pot was filled with American dollars that Martha now took out by the handfuls and held pleadingly out to Ruth.

Ruth took a step backward, disgusted.

"I beg you!" Martha pleaded. "Please! Have pity on an old woman who is all alone, who only wants the best for her grandchild."

Ruth shook her head scornfully, turned, and walked toward the door. This gesture brought about a complete change in Martha.

"Hold it right there, Miss Righteous!" she screamed. "Let's call a spade a spade. Your sister abandoned her child. Here. Here with me. She left that camp and headed west without her. She never gave that child a thought. And now she's mine. Mine!"

Ruth, already at the door, froze and turned. She took a step toward Martha and slapped her hard. At the sound of the slap, Pauli winced, then smiled a very small smile.

Ruth's voice was cold as ice. "You bitch! You were going to let her die in that miserable camp, you miserable old hag, you."

Martha rubbed her cheek with eyes full of hatred, her right hand clutching American dollars.

"Oh, what's the point," Ruth said. "Hannah was right. It's not worth it."

Once again, she headed toward the door.

"You're not going to get away with that!" Martha yelled. "We'll sic the whole Russian army on you! You're not gonna get out of Berlin with her, I promise you that! Karl's got connections, and…"

Ruth turned back, surveying all of Martha's miserable figure.

"I'm not afraid of you, Martha Hiller. I have never been afraid of the likes of you, though, Heaven help me, I should be. I've been through hell and come out the other side, and nothing, not you, not Karl, not the whole damn Russian army can stop me from taking that child home to Hannah. And you, you bitch, can go to hell."

She was about to walk out when Martha attacked her from behind. But Ruth was younger and stronger. She freed herself from Martha's claws that had dug into her shoulder. Fueled by indignation and fury, she gave her a violent push. Martha stumbled backwards and fell hard.

Ruth, running out of the kitchen, almost stumbled over Pauli who was dissolved in tears. But Ruth couldn't deal with that now. She merely picked up the child and the pack and ran out of the house, Martha's fury, loud and vengeful, following their exit.

"You're are not gonna get ten yards with her…the police…the whole Russian army…You gonna rot in Siberia the rest of your life…"

But Ruth opened the front door, not bothering to close it, and ran down the stairs and into the street and kept on running, with the child in her arms.

The Jeep passed the house just as Ruth ran out, but the tall shrubs hid her from view, and the soldiers did not see her. They passed the house slowly, turned at the next corner, and Carter said:

"We best head to the base, guys. I expect the Soviets here any minute. We aren't even supposed to be in this area."

Stettman and Wilson consulted with their eyes, encouraging one another to speak up.

"Maybe one more time, Sarge?" Wilson asked.

Carter did not answer, but at the next corner, to Stettman's and Wilson's great relief, he turned right as if going around the block one more time. They ran into Ruth at the next block. When the Jeep roared toward her out of the side street, Ruth instinctively pulled Pauli close to her. Recognizing the soldiers, the whole of her body slumped with relief and she let go, for just an instant, of the strain of that last hour.

33

Dead End

The street in front of the station was even more crowded now than when she arrived. Carter brought the Jeep to one of his elegant stops and Wilson and Stettman helped Ruth and Pauli out.

Spontaneously, Ruth hugged each of her Good Samaritans and looked after them wistfully when they pulled out. When they turned to wave, she smiled brightly for their sake, but as she made her way into the terminal, she turned somber. She had barely entered the station, when she found, horrified, the whole of it crammed with people packed like sardines. For an instant, she felt panicky. She picked up the child and turned, expecting the roar of the tanks and trucks of the Russian army pulling up behind her. But then she bravely dove into the crowd with the child in her arms, working her way to the edge of the frantic mass of humanity, pushing her way ever so slowly until she reached the ticket and information office.

When she got there—the door was still closed—a hand reached up as if from the ground and tugged at her slacks. Startled, she looked down and recognized the melancholy man with the crutches to whom she had talked when she got off the train earlier that day. Pleased at seeing one another, both spoke at the same time.

"Fancy meeting you here."

"What are you doing here?"

"Legs finally gave out," he smiled.

He had made himself comfortable on the narrow stoop, cradling his crutches and his pack. He looked utterly exhausted, but his eyes were bright with pleasure at seeing her. As they talked, people shoved and knocked against Ruth in their desperate attempt to get close to the train tracks.

Pauli studied the man with the sincere fascination of children confronted with an infirmity. Arno smiled at the child, then turned his attention to his legs. Moving his good leg off the stoop, he grabbed the other with both hands and bent it close to his body. He patted the small space he had created.

"Make yourself at home. By the way, I'm Arno von Hesse."

"Ruth Karstens," Ruth said as she put the child into the space he had made and then stood protectively in front of her.

"I'm surprised they haven't sent the Army yet," Arno said, unsuspectingly. Ruth stared at him wide-eyed.

"The Army?"

"Of course! The Soviets hate nothing more than crowds. Particularly, crowds with freedom on their minds."

Ruth shot him a quick but absent smile. Her mind was working furiously. For a moment, she studied the crowd. It was obvious that those closest to the tracks were defending their positions vigorously.

"I absolutely have to get out today. I just have to," she said. But that seemed more and more unlikely as she watched the mayhem.

Arno grinned. "You could. If you had a First Class ticket."

"A First Class ticket?"

He nodded and pointed with his thumb in the direction of where the train would be headed.

"They have a whole VIP area staked out over there. Hardly anybody there. I checked it out earlier. Problem is, the ticket office is closed, and they won't even let you get close to that place without a first class ticket. I mean, I'd have hocked everything I have." He shrugged. "But."

Ruth's face lit up.

"Let's go."

"You have a first class ticket?"

"No. But I have money."

"Not me, dear lady. I'm washed up."

Ruth picked up Pauli who, fearful of the mad humming of the crowds and of being stuck in a very tight place between a door, her aunt, and a strange man, had been clutching her doll with one arm and hung on for dear life to Ruth's leg with the other.

Ruth pulled at Arno's arms to pull him up.

"We may need you. Let's go. We don't give up around here. Who knows, someone might take pity on you and give you an advantage. So don't you give up."

"Pity?" he asked, incredulously.

Ruth frowned. "So what? If it gets you out of here, what does a little pity matter? Take your crutches, man, and…"

Arno burst out laughing and struggled to get up as the rest of Ruth's words were carried away by the roar of a train that raced into the station. All heads flew into the direction of that sound and pandemonium broke out. Arno and Ruth pressed close to the door, their only protection from being swept away or trampled to death by the frenzied forward surge of the people.

The train was crowded to bursting. Those trying to get off struggled desperately to achieve that feat as those trying to board desperately fought their way on. But the train was already moving again, slowly, then faster. The angry roar of the crowd swelled to a single mad crescendo as the train moved faster and faster out of sight.

Ruth and Arno waited until the agitated crowd had settled down once more into its inevitable waiting before they began their excruciatingly slow journey along the station buildings to the area down the tracks which had been roped off for the more affluent passengers.

34

Compassion

Back in Wiesbaden, Ted Whitman grew more and more concerned about the political situation. The possibility of war lay in the air. The Russians were dead-set against a major German currency reform. They had begun to make preparation to cut off the East. Hannah was troubled all that day. Some time in the afternoon, Whitman rang the bell at Mrs. Garske's apartment door. The strain of having negotiated five flights of stairs with his cast was written on his face when Mrs. Garske opened the door. Recognizing him, her demeanor became instantly forbidding and hostile. Having seen her only a few times and never having spoken to her, he was, at first, a bit startled at her expression, as she had never seemed to him antagonistic. But he had seen such expressions on the faces of other people he dealt with: he was, to her, the enemy, and for her tenants to engage in any a kind of dealing with him was more than she could handle.

"Hello," he said cheerfully, in spite of her obvious repugnance, "I've come to see Mrs. Hiller."

But Mrs. Garske made no motion to open the door further to let him in. She merely regarded him impertinently from head to toe and was about to retreat and, he assumed, slam the door in his face as if she had enough of his repeated visits and she was determined to put an end to them.

Whitman put his free hand on the door to prevent her from closing it, studying her frankly and sincerely. Even with his cast, he was much stronger than that sinewy, skinny creature, and it was almost laughable that she actually thought she could keep him from seeing Hannah. But then something happened that made him change his mind about her adversity to him as an American officer: she threw a quick, almost imperceptible look at the bag full of groceries that he carried, and then he understood. Much like Hannah and Ruth, she too was dependent on the meager handouts from the relief center which provided just enough to keep one from starving. The few staples that had begun to appear in the stores were to be had only with the ration cards and money, if one had it. She must have looked upon the wealth of food that her poor tenants suddenly enjoyed with a great deal of envy and resentment.

Whitman reached into the bag, got out a can of soup, and put it into her hand. Mrs. Garske was so surprised, she looked at the can and then at him as if she couldn't quite understand just what had happened.

He reached into the bag again and put a can of something else into her other hand. Then he tucked some chocolates under her arm. He did all this with the greatest sincerity, while she stood as if turned to stone. Looking away from him and at the food in her hands, her eyes filled with tears that slowly ran down her cheeks. Whitman kindly stroked her arm, pushed the door open, passed her, and knocked on the door of the attic room.

Hannah, joyfully expectant, opened the door. Her expression changed quickly to one of disappointment and once again to joy at seeing him while the children clambered off the bed and came running to the door. Not at all shy, they threw their arms around him when he bent down to greet them which greatly moved him. Hannah smiled at the scene, but her eyes were troubled. Whitman handed the bag of groceries to the children who dug into it immediately and piled everything, laughing and chattering, onto the table. He turned to Hannah.

"You didn't expect Ruth already, did you?"

Hannah shrugged.

"I didn't and I did. I know it's stupid, but…"

Whitman gave Hannah a consoling smile. "She's probably just now left Berlin. I have absolutely no clue when the trains run."

"I'm worried sick!"

"You're worried sick? What about me?" But he grinned as he said it. Consolingly, he took her hand.

"All's not lost yet. If she could get the child right away, there's a good chance for her to get out. Although and unfortunately, my unit goes on alert at six," he said, instantly frightening Hannah.

"Alert? Why? What happened?"

"Nothing yet. But the Soviets are planning something. That's confidential, of course."

Horrified, Hannah stared at him.

"If something happens to her, I don't know what I will do." Looking at the children, she smiled. "It would be ironic, wouldn't it? Here she's stuck with my child in the East, and I'm here with her children in the West."

"Let's hope all goes well. You will go to the station tonight, right?"

"Oh, of course. I don't know which train, but that doesn't matter."

"Sorry I can't take you."

"I can walk. I'd walk miles. I don't mind. I'll go again in the morning, and then again at night. The children like getting out, and they like the trains."

"What about work?"

"I told him the truth. His wife will help out. They are very good people. They understand. But if she isn't here in two days, I'll have to go back to work. I can take the children with me. The baker doesn't mind."

"Good." Whitman got up awkwardly. "Gotta go. Take care of yourself out there. Let's hope they won't keep us on alert too long. Then I can come and take you to the station. The kids might enjoy a ride in the Jeep."

Hannah smiled, but her eyes remained troubled. She saw him to the apartment door to say good-bye when Mrs. Garske's kitchen door opened ever so slightly and she stuck her gray head out.

"Madcher Whitmen," she said in her heavy Germany accent, "ssank you ferry much." Grinning, he gave her a mock salute.

35

The Great Escape

As they made their way along the station walls, Ruth stopped to put the doll into her pack so it would not be torn out of Pauli's arms. The crowd that seemed, at times, like the inner chambers of a beehive, was a constantly moving, pulling, pushing force of intensity. Only the head of the doll stuck out, because Pauli was afraid that it might suffocate if it were stuffed deep into the pack. As Ruth pushed her way through the masses, the doll's lids fluttered nervously and startled the people who came suddenly face to face with what seemed, at first glance, a child. Arno, who occasionally turned back at Ruth and saw the sudden shock on people's faces, laughed.

"You've become, unwittingly, a ghostly puppeteer," he shouted over the roar of the crowd.

"Me? Why?" she shouted back.

He shook his head. It would take too long to explain while shouting.

They finally made their way to an open area just beyond the station buildings alongside the tracks. There, a solid line of East German policemen and Russian soldiers kept a weary eye on the crowds within the station proper. Beyond the police line-up, a gravel area with benches had been created for VIP's and Russian officers. This haven was also crowded, but the people there displayed none of the hysteria and desperation of those within the station.

The people here were more elegantly dressed and their luggage was finer. Their faces were placid as if they were thoroughly disgusted with the inconvenience of it all while the policemen looked, throughout, brutal and indifferent.

A forced calm, brought on by the presence of soldiers and police, had infiltrated the fringes of the crowd that waited there. For awhile, Ruth observed the scene as if casually, careful not to make eye contact with either police or soldiers. It seemed impossible to break through the line of them, because a thick rope had been strung from the end of the building to a lamp post close to the tracks, and five policemen stood behind it, shoulder to shoulder.

Arno turned to her, the exhaustion of having made his way through mad crowds on his crutches was written in his face.

"Now what? Should I kiss one of those guys?"

Ruth thought it over.

"Can you fall?"

"Fall?" he asked, incredulously.

Ruth nodded vigorously. "If you could fall somehow on the other side of the rope," she mouthed.

Arno grinned, shrugged, and started wobbling. He dropped a crutch and clutched in faked helplessness at one of the policemen as he fell over the rope, taking the man with him to the ground.

Ruth feigned shock and cried out. All heads turned in their direction as some of the policemen drew their nightsticks and tore at Arno's arms to get him up. Arno, with surprising quickness slipped away from them, and rolled off the foot high concrete platform onto the tracks. Two of the policemen grabbed Ruth's arms to keep her from rushing to Arno, even though she was still behind the rope. Pauli, petrified, started screaming, and the roar of an approaching train spelled disaster.

Ruth, quick-minded, used the momentary loosening on her arms at the roar of the train to tear herself away and slip under the rope and rush to the tracks. She put Pauli down on the platform—the child became instantly hysterical—and jumped on the tracks herself to help Arno up. Two policemen towered over him, their nightsticks drawn, suspecting a trick even though one of the crutches had made it to the tracks with him.

The train's urgent whistle foiled their plan. They grabbed his arms instead to drag him off the tracks but his leg seemed caught. As they tore at him to get him up and themselves out of danger, a Russian officer bellowed a command that was audible even over the roar of the crowd, the hysterical child, and the persistent whistle of the train. Some soldiers sprang into action, jumped on the tracks, and pulled Arno and Ruth to safety. Lying on the gravel, Arno was badly shaken and so was Ruth who tried to help him up while Pauli, still hysterical, raised her arms to Ruth, sobbing uncontrollably. Arno raised his head.

"Good God, woman! You almost got me killed," he said calmly, a smile in his eyes, in all that commotion. But Ruth could not smile. Mournfully, she shook her head.

"I'm sorry. God, I never thought a train would come. I never," she mumbled, helping him as he struggled up while the illustrious passengers, soldiers, and policemen watched them disdainfully or suspiciously and no one lent a hand. Once again, the Russian officer bellowed a command, and the soldiers came to her aid and helped Arno on his feet and handed him his crutches.

The engineer, having seen the commotion on the tracks, had slowed the train to a crawl, and a hundred hands fingered its iron skin to get a hold somehow to climb on, but the train inched forward with its doors shut.

Ruth picked up Pauli. Her eyes searched for the helpful officer. She smiled, and for a moment, the two looked at each other over the crowd, and for a moment it was as if the madness that surrounded them was gone. For just a split second, a man and a woman looked at each other, their human-ness and their humane-ness, for just an instant, recognized, and if only by one another.

Then things happened very quickly. The train rolled in, the First Class coaches stopping just at the VIP area.

Ruth realized the opportunity as the rear door of the coach stopped right where she stood. She pulled Arno toward it without even thinking. Unsteady on his feet, he stumbled but as if she could command him to follow, she kept tugging, straining toward the door that was now opened from inside.

"Let's go! Let's go!" she shouted.

But the crowd inside the station proper now roared louder than the train. The policemen and soldiers had their hands full trying to hold back those from inside the station that strained to get to the First Class coaches. From the open windows, urgent voices fell down on everyone.

"We're full! Full! Full!" But someone reached out from inside the coach and pulled Ruth and the child inside. The crowd within the station, now desperate, crashed the police line and surged toward the coaches. Their force crushed people against the train.

Ruth, just inside the crammed coach, could not go further. She turned, the desperate fear of being crushed in her eyes and realized that Arno was helplessly pinned against the train just outside the door. More hands appeared from the inside and tugged at her clothes to pull her in further. She gave Pauli over to these hands and turned again and screamed.

"My husband! My husband!"

The cry was so heart wrenching, a large man who had been pushing from behind reached for Arno, nearly picking him up and stuffing him into the train behind Ruth, then pushed himself on. The hands inside the train now pulled Ruth up, when, seemingly from nowhere, a large contingent of East German police, their nightsticks drawn, started to pull people away from the coaches. The desperate forward push of the crowd ceased for an instant, and the large man pushed Arno into the train. But before he could squeeze himself on, the policemen pulled him away and slammed the door shut behind Arno.

36

A Precarious Haven

Ruth and Arno found themselves packed like sardines. Ruth reached for the sobbing Pauli who was being held by a kindly, elderly woman.

"Thank you. Thank you so very much."

"This is insane!" the woman said, smiling, as she handed Pauli over. Ruth turned around to Arno who was wedged between the door and herself. He was obviously in pain, but the admiration in his eyes was boundless.

"Thanks, hero," he said, making her smile. She shrugged.

"It worked, didn't it?" Arno could only stare at her. He shook his head, deeply moved, and his eyes filled with tears.

"Stop that!" she said. "You would've have done the same for me."

"I doubt it!" he said, raising one of his crutches to show her how useless he really was.

"If that's what you think," she said, "then that's what you'll be. And you know better. You just saved our lives because of those crutches."

The packed coach was incredibly hot in spite of the open windows. People fanned themselves with whatever was handy. Some moaned, at the verge of passing out. Voices close to Ruth and Arno called for more space that was miraculously provided though sparsely. Soon Ruth and Arno were able to sit on the steps of the coach, trying to get comfortable as best they could as the train moved faster and faster and left Berlin just as the sun went down.

Barely out of the city limits, it stopped. Alarmed, Ruth looked at Arno who shrugged. But something outside the coach door caught his attention, and he strained to see more clearly. Pauli, now feeling safe, was unfazed and played with her doll.

"Look!" Arno said.

A number of trucks were lined up on a nearby road. Some of the trucks were empty, but others carried soldiers who now scrambled out. The inside of the train came instantly alive.

"Russians! A whole army of them!"

Ruth slumped. But only for a moment. She reached for the child's face and turned it toward her to get her full attention.

"This might be it. Give me the doll, Pauli," and the child handed the doll over without an argument. Ruth frantically stuffed it into the pack.

"Get on Arno's lap. Put your arms around his neck."

Arno had no idea what was going on but her eyes were wide with terror as she helped the child into his lap.

"If they arrest me," she said, "take Pauli to Hannah. Hiller. Wiesbaden."

Pauli, her arms tight around Arno's neck, whispered: "Hold me, or I'll have to go back to my Grammy. An' I don't want to."

"Oh," Arno said, not understanding a thing. A second later, the door of the coach was ripped open, and a police officer stared directly at Ruth. She returned his stare, horrified.

"Everybody out! On the double!" the officer hollered. "Document check!"

Ruth was dumbfounded with relief.

"Let's go! Let's go!" the voice hollered again. "We don't have all day."

Pauli, petrified, started wailing. Ruth reached for her with a relieved smile as Arno struggled with his crutches. She climbed out of the train, but Arno had trouble getting up.

The officer yelled at Arno, "Come on! Come on! Hurry up!"

Ruth regained her composure as the paralyzing fear of a moment ago turned to bright anger.

"Why don't you help him! He lost his leg for you, you bully!"

The policeman glared at her, but he did help Arno out.

"Everybody line up," a loudspeaker now blared. The passengers were slow in obeying that command but finally were lined up alongside the train. It was deathly quiet as the police, watched attentively by the Russians, walked from passenger to passenger to study their documents. Occasionally, they ordered people to step out of the line. Sometimes, whole families—men, women, and children—were asked to step forward. Some sought to argue but were silenced with shouts or a raised gun. An old man beside Ruth was especially agitated and, with his eyes closed, mumbled petrified prayers until a policeman slapped his shoulder. The old man opened his eyes and handed over a document.

"Step forward!" the policeman hollered. The old man fainted. Two Russian soldiers came up and carried him to one of the waiting trucks while the officer reached for Ruth's papers.

"Do they think we're stupid?" the policeman snapped at no one in particular. "No ticket, no trip."

Without looking at Ruth, he checked her passport and visa and then walked away with them. Ruth's apprehension was visible only in her eyes as she turned to Arno and whispered:

"No papers, no get home."

"More importantly," Arno whispered, "does he know the difference between a first class and a second class ticket? Or we'll both be on these trucks."

Ruth looked at him horrified. Arno smiled reassuringly as a Russian officer approached Ruth.

"*I'm an old man now*," Arno whispered, quickly. "*I have seen much trouble. Most of it never happened.* Mark Twain. In case you didn't know."

The Russian officer now stood in front of them, scrutinizing Ruth.

"We do not recognize Allied visas here," he said, in broken German. But he had not counted on a feisty Ruth to whom the learning of languages had been a breeze in high school. She answered him in Russian, and she answered him according to the good old maxim that the best defense is a good offence.

"I was told," she said, her voice raised and her eyes proud, "that this visa was sufficient, regulated by Allied agreement. Surely," she added contemptuously, "I wouldn't have traveled here without the proper documents. I mean, who would?" She looked around disdainfully. Arno's eyes were wide with surprise. "Besides," she said haughtily, "it was signed by Commander..." She leaned over the piece of paper, her finger wandering a little. Not only was she looking at the document upside down, but she was also a little far-sighted. She squinted. Squinted harder.

"By Commander B..." She stopped, astonished, and looked straight into the Russian's eyes.

"Commander Whitman himself. You see here?" She pointed, squinted. "Under this line. It says 'Commander.'"

The officer seemed uncertain. He studied the document again. He looked at Ruth who, feisty, stared straight back at him. He smiled when he handed visa and passport back to her. Her display of courage had, it seemed, won his respect.

"Should you travel here again," he said, "I suggest you get a visa from the proper Soviet authorities."

He moved on as Ruth stared dumbfounded at something far away. In her eyes was a smile. She shook her head.

"He signed it himself as commander. That could land him in jail," she said to Arno who did not in the least understand the significance of that remark.

Ruth kept shaking her head, smiling. When she came home from the club that night, Hannah had waited up for her, wanting to know every morsel of every moment of that glorious date. Excitedly, Ruth had shown her the visa, and they both had poured over it, making sure Ruth's name was spelled correctly, and Pauli's, and their addresses. Neither had given any thought to the authorizing signature that was obscured by a seal to boot and seemed irrelevant anyway just as long as they had the visa. Even Hannah was swept away by the excitement that night, convinced that this visa that had been so illusive was a very good omen, and Pauli was now but days away.

37

Night Journey

The train was less crowded now. People had found ways to make themselves comfortable as best they could in the compartments or on the floor, and, after awhile, the metrical rocking of the train's motion had lulled everyone into an uneasy trance. But every change in the train's rhythm startled them anew. Now and then, the train stopped in the middle of nowhere, jarring the passengers awake, and they looked around with fearful alertness before settling back again.

Ruth and Arno had made themselves at home on the steps of the coach entry where Arno could stretch his legs. Pauli had fallen asleep on Ruth's raincoat on the floor behind them. Arno offered Ruth a cigarette, studying her face in the flame of the match.

"What would you have done if there had not been a war?"

Ruth shot an amused glance over her shoulder, scanning the train's interior.

"Actually, I always wanted to travel."

Arno burst out laughing as Ruth, dreamily, studied her reflection in the door's glass pane.

"I wanted to see the world. Egypt. Greece. Australia." She shot a quick glance at Arno. "And write about it all."

"Quite ambitious for a young woman."

Ruth looked at him reproachfully.

"This is the nineteen-forties, Arno. Why shouldn't I have a career?"

Arno was greatly amused as Ruth, sadly, dismissed the dream.

"But then the war came. And then I got married."

Arno laughed. "Now which was more detrimental to that dream? War or marriage?"

Ruth did not get a chance to answer as the train suddenly slowed, then stopped. Everyone turned toward the windows where there was some commotion and loud voices, and finally they all heard the familiar pounding on the doors, and an unknown voice hollered: "Everybody out!"

"Here we go again," Arno said as he struggled to get up.

The passengers were, once again, lined up alongside the train. With the headlights of the invariable trucks shining disembodied into the night, the authorities ordered some of the people out of the silent line-up.

"We should be close to the border," Arno whispered, but Ruth was not cheered. Gloomily, she watched those that had been asked to step forward and were being herded into the waiting trucks.

"I don't think I can take much more of this," she whispered back, although this time, her paperwork had been accepted as valid and without question.

The document check over, the passengers reclaimed their precarious haven once again, and the train continued through the night while the petrified travelers tried to sleep as best they could. Unbeknownst to them and not far away, a Russian military truck left a country road, drove through a meadow, and stopped on top of the train tracks. The driver maneuvered the truck in such a way that its headlights could not be missed by the oncoming train, blinking them on and off in quick succession as the train approached and stopped. Two Russians climbed out of the truck and walked up to the engineer. They talked with him briefly, climbed back into the truck and left.

When the train stopped, Ruth and Arno strained to penetrate the pitch-black night. But there were none of the trimmings of another document check. When they saw the lights of the truck leaving, they looked at each other, troubled. But all stayed quiet, and they relaxed a little.

38

History

Ruth, picking up the threads of their earlier conversation, pointed to his legs.

"But you...you must had been right in the middle of it all."

Arno shrugged. "Not really. Try to imagine a med unit crammed with wounded soldiers. Try to imagine me, busy stitching up a soldier. The place is a madhouse with orderlies trying to help the mangled masses of humanity that were brought in constantly. Try to imagine the moans and cries and the orderlies shouting for me. And then try to imagine a bomb that hits, and the unit becomes an instant blood bath."

He stopped, squinting at something far away.

"Yes, I was in the middle all right. But nothing heroic. Just in the middle of bodies all shot up and mangled beyond recognition, some of them. They drafted me a year into my internship. It gave me the privilege of seeing the war from inside one med unit after another."

He lit a cigarette and smoked silently for awhile.

"All war mongers should spend just one week in a med unit. That would learn'em in a hurry."

Ruth studied him with deep compassion.

"I came home, like this, and she left."

"Your wife?"

He nodded. "She's quick and pretty. She has the mind of a business-man. She never had any patience with pain, blood, or hunger."

He stopped again and shrugged resignedly. "She's in Frankfurt now. She wants me to come." He paused. "And I have nowhere else to go. Staying here would be like jumping from the frying pan into the fire."

39

Morning

Ruth was fast asleep, her head resting on Arno's shoulder while he stared pensively out at the dawning day. When he shifted his arm, she woke up. The happy and persistent song of birds filtered in through the open windows, and soon the train was alive with movement and voices. Pauli tugged at Ruth.

"I'm hungry."

Ruth gave Arno a comical look.

"I hate that word!"

Arno laughed. "They should ban it."

The sudden, loud banging up and down the train startled them and a male voice hollered out:

"Everybody wake up! Everybody! Listen! Folks, listen. The Russians have blockaded Berlin. They stopped all trains, trucks, buses. Right now, nothing's moving."

There was a discernible instant of utter silence, then the train began rocking with people clambering through it and shouting and climbing off. They surrounded the engineer who knew as much as they did.

"How will we eat?"

"What will we feed the children?"

"What about water?"

"How long will we be here? They can't leave us in the middle of nowhere without food and water."

The engineer raised his hands.

"Hold it! Hold it, folks! I know as much as you do. They came last night in a truck and told me to stay put. Nobody is to leave the train. Well, or the vicinity of the train, and that's all I know, folks."

But when the passengers crowded even more urgently around him—surely, he must have some kind of an answer—surely, it was not right that they should be abandoned like this—surely, the train would move again soon—he tipped his hat, pushed his way out of the crowd and climbed into his caboose, not to be seen again.

Ruth stared at Arno horrified. He shook his head. "Right this minute, I'm fresh out of ideas."

As he spoke, the calm and then more forceful roar of airplanes filtered down to them. The company of stranded passengers became deathly quiet and looked up at the sky. An old woman beside Ruth crossed herself, burst into tears, and began wailing.

"The war! They've started the war again. They'll bomb us all." Ruth consolingly stroked her arm as Arno tried to make out the planes, listening closely to their roaring.

"American planes, I think," he said, finally. "Maybe the war did start again!"

Ruth's eyes were full of terror. Arno laughed.

"Either this or they are airlifting stuff to Berlin. They said they would. I hope that's it. Unbelievable that they'd do it. When you think about it. I mean, real guts."

40

A Picnic in the Meadow

The morning dew on the meadow grass had not yet dried, but the sun lay cheerfully on the grass, the passengers, and the train. The day promised to be warm and sunny and cotton clouds sailed in a deep blue sky. The stranded passengers had staked out small territories on coats and blankets in the meadow alongside the train and finally settled into the inevitable. Were it not for the colossus of the train that snaked itself down the tracks, one might get the impression of an immense family picnic. At regular intervals, the quiet roaring of the American planes filtered down to them.

Ruth, Arno, and Pauli had made themselves comfortable beneath a distant tree. Ruth opened her backpack and pulled out the small loaf of bread she had brought from home and a kitchen knife as Arno began digging in his own pack. Ruth cut off a piece of bread and handed it to Pauli who studied it for a moment disdainfully, then bravely bit into it. The bread was hard, but she kept chewing away at it.

"I'm sorry," Ruth said, watching her, partly amused, partly sorrowful. "But that's all I have." She cut another piece and was about to hand it to Arno who had just pulled a small package out of his bag.

"Wait!" he said. "Men do not live by bread alone."

Almost reverently, he unwrapped the package and pulled out a small salami and a chunk of cheese.

"My God, where did you get that?"

Arno looked at the food with some regret. "Buddy of mine traded it for me at some farm. It cost me my camera, a first edition of the Gutenberg Bible, and a radio."

Ruth gave him a disbelieving look. Arno grinned. "My dear, material things don't mean beans when you're hungry. And we can't eat the Gutenberg Bible, or any other Bible, for that matter—first edition or not. Romantics and idealists would had us believe otherwise, but the sad truth remains…"

He pulled out a pocketknife, sliced an inch size piece of the salami and handed it to Pauli. Ruth reached for it in a flash.

"Not so big! Who knows how long we'll be here."

She cut the piece in half, handing one half to Pauli, the other to Arno.

"Just a tiny slice for me," she said.

"Let's not mince salami here." He handed the piece back to her. "Here, you take this, and I'll cut myself a thin slice."

He cut three thin slices of the cheese and Ruth shared the bread and so they sat and ate and looked contentedly around them. Some of the children had begun to play catch, and as they ran by, they called out to Pauli.

"Wanna play?"

Pauli looked at Ruth who smiled encouragingly, and Pauli ran off. Ruth dreamed out over the landscape as Arno dug for something in his pack and pulled out a book. It was a thin volume of poetry.

"I will read to you."

He held up the book.

"By the way, it survived the bomb. Funny, isn't it. A little tattered. Like me. But very much alive." He leafed through the pages. "How about…It's in English. You speak English?"

Ruth nodded, and he began reading Matthew Arnold's *Dover Beach*.

Ruth stretched out in the grass and closed her eyes and let his voice and the slight breeze that had come up wash over her. When he came toward the end of the poem, he raised his voice a little:

"...Ah, love, let us be true to one another!
for the world, which seems to lie before us
like a land of dreams, So various, so beautiful, so new,
Hath really neither joy, nor love nor light,
Nor certitude, nor peace, nor help for pain;
And we are here as on a darkling plain
Swept with confused alarms of struggle and flight
Where ignorant armies clash by night."

He had barely finished when the sudden roar of trucks on a near road startled them. The mood of the idyllic 'picnic' changed instantly. People jumped up, reached for their baggage, picked up blankets or coats or whatever they sat on as the children scattered in search of their parents.

Ruth and Arno watched, alarmed, as the trucks lined up on the road.

"I'm getting out of here," she sighed as Pauli came running and threw herself into her arms.

41

Walking Away

Once again, the passengers had to line up. Once again, there was a document check. Once again, people were herded into the waiting trucks that soon left with their pitiful cargo.

The children, recovering quickly, began to play again while the adults, haltingly and distressed, returned to the places they had previously staked out. But the cheerful mood that had characterized the involuntary picnic had made way to silence and somberness.

Ruth and Arno had returned to the tree and sat down heavily.

"How far, do you think, is the border?" Ruth asked.

"Twenty kilometers or so. Not that far."

Ruth thought this over.

"Let's walk out! We can do it in a day. Two at the uppermost." Arno slumped, but the more she considered the idea, the more she liked it, in fact, she felt downright enthusiastic over it.

"What do you say? Let's do it!"

Arno turned toward her and took her hands.

"I can't. I really can't, sweet Ruth. Look at me. I would only put you in danger. We've saved each other once. Let's not tempt fate."

His voice trailed. Briefly, he kissed her hands, then let go.

Ruth opened her mouth to protest but he put his finger over her lips. "And if you're going to leave, go now. I'll say you went to look for berries…"

Ruth studied him silently. If she left him here, he might well end up on one of the trucks. But if she took him with her, their progress would be awfully slow, and no one knew just what the Russians were up to.

"Your task is to take Pauli to Hannah," Arno said. "Your task is not, and never was, to save me. I'm a big guy. I might be crippled, but I can take care of myself. I always have. I can do it now. Go!"

"All right."

Ruth got up and called to Pauli. As the child came running, she gathered their things. When she was done, she squatted down, took Arno's hand and put it briefly against her cheek.

"I wish you luck. And only good things."

Tears welled up in Arno's eyes, but he smiled. "Don't cross the border without a guide. There are mines. And don't be reckless. Remember Falstaff—prudence being the better part of valor and all that. Go!"

Ruth handed the doll to Pauli, took her by the hand, gave Arno a last smile, and walked into the meadow. Arno looked after them mournfully. But they did not get very far before Pauli stumbled and fell and dropped the doll. Ruth squatted down to talk to her, and then they turned back and came back toward him.

Ruth carried the doll, and Pauli looked cross. Arno, assuming that Ruth had changed her mind, tried to look severe. But she said: "I don't think it would be good for us to carry the doll. Martha has, undoubtedly, described it to her troops. If she has troops."

Arno took the doll.

"I'll bring it," he said. He looked at Pauli and grinned. "Don't worry. I'll treat her as my own."

An unwilling smile crossed Pauli's face at the mere thought of Arno playing with a doll.

"Good bye, Princess!" she said, threw the doll a kiss, quickly took Ruth's hand, and pulled her away. Arno looked after them as they moved further and further away, pretending to look for berries. Finally, they disappeared in a grove of trees.

42

Thunder and Lightning

Having neither a watch nor a compass nor a map, Ruth tried to orient herself by the position of the sun. But their progress, heading west, was slow. Trying to avoid the roads where there might be soldiers, they stuck to paths alongside the meadows that, the grass being high, provided cover. It seemed to Ruth that they had not come very far when, that afternoon, tired and dirty, they climbed a path that ran up a low hill crowned with pines.

Ruth, who had been singing softly as they walked, said: "When we reach those trees, we'll rest a little. Can you make it?"

Pauli did not answer, just trotted along, hot and tired, hanging back a little as if she were about to drop. When they reached the shade of the trees, the exhausted child simply sat down.

Ruth pulled the handy raincoat out of her bag, spread it out, and coaxed Pauli onto it. She watched her, tenderly and with concern, until she was fast asleep. Then she got up and walked the path to the other side of the grove. The path wound its way down the hill, passed an old barn, cut through tilled fields, and ended in a small village. A farmhouse stood where path and village met, and Ruth saw a woman working with a hoe in what looked like a vegetable garden. A nearby clothesline full of laundry whipped gaily in the summer breeze. Beyond the village, farmland and small forests stretched to low mountains in the distance.

Ruth mused that the problem with villages was that everyone knew everyone else. She and the child would stand out like sore thumbs walking down the street, and as far as she could tell, there was no other way but to walk through the village if she wanted to get to the mountains. Walking around it might take them hours out of their way. She could, of course, say that she was headed toward her sister's house in the next village, provided someone stopped and asked where she was going, and then she'd be hard pressed to give the name of that village, not knowing the area at all.

I'll think of something, she thought defiantly and, resolutely, returned to Pauli. Taking but a corner of the coat for her head, she lay down and promptly and soundly fell into a deep sleep.

A sudden clap of thunder woke her abruptly, and she sat up, startled and confused. For an instant, she didn't know where she was or what she was doing on the ground. But an instant later, she was fully awake, quickly realizing the danger they were in if they remained among the trees.

She shook Pauli. "Wake up, honey! We have to go. A storm is coming."

Drowsily, Pauli sat up. Ruth moved her gently off the coat, put it on, shouldered the pack, and picked up the sleepy child. As they headed out of the trees, the wind became fierce, tearing at their hair and clothes. Ruth had a hard time wrapping her coat around Pauli to keep her warm as she walked briskly toward the village.

The woman who, earlier, had been busy in the garden ran out of the house and worked frantically to get the wash off the line. She was only half done when Ruth reached the fence.

The woman looked up, startled and afraid. Realizing that there was a child, she came quickly to the gate and opened it. The wind was howling now, nearly tearing the laundry off the line and the first thick, heavy drops of rain began to fall. The woman was momentarily undecided as to what to do, then she pointed to the house where there was an overhang above the backdoor.

Ruth ran to deposit Pauli there, then ran back to help the woman with the laundry. They were done quickly, and Ruth picked up the basket as they ran toward the house. They reached it just as the rain started falling like a torrent and thunder and lightning descended on them.

The woman opened the door to the farmhouse and, windblown and wet, they rushed into an ample country kitchen with a large table square in the middle. Ruth put the basket on it and shook herself just as the woman exclaimed, horrified:

"The windows!"

She run out and the sound of windows being shut loudly somewhere in the house fell into the quiet kitchen. Pauli pulled out a chair and sat down.

The woman returned, looking her visitors over. She was in her fifties, at once warm and a little apprehensive. Her face spoke of grief.

"So," she said, smoothing her gray hair that was gathered in a bun at the back of her head and was now wholly in disarray, "may I help you? What is it you have?"

Ruth was confused, and so they stared at one another for an instant, until Ruth gathered the meaning of the question.

"Oh, no. I didn't come to barter. I'm on my way to…" She stopped. It was probably not wise to reveal too much too soon.

"Refugees?" the woman asked.

Ruth searched for an answer as the woman, glancing at Pauli, could not hide a thin smile. The child had put her head on her arm, studying the women with a tired sideways look.

Ruth decided to level with her host. "I came from the West yesterday, Wiesbaden, actually, and on the way home, they started the blockade and stopped the trains. So I decided to walk home."

The woman shot her an incredulous look.

"You are going to walk all the way to Wiesbaden with this child?"

Ruth laughed.

"Not all the way. Just across the so-called border into the American Sector. I can get a train from there. I hope. But what I urgently need is a guide to take me across the mountain. I've been told that there are mines."

The woman studied Ruth's muddy shoes and socks, the pants that were not very clean, the dirty hands, then the face, then the child. Gradually, her suspicions waned, and she held out her hand.

"I'm Anna Mohr."

"Ruth Karstens. And Pauli, my niece."

The woman stroked Pauli's hair.

"Niece, eh? Are you hungry, little Pauli? Would you like a little milk? A sandwich even?"

She walked into the living room and closed the panels of the sheer curtains decorating the window.

"People are too nosy nowadays. If you want to wash up…"

She pointed to a door that led into a corridor, then busied herself at the icebox and the stove.

Ruth put down her wet coat and pack and left the kitchen while Anna poured a glass of milk for Pauli. She took a loaf of bread out of the cupboard, sliced it, spread the slices with butter and jam and put them in front of the child.

"Strawberry jam. Fresh from the garden, sweetheart. Do you like strawberry jam?"

Chewing happily, Pauli smiled and nodded just as Ruth returned to the kitchen. She could not help but smile at the scene of Pauli biting into the sandwich.

"This looks so good."

"Want some?"

Dreamily, Ruth studied Pauli's sandwich.

"I haven't seen jam in years."

43

Respite

After their meal, Ruth and Anna folded the laundry at the kitchen table while Pauli, who had found a basket with kittens beneath the stove, interrupted their conversation with loud cries of delight that made the women smile.

"Klaus will know somebody," Anna said. "He went to help his sister, in the next village, but he'll be back soon. Not my kind of woman, she. But he needs to find things to do. Besides, she has cows. And she gives us milk for his help."

Anna began folding more determinedly, and, curiously, Ruth looked up.

"Our son was killed in action. Then our daughter. In Dresden. He hasn't been the same since."

She tried not to cry, folding furiously. But the tears came just the same. Finally, she used some garment she'd been folding to hide her face. Deeply moved, Ruth reached out to touch her arm. Anna wiped her tears and squared her shoulders.

"I tell you this…if ever I have sinned, if ever any of us women have sinned, we have paid for it dearly—body for body, soul for soul—with the death of our children, our men, our women. And that's all I'm going to say on the subject." She smiled through her tears. "And now we're going to concentrate on getting you across. That's what's important. That's what we'll think about."

Just then, the backdoor opened, and Klaus Mohr, wet and wind-blown, walked in, not looking up, still battling the elements at the moment of his walking in the door. Not expecting visitors, he did what he obviously always did, he took off his cap, shaking the rain off of it before closing the door—and hung the cap and his wind jacket on a hook behind it. When he turned and looked up and faced them, Ruth and Anna couldn't help but laugh at the startled expression on his face.

"Well, " he said, wide-eyed. He was a short, squat man with bright blue eyes that now surveyed Ruth, Anna, and the child.

"Meet Ruth Karstens and her niece Pauli," Anna said.

Klaus limped to the table.

"He needs hip surgery," Anna explained as Klaus held out a square, callused hand to Ruth, throwing an inquisitive sideways glance at his wife.

"Ruth needs a guide to get her over the mountains," Anna explained. "Tea?" she asked, already getting up, knowing the answer, and putting on the kettle.

Klaus sat down, studying Ruth quietly for a moment. It seemed to her that, no matter whoever his wife took in or what she said, he liked to make up his own mind about a person or a situation. After awhile, his eyes smiled.

"See what we can do," he said.

He finished his tea, listening to Anna's explanations, asking Ruth questions now and then, such as when exactly she left the train and how long, exactly, she had walked. Ruth, having no watch, said that she had kept an eye on the sun to give her a sense of time. Klaus, knowing the country, seemed satisfied that she told the truth. He finished his tea and got up.

"Gotta see someone about a cow," he said and went to put on his jacket and cap. Anna winked at Ruth. He would, that wink meant, go out and talk to someone he could trust, see if that someone knew of a guide that was dependable.

"Not all of them are, of course," she said. "Some take you half way across and leave you stranded there. Some even rob you. Not all. But some."

44

An Evening at the Mohr's

That night, after a simple dinner of canned sausage and garden vegetables, Ruth, Anna, and Klaus sat at the kitchen table. For Ruth, merely to have meat and fresh vegetables was a rare treat—her dinner with Whitman the rarest of exceptions—and she had eaten slowly, savoring every morsel. Anna cleared the table as Ruth washed the dishes, savoring this as well. The mere luxury of having hot tap water and being able to rinse the dishes was something she did not have in the attic room where the dishes were washed in a bowl of water warmed in Mrs. Garske's kitchen and then rinsed in cold water in the bathroom sink.

Soon after they had eaten, Pauli, playing with the kittens, nodded off in the corner where the coal stove was. Anna directed Ruth to a small bedroom upstairs to put her down. Coming back, she could smell the scent of coffee halfway down the stairs.

"We usually make coffee on Sunday," Anna said, beaming. "But today is special."

She put cups and saucers and cream and sugar on the table, and Ruth sat down, feeling, for the first time in a long time, at home somewhere.

Klaus had come back from his errand shortly before supper. "Someone will be coming," he said. "They say he's rough but they think he's reliable. He's always come back, anyway, or, in other words, he couldn't show his face in the village if he tried something funny. People would find out after awhile."

Anna had barely poured the coffee when Klaus got up and turned off all the lights in the kitchen, opened the window wide and leaned way out as if to make sure that no one was hiding beneath the window to hear what was being said in the kitchen. He came back to the table and offered Ruth a cigarette, shading the flame of the match with his hand as he lit it.

"You picked a nice time to get the child, Mrs. Karstens," he said. "A week ago, it would've been easier. If the Russians put a real border here, we're gonna be stuck behind it."

"Can't you leave?"

He looked at something beyond her for awhile. "And where do you propose we go? The farm has been here for three hundred years. My father had it before me, and my grandfather and my great grandfather, and so on. Besides, once everybody calms down, it may not be so bad. A farm is a farm. At least, we have food. And life on the farm is always the same, no matter who rules the country. Of course, they been talking about co-ops, quotas, and who knows what else. Something like what Stalin did in Russia, doing away with personal property. But the farm isn't large, so we may be saved from that. But who knows what's gonna happen. Except there'll be no Marshall Plan for us if they close that border. This much I do know."

He stopped abruptly, listening to the determined footsteps coming down the sidewalk. They stopped beneath the window, then went on a step or two. Klaus got up, looked out the window, closed it, and let the shade down.

"Turn the stove light on," he said to Anna. "It's him."

45

An Incredulous Confession

That same evening, Hannah and Whitman sat at the table in the attic room which was as hot as an oven. Summer had finally come, and even though Hannah had opened both the attic room door and the door to Mrs. Garske's kitchen directly across to take advantage of the slightest draft between the window there and the meager skylight, the heat was unbearable. The children had long fallen asleep in the old bedstead where Hannah had put them down when she came back from the train station without a sign of Ruth.

Under the pretense of having to run an urgent errand, Whitman had been able to leave his unit for an hour. Now and then, he glanced at Hannah and opened his mouth as if to say something but he kept changing his mind.

"And you checked the trains?" Hannah asked, thoughtfully stirring her coffee. She was referring to the precarious schedules that had characterized train travel these last few days.

"No trains from the East since day before yesterday," Whitman said.

"I'm worried sick. I shouldn't be, I know, because she's so clever. And her papers are in order. So there shouldn't be any trouble, but if there are no trains, how's she going to get back? Maybe Martha did something. But what could she do?"

Whitman finally got up enough nerve to say what he came to say. "Her papers are no good."

"What do you mean they're no good?"

"I signed 'em."

"Shouldn't you?"

Whitman shook his head. "No. But when they denied her the visa, I made one up. I thought, fat chance that anybody would notice." He shrugged. "But if they check and there is no commander Whitman…"

Hannah stared at him horrified.

"You forged the signature?"

"No. Not that. I just signed Thaddeus A. Whitman where it said 'Signature of Commanding Officer' which I'm not."

"Is that very bad?"

Whitman laughed.

"Enough for a court martial, that's for sure. But what was I gonna do? She needed that visa. I thought the blockade was days away, and she'd be back way before then." He looked quite crestfallen which did nothing to alleviate Hannah's horror. "Funny thing," he said, "I'm not in the least worried about myself. Let 'em bust me. But I am worried sick about her. If I hadn't signed that paper, she'd be here."

"Oh, my God!" Hannah said. "What if they arrest her?"

"That's what I'm afraid of."

46

A Visitor with A Purpose

Klaus came back into the kitchen with a short, stocky man whose small eyes lit up momentarily when he saw Ruth. He shook hands with her and said: "Call me Ishmael."

This amused Ruth. "Call me Moby Dick," she said, smiling. But the man was not amused.

"This was no joke," he said, aggressively. "You don't know my name. You want me to take you across, you call me Ishmael. Too dangerous to know someone's name."

Troubled, Klaus and Anna look at one another. This was not the kind of man they hoped to find.

"Where's the child?" he asked, looking around.

"Upstairs, asleep. Did you want to leave now?"

Ishmael looked at her with contempt.

"There's a moon in an hour. Nobody walks across with a moon. Unless, of course, you wanna get shot."

"Oh," Ruth said. The more he talked, the less she liked him. But she had to cross the mountains somehow, and he seemed the only recourse that moment.

"How old?"

"Who? The child? Five. She's a very sensible child. She walked with me since we left the train, and you can trust..."

But Ishmael interrupted her. "I trust no one. All we need is for her to cry and whine an' talk when she shouldn't, and we're all done for. And since there's a child, it will cost more. A hundred for you, fifty for the child. We leave in a week. Got a couple of other people."

Ruth's eyes were wide with shock.

"A hundred and fifty marks? And in a week?"

Ishmael studied her thoughtfully for a moment, then turned away and looked at Klaus.

"I thought you said she could pay? I want you people to consider that I'm putting my life on the line here."

"You'll get your money," Klaus said.

"Oh, no, Klaus. Never!" Ruth cried out.

Ishmael looked from one to the other.

"If you don't have the money, and if you're not gonna take his, maybe there's something else you have, jewelry, watch, whatever."

His eyes slid very, very slowly over Ruth's body. "I prefer money, but…" He paused for a moment, letting a second lewd look glide over Ruth's body. "There've been other women who didn't have the money. We came to an agreement."

Ruth blushed at the brazenness of the offer and looked him over calmly.

"Thank you very much for coming, Mr. Ishmael, but I don't think I'm interested."

"Listen, lady! I can't wait. There are other people waiting to get across. And these mountains ain't easy. This thing needs to be planned."

"I'm sure it does. You go right ahead and plan, but without me."

Ishmael turned to leave and turned back.

"All right! All right! I'll do it for a hundred. Half of it now, half of it when we're across."

"No, thank you. I walk across by myself if I have to."

"You crazy? But fine, fine. You don't want my services, fine." He turned to Klaus and Anna. "Next time, don't waste my time."

He stormed out and slammed the door. Stunned, Anna looked at Klaus. Ruth paced the kitchen floor. "Now what?" Anna asked.

Klaus thought it over.

"I could ask Marie. She knows Peter Singer, and I know he took people across a couple of times last year."

"Marie?" Anna laughed. "His sister," she said to Ruth, and then to Klaus, "She wouldn't help anybody."

But Klaus was stubborn. "I'm not asking her to help. Maybe she'll have to put Ruth and the child up for a night. In the hayloft, probably, knowing her. All I want to know from her is where we can reach Peter."

"All right," Anna said, resignedly. She didn't like the plan, but there was no other if Ruth wanted to get home.

"We'll set out before sun-up," Klaus said. "Let's turn in." He left the kitchen, leaving it up to the 'womenfolk' to clear the table and to lock up. Anna lent Ruth a nightgown, and before the women went to bed, they washed Ruth's and Pauli's clothes so that they wouldn't look, as Anna said, like hoodlums when they went to see Marie.

47

A Hayride

The next morning, they got up at daybreak. Anna made breakfast and soon after Klaus went out to hitch his old horse to a wagon and to load hay. Pauli, who found the farm exciting, had run out with him into the yard to watch what he was doing. But then she got a kick out of chasing the nervous chickens that roamed freely and the quick cats and ever more kittens that were in the barn. Finally, Klaus caught her, picked her up, and put her way up on the seat, promising her that she could drive the wagon if, until then, she held the reigns so the horse wouldn't suddenly take off. This made her feel terribly important, although the real reason for his kind act was that she got under his feet and if he was going to get Ruth out of the village before people were up, they had to get going.

In the kitchen, Anna handed Ruth a package wrapped in brown paper and a bottle with some pale liquid.

"You guys will need something to eat and drink. A little tea. That's all there is. And there's some strawberry jam in there for your sister and the girls."

They hugged, crying just a little.

"Thanks for everything," Ruth said. "I will never be able to repay it."

"What goes around, comes around. Take care of yourself."

Tears in her eyes, she walked Ruth out and then walked quickly back into the house as if she could not handle good-byes in the least.

Klaus and Ruth climbed onto the wagon. Klaus took the reigns out of Pauli's hands. "You'll get them back in a minute," he said as he guided the wagon out of the yard and down the street which was quiet, and then down a country road where he returned the reigns to Pauli once the horse was in a quiet trot.

The morning was clear and crisp. The storm of the day before had left some errant clouds behind that were tinted red by the sun which was about to rise. They had not gone far when, coming from the next village whose red roofs they could see in the distance, a car approached at great speed, creating arced sprays of mud and rainwater in its wake.

"I wonder who's in such a hurry this early in the morning?" Ruth laughed.

"Get down!" Klaus said, reaching up, grabbing the reigns with one hand and pulling Pauli down to his feet with the other. He reached up again and pulled Ruth's head onto his shoulder. Even from that distance, he had spotted the red dot on the hood of the car, which, as it raced closer, turned out to be a Russian flag.

Fine sprays of water and mud settled on the travelers as the car raced by. Ruth, wiping her face, started laughing.

"And Anna let me take a bath! And helped me wash the clothes. A lot of good that did."

"You'll probably look worse once you get across," Klaus said laconically, and, to Pauli, "It's all right, child! You can come up now."

The wagon rolled into and through the village and down a rutted path into a good-size farm that sat on the outskirts. It was expansive with a large barn and various sheds, the house itself squat and solid, its windows sparkling in the morning sun. The whole of it was surrounded by neatly tilled fields that ran as far as the eye could see.

As they drove into the barnyard, a woman, wearing rubber boots, a dark dress, an apron, and a kerchief wound around her head, came out of the barn. Expecting her brother, she was about to walk up to the wagon but stopped short when she saw Ruth and the child. Klaus climbed off the wagon.

"Morning, Marie."

Uncertain and unfriendly, Marie studied Ruth and Pauli, wiping her hands on her apron.

"Morning!"

Klaus helped Ruth and Pauli down, then walked up to his sister.

"Let's go in the house."

Marie continued wiping her hands, eyeing Ruth and the child suspiciously for a while longer before turning and walking sullenly ahead of them into the house through the back door.

They entered a kind of mudroom where boots lay against the wall and work clothes hung from hooks. Marie opened a door that led into a small and dark kitchen where she rudely turned away from them and began stirring something in a pot on the stove. On the table sat a large cookie sheet with freshly baked rolls glazed with sugar icing.

"These two young ladies," Klaus said, "need to get across the mountains to the West. I know that Peter Singer takes people across. Have you seen him?"

"I don't know any Peter Singer," she said sullenly, stirring whatever it was she was cooking which looked to Ruth like vegetable soup with a good layer of fat and big chunks of meat.

Klaus didn't catch what Marie tried to tell him.

"What do you mean? You guys went to school together."

Marie turned around and shot him a fiery glance realizing at the same time that the child's eyes were glued to the tray of sweet rolls. She stopped stirring the pot, took the cookie sheet and put it on a shelf above the stove.

"I just told you that I don't know any Peter Singer. I have never met the man and I don't know what he does."

"All right! All right! Do you know anyone else?"

Just then Pauli piped up, "I have to go to the bathroom."

Marie pointed with the cooking spoon to an open door that led into a hallway.

"Last door to the right." Ruth took Pauli down the long hallway, waiting outside the door after the child said: "I can go by myself."

She leaned against the wall and even though the bathroom was some distance from the kitchen, the voices were loud enough for her to hear every word.

"Are you crazy bringing these people here?" Marie asked, belligerently. "You know very well that Dieter is delivering milk to the Russians. That's why they let us keep the cows. Do you know what it means having those cows? The milk you drink comes from them too, just in case you forgot."

"Come on, Marie! How much danger to your ten cows can a woman and a child be? All they need is a place to stay until she can get a guide. Put them in the hayloft, for God's sake. Come on! Have a heart!"

Now Marie's voice really got loud. "Have a heart! Are you crazy? Do you know what will happen to us if they find out that I'm harboring refugees? They don't ask questions. They either shoot you or send you to Siberia. You know that as well as I do."

"Listen. She's from the West. She has the right papers. They stopped the trains, and who know how long they…"

"Why should I worry about that? Who worries about us? In these times, you can't be too careful. What if she is a spy? What if this is a set-up? Have you thought of that?"

Ruth had heard enough. When Pauli came out of the bathroom, Ruth walked resolutely back to the kitchen, her steps purposely loud on the hallway tiles. Marie, who was still standing by the stove, stopped talking.

"I could not help but hear," Ruth said, and, turning to Klaus, "If you point me in the right direction, we'll just go on."

Klaus Mohr stared at his sister's back but she did not turn. He shrugged and walked to the stove, holding her hand to prevent her from stirring. She looked up as he stared at her, his head cocked side-ways, pleading with his eyes as he well may have done when they were children. Their eyes locked in a brief, non-verbal exchange, but she did not yield. He reached above her to the shelf, took a roll, and handed it to Pauli.

"Here, child!"

Pauli took the roll but looked uncertainly at Marie as if the woman might tear it out of her hands in an instant.

"Keep it," Klaus said. "It was mine, and now I'm giving it to you."

Pauli smiled gratefully and bit into the treasure.

"They can go through the barn if they want to," Marie said. Ruth took Pauli's hand and walked out, not bothering to say good-bye. She took the pack out of the wagon, adjusting it so it would be comfortable on her back on their long walk home, when Klaus came out of the house.

"I'm sorry," he said. "She's weird that way."

Ruth shrugged. "I guess we shouldn't blame her. These are dangerous times, and she has to live somehow."

"Go through the barn, and you'll see the path. It goes about eight kilometers or so, through the fields and some forest and dead-ends by a road. Once you cross the road, there's no more path and you're on your own, climbing the mountain. Seems to me, that's the best place to cross, I think. Not too steep. If you take a left at the road, it'll take you to Berns, a village, not quite a kilometer down that road."

Ruth held out her hand. "Thanks so much for everything."

"I'd take you myself, but the bastards won't let anyone go anywhere without a permit. I can come here, because she's my sister."

He held on to her hand for a long time without saying anything. Then he turned, took a pitch fork, and began unloading the hay.

Ruth called Pauli who had been investigating the yard and together they walked through the barn that held a number of penned up cows which they had not expected. Pauli kept fearfully close to Ruth.

"Are you scared? Haven't you ever seen a cow before?"

"In my picture book. But they weren't that big. And they didn't smell," the child said, making Ruth laugh

"You want to touch one?" she asked. But that took more courage than Pauli had because she clamped her arms even tighter around Ruth's leg and vigorously shook her head.

The gate out of the barn led to a grassy area from where Ruth could see the path that was rutted by wagon wheels and pockmarked by time and the weather. Rain pooled in the ruts and holes and the rest of it was muddy. Staying close to the crop line of a tilled field which had grown weeds and grass and was less muddy, they set out, with Ruth beginning to sing softly, and Pauli skipping behind.

48

Hiking Through the Countryside

From a distance, the mountain range stretched its rippled crests along the horizon like a long, green dragon resting calmly. But as they came closer, Ruth realized that their climb would be more difficult than she had anticipated. The rise directly ahead of her was densely wooded and seemed wild and impenetrable, and the broad band of meadowland at its base was scattered with ragged rocks, split boulders, and dead timber. She could not see the road they would have to cross to begin their ascent, but it would not be far.

From the position of the sun she figured that it was about noon or a little after. She decided that they should take a good break to be rested enough for their climb and stopped at the edge of an untilled field that, untended in years, had turned into a meadow wild with flowers. Over the tall grasses, she could see the roofs of the village Klaus had mentioned earlier but, thankfully, the grass was tall enough to hide her and the child from view.

Pauli, tired and cross from their hike in the sun, now discovered the flowers and, with cries of joy, dashed into and out of the meadow picking wild daisies and yellow mustard grass and blue cornflowers and red poppies that were nearly done blooming.

"When you have a good bunch," Ruth said, spreading the raincoat, "I'll show you how to make a wreath for your hair."

And so they sat peacefully in that tranquil place, fashioning two wreaths, with no sound other than the humming of the bees, the occasional chirping of birds, and the rushing of a soft wind in the tall meadow grass. Now and then, the faint droning of the American planes that had begun to deliver food to Berlin filtered down to them as if from a great distance. Using each other as mirrors, they exclaimed, laughing, that they both looked stunning.

"Let's have a little lunch," Ruth said, "and then we both can take a small nap. It might do us good before we climb. Who knows how long that will take."

They shared a little of the bread and the tea Anna Mohr had packed for them. The butter on the sandwiches had melted in the heat and the tea was warm, but they both agreed that all was delicious anyway. Pauli touched her wreath just one more time to make sure it would not suffer when she lay down. She fell asleep instantly while Ruth lay, with her arms crossed behind her head, staring at the mountain, studying the long slope they would have to climb, trying to discover a gap in the impenetrable wilderness that would indicate a path. But all seemed solid with trees and underbrush.

She looked up at the sky that, gradually, had begun to gather pale, gauzy clouds. She closed her eyes and fell asleep until something startled her awake. A cool breeze had come up and she shivered. The sky had turned dark.

"Oh, for God's sake!" she said. They'd have no choice now but to seek shelter in the village which had been the last thing she wanted to do. But if they didn't want to be caught defenseless in the meadow in a storm, they best head there.

"Wake up, honey!" She shook Pauli awake. "We have another storm."

"Not again," Pauli sighed and turned over, trying to go back to sleep. Ruth took a sweater out of the pack that the child, in wise foresight, had stuffed into it at Martha's house.

"Here, put this on. Want some tea?"

Pauli nodded, cross from having been woken out of a deep sleep. Ruth handed her the bottle.

"But just a small sip. Don't know when we'll get more." Cautiously, the child took a few small sips as Ruth got up carefully, looking out over the tall grasses. No one was in sight. No farmer, no wagon, no one in the vast sea of green that was between her and the village. She stowed the bottle away, decided to carry the coat, and shouldered the bag.

"I think," she said, reaching for the child's hand, "we should take this path to the road. Hopefully, there is a road, and then go left." They set out. "If Klaus was right. I hope he was right." She looked up at the sky because the sound of thunder, though distant, was now unmistakable.

"Can you walk?"

Pauli shook her head. Ruth picked her up and headed out of the meadow toward the road that was washed out in part and had, it seemed to her, seen bombing hits during the war. She walked fast now, the thunder coming ever closer. Just as they reached the outskirts of the village where an abandoned gas station sat looking desolate with its doors and windows boarded up, the storm broke. She merely glanced across the street at a whitewashed house adorned with flower boxes and bright flowers. Her glance was one of caution rather than curiosity, but even if danger were to come from the house, nothing could be done about it now.

She rushed to find shelter under an overhanging, broken roof close to the front door of the gas station as the wind kicked up and whipped some of the rain toward them. Pauli began to shiver. Ruth pulled the raincoat over the child and herself as best she could, holding her close to her own warmth, and so they sat, wet and desolate, in a desolate place while the rain came down in torrents. The village, it seemed to Ruth, consisted of not much more than a long road with simple and solid dwellings running the length of it. The whole of it was deserted. Once again she studied the house directly across wondering whether or not she should make a dash for it. The overhang above the door there would provide much more shelter than where they were. Mulling it over, she stared at the front door that slowly opened. At first, she thought the driving rain played tricks with her mind. But no. Ruth held Pauli even closer, watching the door with great concern.

An instant later, an old man took a cautious step out the door, quickly looked up and down the street and then waved Ruth to him with some urgency. Ruth hesitated. But the storm was fierce, and Pauli shivered violently. Ruth decided to take the gamble, picked up the child, and ran across the street. By the time they get to the house, they were soaked. The old man pulled them inside and closed the door behind them.

49

Nikolas

They found themselves in a small, cozy foyer, a living room off to one side, a hallway with a staircase straight ahead. The old man, a little bent by either age or sorrow, regarded them with a quick, kind smile. "Here! Give me your coat," he said. "And your sweater, little one."

He opened a linen closet and pulled out two towels. "Here! Dry yourself off. I'll hang this up right here on that hook. I saw you from the window. This is no weather for a dog to be out in, much less a woman and a little one. You're not from here. Could tell that much." His voice trailed off as he watched, his hands itching to help anyway he could.

"Thanks so much, that's better," Ruth said. He made a formal, inviting gesture toward the living room as if he were pointing them toward the ballroom of a castle.

"In here! I live alone, so you must excuse the disorder—I…"

Ruth and Pauli walked into a room that was filled with books which spilled out of shelves, were stacked on the floor and on chairs, on the coffee table, on the couch. The armchair by the window was free, but an open book there had obviously just been left. Somewhat embarrassed, the old man busied himself with making room on the couch.

"I don't get much company. We sit in the kitchen when I do. Most everyone here has gone over the mountain. Village's near empty. I'll go make some tea. You'll catch pneumonia otherwise, you and the child."

Ruth was at once amused and moved by his embarrassment and his ardent desire to help them. But at the word 'tea' she protested.

"Please, don't! I'm sure it won't last long, and then we can go on. Please, don't go through any trouble for us."

He was done clearing the couch and pointed to it, pleading almost as if, once they sat, they wouldn't be so eager to leave.

"It's no trouble. This is pleasure. Trouble is when they burn books. Please, do sit down!"

He shuffled out of the room. An instant later he came back with a pair of thick socks.

"Here, put these on. Then the others can dry. No point getting sick. If you want to change the child...I'll wait in the kitchen. Call when you're done."

He turned to leave, turned back, held out his hand that Ruth took, a little baffled.

"Nikolas Wagner," he said, chuckling. "You wouldn't know who to call otherwise."

"Ruth Karstens. And this is Pauli."

He nodded, pleased, and shuffled out again.

"Nikolas?" Pauli giggled.

"Shh," Ruth said, digging in the pack for dry clothes for Pauli. The child looked around, absorbing everything in the room as Ruth took off her wet clothes and put on dry ones, changing her socks, wiping her shoes inside and out with the towel.

"I hope they'll dry enough for us to go on. You did a great job packing, but unfortunately you didn't pack another pair of shoes."

"I can go barefoot."

"Sure. In this weather."

"Well, then you only have to wipe off my feet."

Ruth laughed. "That would be easy enough, I guess," taking off her own shoes and socks, putting on the thick ones Nikolas had given her. "This does feel much better, but how am I going to get the rest of it dry?"

"This is a mess," Pauli said.

"Shh! He is probably a lonely old man and these books are his friends."

"You can't talk to them."

"Of course, you can. I do."

Pauli gave her an uncertain look.

"You do?"

"Of course! Not out loud, of course, but in my mind I talk to all the people I read about."

Nikolas came back, carrying a tray, and Ruth, accommodatingly, jumped up to help even though there was nothing she could do as he carried the tray just fine, putting it on the low coffee table.

"Thank you, thank you. That's all right. Do sit down. I can handle this. A little rheumatism in the back, but the rest is still quite functional."

He put cups and teapot and a plate with slices of dark bread on the table.

"No butter. No sugar. But I have honey. I have a couple of hives up in the woods. No one touches them." He chuckled. "Too scared of being stung. But the honey comes in handy when there's no sugar."

He pulled up a chair after moving books off of it, sat down, and poured the tea. Holding up the plate, he offered a slice of bread to Pauli.

"The honey's seeped into the bread so you can't see it, but it's quite sweet."

Pauli cautiously took a slice and just as cautiously bit into it.

"Hmmm," she said, nodding, "like cake."

"I know. I know," Nikolas said. "So I trade my honey for books. I can't forget those books burning in a pile huge as a house, just about. Here, have some yourself." He held the plate out to Ruth. "And drink up, drink up. It's good and hot. I put honey in it too."

Satisfied that his visitors were well taken care off, he got up to settle in his armchair by the window.

"More comfortable for my back," he explained. He looked briefly out the window where it was still raining fiercely.

"You'll be here awhile, I think." He turned back to Ruth. "So then, where'd you hail from and where're you headed?"

"Across the mountain," Ruth said, smiling, remembering his reference that most everyone in the village had headed over the mountain to the West.

"Ah," he said. "And where is home?"

"Also over the mountain. I came from there two days ago, and then they stopped the trains."

"Ah," he said again.

"What's it like there, in the West?"

"Not much different than here, actually. Maybe a little freer because you can go from place to place in the American sector. But there still is little food and everything is bombed."

"Are there books?"

"There must be, but I have seen few."

Pauli, having wolfed down three slices of bread and having finished her tea slid off the couch, her eye on a large picture book that lay on top of a stack of others beneath the dining table. She crawled to it and, with a quick, cautious look at Nikolas who pretended not to notice opened it.

"So I trade my honey for books, as I said," Nikolas said. "Like I said, I can't forget those books burning in a pile. All that wisdom going up in smoke. All that truth."

The memory made him sad, but then he smiled and pointed to a shelf.

"I was going to built a library in the village. That was my dream. The greatest evil, Socrates said, is ignorance. There will be no books in these parts when they close that border for good. There'll be night here. Permanently. In the mind."

"You could have a library right here in this house," Ruth said, smiling.

"I could, but when I die, they'll burn the house and the books with it. So I give them to the people who head west. They can't take much, but they are always willing to take a book or two. I have a hunch you might be a candidate when I saw you sitting there."

Ruth laughed. "I'd be glad to."

"But books are heavy," he mused. "And you have the little one. We'll have to give you just two or three. Books that are light. When the trains still ran, I used to go to the station. I have a small hand wagon. Packed it full of books and handed'em out to the people going west. One day, the police stopped me and took all my books. That was a very sad day. Very sad. I worry about them."

"I can take more, if you like."

"No, no. You have the child to worry about. Sad times we live in. And never learn a thing. We poison Socrates, nail Christ to the cross, shoot Gandhi, but we'll follow a war mongering madman any day." He turned away from her, staring out the window, thinking.

"You might have to spend the night," he said. "It's getting worse. There's plenty of room. My sons went west. I have three. I was lucky. They all came back from the war. They all were shot, and they all survived. My wife would have liked that. But she died. Four years ago."

"Why didn't you go with them? Wouldn't this have been better than staying here?"

"Maybe. But I couldn't leave the books. What would have happened to them? You can't take anything with you. And you can't go anywhere without a permit. Not on the trains, not on the busses. Not even on foot, unless you know the back roads. You know how it is."

Under the table, Pauli held a loudly whispered conversation with the pictures in the book. Ruth and Nikolas looked at each other.

"See," he said, "that's why I couldn't leave. They are more important than eating."

Ruth laughed. "I know a man who would not agree with you," she said, thinking of Arno who, unless the Russians brought in food, would be nibbling on what was left of the Salami and the cheese, having no bread, for as long as the trains were not moving.

"By trade," Nikolas said, "I was a carpenter. I would have built beautiful shelves for the books. Real smooth. Nice wood. Warm. I can still see that library in my mind."

"Sooner or later," Ruth said consolingly, "the trains will have to run again. The Russians can't shut themselves off from the rest of the world forever. And then you can get more of them across, and they'll be in someone's library."

Darkness fell slowly as they sat, thinking, talking occasionally. The rain would not let up, and Ruth had no choice but to spend the night. Pauli, under the table, had discovered more picture books, but as it got dark, she started yawning.

Nikolas went to the kitchen to heat up some soup. "A woman down the street brings it to me once in awhile. They have a small farm. Some chickens. She lost her husband, so I help out once in awhile with the garden. Give her some honey."

They ate, and Nikolas showed Ruth into a small, clean bedroom upstairs that held two beds. Pauli, two books under her arm, had climbed up behind them. Nikolas, smiling, turned on a bright nightlight.

"My two oldest slept here," he explained, and, turning to Pauli, smiling, proud that she valued his books, "don't read too long. Don't want to ruin your eyes."

But the warning was hardly necessary. Ruth had barely tucked her in and opened a book to read to her, when the child fell asleep.

Ruth turned off the light, undressed, and slipped under the cool sheets of her own bed where she lay, for a long time, unable to go to sleep. If the rain did not stop, she'd be stuck for days. She could only imagine what Hannah was going through since she had not come back when she said she would. And the children would ask about her. Hopefully, Hannah had a good and reassuring story, although, knowing Hannah, she'd probably tell them, very softly, the truth, worrying them sick. And Ted. What would he think after he was so kind getting her the visa? No doubt he knew all that happened, would know that she'd have trouble getting out.

Arms crossed behind her head, she stared into darkness seeing, once again, the splendor of the officers' club: the bright lights, the golden mirrors, the marble, the women dressed in clothes she could not imagine ever wearing, the food, the music, all now far away as if it had never happened, as if she had imagined it all. And Ted. So kind. So sensible. She did not want to fall in love with anyone and had fallen in love with him the moment he bribed her with the doggy bag and made her laugh. How could she not, she thought, fall in love with someone so handsome and caring and courageous? The thoughts of him made her smile into the darkness. But it was impossible.

If ever their relationship came to anything, she would forever worry that, one day, he would be aware of that they were worlds apart. How could he ever understand what she had gone through? And even if he could, how could she ever, if it came to that, go to the States. There would be women like Sheryl everywhere. And she, Ruth, would forever have a German accent, and everyone would forever remember the war and no one would ever want to know that she was but a young woman who had wanted nothing more than to have a small house and two children, or maybe even three, who loved good clothes and who loved her garden. Or hoped, once the children were bigger, that she could take them to England and France and Italy. Who had wanted nothing more than to be happy. No, the idea of Ted and her was quite out of the question.

She huddled into the sheets and, listening to Pauli's quiet breathing, she fell asleep.

When they came downstairs the next morning, Nikolas had already made tea which he kept warm beneath a tea cosy and had set the coffee table for breakfast with the same bread spread with honey. The sky had cleared and though rain drops glistened in the trees that stood along the street, the day promised to be splendid.

Nikolas gave her three books. A tall one, not very thick, of the story of Parzival with beautiful color plates which Pauli leafed through curiously, and two volumes of poetry by Goethe and Schiller. Ruth stuffed those into her pack since Pauli insisted on carrying the *Parzival.*

"Good bye, my dear," Nikolas said. "I will be thinking of you all the way. Good luck! And remember, walk the road for about a kilometer from where you came in on that path. You'll see another one that climbs the mountain where it isn't so steep."

He bent down to hug Pauli. "When you get home, send me a postcard and draw me a picture. Will you do that? I don't know when I will get it, but eventually, I will."

"I can write my name."

"Well, that's even better."

He kissed the child as Ruth opened the front door. Though bathed in the morning sun, the boarded up gas station across the street looked as desolate as it had the day before.

"Ready?" she said.

Pauli nodded, the *Parzival* under her arm.

50

Of Love and War

They walked out of the twilight of Nikolas' somber house and the daz-
zling light nearly blinded them. The morning sun, as if to amuse itself
with its own brilliant reflections, had created a dizzying array of mirrors
out of the meanest objects and surfaces, flashing back brilliant bundles
of blinding light from puddles, window panes, metal gutter nails, pol-
ished shutter hinges, and roof shingles.

"Sunglasses would be a blessing," Ruth said, turning back, thinking
Nikolas in the door, but he had walked away to somewhere else in the
house as if he couldn't bear watching them leave. More out of habitual
caution than curiosity, Ruth cast a quick glance down the tree-lined
canyon of the street whose dwellings had been obscured by the cloud-
burst the day before. They were unassuming dwellings, docile and simple, and their inhabitants were nowhere to be seen. Only a lonely cat
sunned itself on a ledge outside a window.

Ruth took Pauli's hand and, turning back the way they had come,
they walked briskly out of the village while fat, diamond colored raindrops let go of sopping wet leaves and exploded in their hair and on
their shoulders, startling them and making them laugh. But soon, they
left the trees behind, and even though it was early morning, the sun
burned down on them and promised an even hotter day. Now and then,
Pauli dashed into the wild meadow where they had rested the day

before to pick a cornflower here or a daisy there, disappearing entirely at times in the tall grass, calling out sweetly, "Come and find me."

But Ruth was not in the mood to play. If they were to cross the mountain in a day, they would have to keep moving. Suddenly, the idea of walking home with the child, which had seemed manageable at the time, seemed now reckless and foolish. If Ishmael was any indication, she'd be in deep trouble if she met a man like that on the mountain, and she had not even thought of the wildlife that roamed in these woods. And what if they couldn't cross the mountain during the day and she'd have to spend the night in the wilderness with a small child, having no weapon to defend herself against whatever might come along?

Without breaking her pace, she began searching the field of dead timber to her left for a good sized stick that she could use as a club if it came to that. Briefly, she considered turning back. Nikolas, she knew, would love to have them, and she could make herself useful, helping him sort his books and keeping house until the trains ran again. But Hannah would not know where she was and the children would be frightened. She was also worried about Martha's threat of sending the Russian Army after her. Most likely, that had been a bluff. But if she stayed with Nikolas until the trains ran again, the likelihood of some-one checking up on the strange woman and child living with him was a real threat. And if Martha filed any kind of a report, the child might be sent back and she, herself, might end up in Siberia. She found a good-sized stick that also made a good walking staff and felt a little safer car-rying that 'weapon' though she laughed and said to Pauli:

"Of course, it's no match for a gun or a knife."

"What gun?" Pauli asked, startled, not having been clued in to her aunt's thoughts and fears.

"Oh, nothing," Ruth said. "I was just thinking of the soldiers."

Pauli shot her a puzzled look. Maybe her aunt was going crazy because there wasn't a soldier in sight.

As the sun climbed, a vast silence settled lazily over the countryside, only occasionally broken by the exuberant trill of birds and the soft morning breeze making a quiet rush in the meadow grass. But when she listened closely, Ruth could hear the somber murmuring of the woods on the mountain.

They had walked about three kilometers when a Mercedes, a small red flag whipping gaily on the hood, came toward them at great speed, bouncing in the ruts and crevices of the road and slowed as it approached Ruth and the child. Ruth looked up as if unconcerned, but her heart began to pound. Not that Martha could possibly know just where she was, but then, the network of spying on people in this part of the country had already begun, and the authorities had their means of getting information out of the populace. What if they had followed her trail to the Mohr's? Or what if Ishmael had gone straight to the authorities after she refused his 'favors'?

"God, I hope they don't stop," Ruth whispered, reaching for Pauli's hand as if to keep her from running out into the road and being run over. The Mercedes passed, the driver looking straight ahead as if Ruth were not there. But his passenger, wearing a uniform, looked at her curiously. The car slowed and speeded up again.

Ruth did not turn but all her senses strained toward the diminishing purr of the engine. When she could no longer hear it, she relaxed. But only for a little while as the car must have turned at the village and came back.

Hearing it come up behind her, scattering gravel, Ruth took a deep breath and stood still at the side of the road, turning toward it as if to let it pass, pulling Pauli out of harm's way. The Mercedes pulled ahead of her and stopped.

"If they say anything, you say that today is your birthday and we're out picking flowers and having a picnic."

The back door opened and a Russian officer climbed out. Ruth, her head high, stared down the officer as if the encounter annoyed her while he merely stood by the car, studying her, taking in her hair, her face, her body, her legs. He brushed his hand over his eyes then, as if, tired, he had seen an apparition. Then he let his hand fall and smiled pensively and came toward her.

"I have not seen her in so long, I forgot what she looks like," he said, in Russian. "But she walks like you, with grace and elegance. And proud. She is always proud. That's what attracted me to her."

Ruth looked at his eyes, trying to divine the meaning of what he said.

"I should, I suppose, ask you for your papers," he said, smiling wearily. "Do you have papers?"

Ruth took her pack off and fished inside. He reached for the documents and unfolded them, but he only pretended to read them as if for the benefit of the driver. Pauli who had huddled close to Ruth with *Parzival* under one arm and the now nearly wilted wildflowers in the other, piped up:

"Today is my birthday, and we are going to pick flowers and have a picnic."

Since she spoke German, the officer looked to Ruth who was not, at first sure, whether or not it was wise to translate. He might find her useful as a translator and pack her in the car and take her along. But knowing Russian had saved her once before, and she translated what the child had said.

He looked at her, puzzled and nodded, making no comment regarding her language skill. Resting his hand on Pauli's hair, he said:

"A picnic? That sounds wonderful. How old are you today?"

Ruth caught her breath. They had not discussed that, but Pauli, quick-minded as if she had a sense of the danger, said proudly:

"Five."

"I too have a daughter," he said, smiling down at the child. "The last time I saw her, she was a baby." He spread his hands to measure out about a foot of space. "She's four now and, I'm sure, as pretty as you are."

He handed the papers back to Ruth, looking beyond her toward the village, squinting as if the sun were blinding him.

"There's been a dispatch. About a woman traveling alone with a child." He paused. "I thought you might be her, but I see that you're not."

The involuntary expression of relief on Ruth's face made him smile.

"Thank you," she said.

"I have a dacha outside Moscow. We used to have picnics there in the summer. And bonfires. We used to sing and dance around the fire. Where did you grow up?" Ruth blushed a little at the lie she was about to tell.

"In Dresden."

"Ah, Dresden! Dresden was a jewel. I wish you luck."

He stroked Pauli's hair, smiling down at her before walking back to the Mercedes. The driver wore the same stony expression he had when they passed the first time. The officer got back into the car. Ruth and Pauli watched as it maneuvered the turn on the narrow road. Ruth was about to raise her hand good-bye, but the officer looked straight ahead without acknowledging her, and the car headed toward the village.

As soon as they were out of sight, Ruth reached for Pauli's hand.

"No more picking flowers. No more playing hide and go seek, sweet thing. Did you hear what he said? A dispatch. A dispatch! That bitch reported us. She actually reported us. Sorry," Ruth said then, remembering that 'bitch' was not quite the word she wanted Pauli to use. Briskly walking down the road with the child in tow, she kept her eyes straight ahead in case another surprise came down the pike.

"And if that happens," she said, "we'll dash into the meadow. On the other hand, this is ridiculous. We stand out on this road like red flags. Who knows where the path is that Nikolas mentioned. We're going up now."

51

Solomon

Their climb was slow and cumbersome. Ruth kept to the right hoping to run across the path that Nikolas had mentioned and soon found a thin trail that had been hewn out of the underbrush. One could just barely call it a path as the forest had already begun to reclaim it, but not having to fight dense scrub made their ascent a little easier.

The woods were very quiet, and their footsteps made but soft sounds on the spongy forest floor. The sun barely filtered through the dense growth while now and then errant raindrops fell on them from the leaves.

Their progress was slow and, Pauli, getting tired, hung back more and more until it seemed to Ruth that she was pulling the child up the hill. Finally, she stopped. The strain of climbing and having to be watchful took their toll on her as well, but she tried to be cheerful.

"Let's take a little break."

Pauli did not answer but merely stood with hanging arms. Ruth dug the old raincoat out of the pack and spread it out.

"Come on. We'll eat a little something. Then you can take a little nap, and then we go on. How's that?" But Pauli simply lay down on the coat and, instantly, fell asleep. Ruth sat beside her, tailor-fashion, watching, listening. Not having a watch, she tried to gauge the time she could afford to let Pauli sleep, feeling more and more uneasy. The forest was much too quiet, and it seemed to her that behind each tree or dense shrub was a pair of eyes watching her. Her uneasiness became a self-fulfilling prophecy when, at first faint, then more pronounced, she heard the crushing of dry twigs and the violent rustle of leaves.

Her body rigid with alertness, she tried to make out the direction of the sound that was neither heavy nor rhythmical and, at times, stopped altogether. She reached for the staff and scooted close to Pauli to protect her from whatever wild animal was about to invade their territory. A kind of heavy breathing now accompanied the other sounds, and just as she raised the staff to hit whatever beast would break in on them, the face of a dog appeared out of the underbrush directly ahead of her.

The tension that had a hold on her now made room to surprise and incredulity. She didn't know if she should laugh or cry.

"God, you scared me!" she whispered. "Go away! Scat!" She waved the staff to wave the dog away and realized just how ridiculous this was. Besides, the dog had no intention of leaving. It merely stared at her antics with equanimity, wagging its tail, glad to have found some company.

Ruth reached into the pack and pulled out a piece of the dark bread. Now hard as a rock, she had a difficult time breaking off a piece as the dog watched and waited.

"Come here!"

The dog came closer. A mutt of indefinable heritage, its hair matted, it looked as if it had been on its own for some time. The bread was gone in one gulp.

"No more. Until we get out of here." The dog let out a quick, demanding bark.

Ruth reached for its face and clamped its mouth shut.

"You bark again, and I'll kill you!"

The dog seemed to have understood that tone. When she let go, it lay down, put its head on her knee, looking up at her with the kind of adoring look dogs have when they know they're home. But the barking had filtered into Pauli's deep and exhausted sleep. Drowsily, she opened her eyes, not knowing where she was. Seeing the dog, she cried out and jumped toward Ruth. Ruth quickly covered her mouth and put her arms around her.

"Shh! It's just a dog."

Still half asleep but safe in Ruth's arms, Pauli studied the newcomer suspiciously. But waking fully, she held out her hand. The dog licked it briefly, and Pauli smiled happily.

"Can he come with us?"

"I don't think we have a choice. He won't leave."

"What's his name?"

"Don't know. Solomon, I guess. He was wise enough to find us, maybe he'll help us find our way out of here."

52

Soldiers and Other Dangers

They sat a moment longer, drinking a little of the tea Nikolas had made for them and sharing some of the honey soaked bread, getting their fingers good and sticky. Solomon was content with the stone hard bread she had brought from home. Ruth hoped that, having bought the dog's loyalty with food, it would bark if someone were to approach them. On the other hand, it had come up to them so trustingly and attached itself to them so easily, it might desert them for another stranger in a heartbeat.

She urged Pauli to finish her bread and grew more and more impatient when the child took her sweet time licking the honey off her fingers since there was no water. Finally, Ruth jumped up.

"You'll just have to lick your fingers as we walk," she said, trying to keep her voice calm as she coaxed the child off the coat. She stuffed the coat and the *Parzival* into her pack. Pauli had dropped the book a number of times during their climb, and it wouldn't be fit for a library if she kept it up. Shouldering the pack, she took Pauli's sticky hand, and they continued their climb. The dog, trotting either beside them or ahead of them, sometimes disappeared in the underbrush and returned.

At times, it seemed to her the winding path would go upward forever, and when they finally reached the crest, she felt as elated as if they had make it up Mt. Everest.

"Almost there," she said, smiling, as they began their descent. But only a short way down the mountain, the dog stopped, its ears up, looking back at them uncertainly. Ruth also stopped, watching the dog, listening. For the first time, she became aware of the noise their walking made, slipping on errant plots of small rock or crushing dead leaves and twigs. Standing still, she heard what she had not heard before: the sound of machinery and hammering that came to them as if from a great distance.

"I guess she was right," Ruth said.

"Who?"

"I met a woman when I waited at the visa office, and she said…" She stopped, realizing that, if she told Pauli of the villages that were blasted out of the way of the new Russian border, she would only be frightened.

"What did she say?" Pauli insisted.

"She said that they're fixing up the villages that were destroyed in the war."

"Oh."

"Let's walked north a little," Ruth said. "I don't feel like going through construction sites where there're lots of people. That would not be a good idea, would it?"

Pauli shook her head. "When are we going to get there?"

"Where?"

"Home."

"Soon. Once we're down this mountain, we should be in the West."

"How far is that?"

"Not far. Just down this mountain, after we've walked north a little."

They walked parallel to the crest for some time with Ruth stopping now and then to listen until she could no longer hear the machinery.

"I think we can go down now," she said, and, cautiously, they began their descent, though she kept an eye on the dog who sauntered ahead of them and whose ears were wiser than hers. The dog now ran carefree enough, but they were quite a ways down the mountain before Ruth relaxed. Finally, she squatted down, directing Pauli's gaze through an opening in the foliage toward a village that lay peacefully in the summer sun some distance away in the open country. Halfway between the village and their vantage point, a farmer tilled a field with an ox.

"See that village?" Ruth asked. "That's already in the West. We can take a train from there and be home in jiffy." Pauli nodded happily, and Ruth felt confident now that they would make it.

She did not know that, at the foot of the mountain, a contingent of Russian soldiers had been busy clearing a wide strip of land that morning. They felled trees, cleared underbrush, and bulldozed what could not be ripped out, creating the very Iron Curtain that was to divide the world into East and West. Just beyond the soldiers and the strip lay the American Sector. It was nothing but lush farm and meadowland that had gone wild. A paved road meandered through the lushness not far away. As the Russians worked, an American Jeep appeared on that road now and then and stopped. The driver would raise a pair of binoculars and would watch the Russians for a moment, then drive slowly out of sight. This game was repeated at regular intervals throughout the day.

The Russians worked their way south and left a lone guard behind who sat on the ground above the cleared border strip, his back leaning comfortably against a tree. He had a good view of the strip that was about fifty yards wide, and of the paved road beyond where, occasionally, an American Jeep appeared and stopped. The guard would reach for a pair of binoculars and study the Jeep. Invariably, he saw an American soldier watching *him* through binoculars and the Russian would grin as if to let the American know that he was not bothered in the least by the surveillance. During one of these encounters, he lowered the binoculars before the American Jeep moved on and struck a match to light a cigarette as if to emphasize his lack of concern.

At the soft sound of leaves being crushed somewhere above him, he looked up. He dropped the match and froze, reached for his gun and rolled behind a tree. The American in the Jeep assumed that the charade was for his benefit, grinned, and drove on. The Russian soldier lay as if frozen, his eyes trying to penetrate the woods.

Ruth and Pauli walked directly and unsuspectingly toward him.

Solomon, having trailed behind, got the man's scent only a fraction before he jumped out from behind the tree, brandishing his gun. Ruth, having turned back toward the dog, wondering what was wrong, did not immediately see the soldier who yelled, "Halt!" and she turned back and turned to stone. Pauli became instantly hysterical.

53

Helplessness and Guts

The farmer whom Ruth had seen from the mountain was a young man, only seventeen. He looked curiously toward the woods when the dog began to bark. The sound came almost simultaneously with the petrified screams of a child. The young farmer stopped the ox as his eyes searched the impenetrable woods. A woman's voice screamed something, then both the barking and the screaming stopped. Curiously, he scanned the whole of the mountain, but all was deathly quiet.

In the din of the dog's frenzied barks and the child's hysteria, Ruth's mind worked furiously. The soldier's hair and face had seen neither water nor a barber in some time. His uniform was filthy, his boots and pants muddy. He kept his narrow eyes on her as he moved his gun from her to Pauli, to the dog and then back to her. Ruth cast a desperate glance at the border strip that was but a few yards away and stared back at the gun. Making a run for it would be suicide.

"Shut up, Solomon!" she screamed, but the dog kept barking at the guard and the guard, it seemed, had enough of that, aiming the gun at the dog, ready to shoot.

"Don't you dare!" Ruth screamed in Russian, hoping that the use of his language would make him hesitate. She took a step forward and raised her hand as if she could stop the bullet. The guard pointed the gun back at her the instant she moved which stopped her dead in her tracks. Slowly, he walked toward her, grinning. His hands were as filthy as the rest of him. He looked over her body, resting his eyes on her breasts as his smile got broader. His teeth were rotten. Ruth stood like a statue, clutching Pauli's hand. Risking a second desperate glance toward the border strip, she saw the farmer who had stopped tilling, his attention directed toward the woods, but the dense leaves of the overhanging branches obscured them from view.

Ruth raised her hand at the soldier in a futile attempt to ward him off for just an instant. She reached for the dog's collar and yanked it which shut the dog up instantly. Holding on to the dog, she squatted down to comfort the screaming Pauli. The guard's gun followed her every move.

"Pauli, honey, listen to me! Please listen to me! You have to run. Please! Please run! You have to stop screaming and run to that farmer in the field over there. Please, Pauli! I beg you."

The child, her head now hidden in Ruth's shoulder, stopped screaming, but her body shook with uncontrollable sobs.

"As soon as this man touches me, you run. With Solomon. It's our only chance. Please do that for your Aunt Ruth!"

"I'm scared!" the child wailed.

"I beg you. Do that for your Aunt Ruth. Your Mommy needs you. Please! You're smart. You're fast. You can do this! Tell the farmer. Tell him to come help us!" Engaging the child's help was a silly, futile ruse, but Ruth hoped that Pauli, if she thought she was useful, would run.

Pauli calmed down a little and, finally, nodded.

"When he touches me, you run."

Pauli nodded.

Ruth got up. The guard tore at her blouse.

"Run!"

Pauli, still crying and petrified, waited, hanging on to Ruth as the guard ripped the front of Ruth's blouse off and tore at her bra.

"For God's sake, child," Ruth screamed desperately, "run!" She was in tears now, but as if a spell had been broken, Pauli let go of her and ran like the wind, and the dog followed.

The guard, interested neither in the child nor the dog, pressed the tip of the gun's barrel to her heart and started tearing at her slacks. Ruth raised both her hands as if to show him that she would oblige him. Frantically, she fumbled for the bra clasp and undid that then pretended to undo the button on her slacks. She risked a glance toward the border strip were Pauli ran, fell, got up, and kept running.

Ruth yanked up her hand, pushed the gun upward and, with a well directed knee, hit the guard smack between the legs. The gun went off and dropped as the guard fell to his knees, holding himself, howling. Frantically, Ruth reached for the gun, hit him over the head with it, and ran.

Behind the plow, in a shallow furrow, the young farmer clumsily held on to the sobbing Pauli. He was quite unfamiliar with comforting small children but, awkwardly, tried his best by saying over and over, "Here, here." Solomon, panting, kept an eye on the woods. When the gun went off, the farmer threw himself on top of Pauli and covered his head. He lifted it just in time to see a woman flying toward him across the field, her breasts bare, brandishing a gun in one hand and a backpack in the other, the remnants of her white blouse whipping from her shoulders like a banner. When she reached them, she fell, out of breath, into the tilled field, the right arm of her blouse soaked in blood. Briefly, she opened her eyes and looked at him.

"Is this the West?"

The young man, a little shy in the presence of a half-dressed woman, grinned and nodded, quickly glancing away from her and then back at her injured arm. The sudden sound of a motor made them both look up. An American Jeep with four soldiers had appeared from nowhere on the paved road, and the base of the mountain was now teeming with Russian soldiers who had somehow materialized. Ruth and the farmer could see the truck that had brought them through the legs of the ox that had stood dumbly throughout the ruckus. Two of the American soldiers jumped out of the Jeep and ran toward Ruth, one of them carrying a green box with a red cross on it. The others kept a close eye on the border strip where a black car had arrived. The unfortunate guard, still clutching himself and bleeding from a head wound, limped forlornly to the car.

54

A Safe Haven

The American soldiers came around the ox and knelt down beside Ruth. One of them opened the first aid kit before he even said a word. The other put his hand on Pauli's hair, searching her with his eyes for injuries, glancing at the young farmer who waved his hands, "Nein, nein, fein," pointing at Ruth.

"Ich dir helfen," the American with the first aid kit said to her in broken German. Ruth smiled.

"I speak English."

"Great," he said, grinning. He took a pair of scissors and, with a sideways glance at her—"You mind?"—without waiting for an answer, cut clear through the sleeve of her blouse, peeled it back carefully and began cleaning the wound.

"Got a little scrape. Nothing bad. Looks good," he said. "This'll sting a little," he said just as Ruth said, "Ouch!" because he had already begun to apply iodine.

"What happened?" the other soldier asked, a notebook ready, satisfied that the child was all right. Pauli, lying in the furrow beside Ruth and now feeling safe, watched them curiously. As they spoke, her mouth moved as if she were about to mimic them, finding the sound of their language oddly twisted. The soldier, aware of the child's scrutiny, reached into his pocket and, winking at her, handed her a piece of gum. She took it haltingly.

"Kaugummi," he said, mouthing the German word for gum. Cautiously, she unwrapped it and stuffed it into her mouth.

"We came across the mountain, and he was waiting for me at the bottom," Ruth said and briefly described her narrow escape. "Ouch," the soldiers said and burst out laughing.

"Depending on your hit, he's gonna be out for a couple of days. He ain't gonna feel too well. Where did you come from?"

"The village that's just across. I don't know what it's called."

"Just you?"

"No. The child and I."

"You came across the mountain with the child?"

"It wasn't that bad." Ruth laughed. "Until I met Gorgeous over there, of course."

The soldiers smiled. "He's gone now." They could see the car leaving while the Russian soldiers that had recently arrived lingered on, keeping their eyes on the Jeep and on what they could glimpse of Ruth and her companions behind the plow.

"Did you see anything that would be of interest to us? Equipment? Weapons? Anything you'd find unusual?"

Ruth tried to sit up.

"Keep your head down," the soldiers said. "We doubt they're gonna shoot with us sitting here, but you never know."

Ruth told them that she had heard some large equipment further down the road, but that was really all she knew. They seemed satisfied.

"We know about that," they said.

Most of the Russians had now climbed back on the truck that, using the border strip for a road, roared off and soon disappeared behind a bend. Those that were left behind stood, their guns drawn, watching what went on in the field.

"Where were you headed?"

"Home," Ruth said. "I came from Wiesbaden a couple of days ago and got stuck when they blockaded everything. So I walked."

The soldiers looked at each other, raising their eyebrows in admiration. "You're quite a ways from home, ma'am. I guess you know that?"

Ruth nodded. "Just being in the West is great."

"You bet." They got up. "Will you be all right?"

"I'll be fine," she said. "I'm sure this young man here will see me to the train station."

The farmer sensing that he was being talked about looked curiously from one to the other, not understanding a word.

"What's your name?" Ruth asked him in German.

"Otto. Stein. Otto Stein."

"We suggest you head out now while we're here," the paramedic said. "So they don't try any monkey business."

They got up and one of them let out a loud whistle toward the Jeep. The driver turned and held up his thumb to indicate something like an 'all clear.'

"They want us to head to the village while they're still here," she translated to the farmer. He looked a little doubtful at the ox and plow and nodded, undoing the plow.

"You walk ahead of the animal," he said. "Go straight."

And so they headed clear across the field, Ruth and the child ahead, as if shielded by the ox who would take the shot should one of the Russians' guns go off 'accidentally'. When they entered the village, Ruth turned. The American soldiers were still standing in the field. She raised her hand, and they waved back. The farmer turned into the yard of a farmhouse where Ruth finally permitted herself to feel what she had not permitted herself to feel since she left Berlin—utter exhaustion. She fell, feeling suddenly weak, onto an old bench that stood in the yard and burst into tears.

Otto and Pauli stood by helplessly, Pauli looking up at Otto as if salvation might come from him.

"Komm," he said. He went into the house to get his mother, realizing that some situations were simply beyond his knowledge and were handled best by women.

55

Home Sweet Home

The Stein family put Ruth up for the night. Otto Stein, Sr. had been killed in the war. The older of the two sons worked in the next town clearing rubble. Young Otto's mother, a short, plump, and energetic woman whose name was Ingrid, went through the village the next morning to find a dress that Ruth could wear on the way home since the blouse was beyond mending. The dress was a little long and a little wide, but that didn't matter in the least. Ingrid even heated up some water so they could bathe in an old iron tub and wash their hair, with help from Ingrid who believed firmly that Ruth should not get her injured arm wet and possibly infected.

Otto took them to the next town, but not before they had decided to leave Solomon behind. The dog had, as they walked into the yard the day before, found his place beneath the bench Ruth sat on and came out only when Ingrid offered it some food, but then it retreated back to that safe spot which they watched with some amusement.

"He thinks he's home," Ingrid said. "Why don't you leave him? From what you tell me, you couldn't keep him anyway."

Otto waited with them at the train station for all the three hours it took for a train to come, finally, making sure that they were settled comfortably, and waiting even until they pulled out which moved Ruth deeply.

The train was nearly empty, and Ruth and Pauli had a compartment to themselves.

"You think Solomon will like it at the farmers?" Pauli asked.

"He'll love it! He would not be happy in our attic room, and every time he needed to go outside, you'd have to climb five flights of stairs down with him and five back up."

Pauli looked at her doubtfully as if she could not imagine five flights of stairs.

"How do Penelope and Eva go out to play?"

Ruth laughed. "They climb down five flights of stairs and five back up."

Pauli was about to ask more but then something outside the window caught her attention which gave Ruth a chance to settle back and close her eyes for a little while.

She felt both drained and elated. What a harebrained idea it had been to go and get the child. Reckless and impulsive. She could have been stuck behind that border forever, as Whitman had pointed out. Both of them could have been shot, and then what would Hannah have? She shuddered at the memory of the Russian's face. The disgust she had felt and the terror. She opened her eyes. That face and the point of that gun at her heart would be with her for a long time. She looked at Pauli who was busy counting the homes of the small village they traveled through. Ruth smiled. But it had turned out well. It may have been reckless and impulsive, but it turned out well. Ruth smiled in anticipation of seeing Hannah's face when they got home.

When the train pulled into their station, Ruth got up and took the pack out of the rack above her head. Her right arm, still bandaged, gave her some trouble.

"A shame that your Mommy doesn't know we're coming today. I can't wait to see her face."

Smiling, she shouldered the pack and, inadvertently, looked out the window. Hannah, the children beside her, frantically searched the train's windows for Ruth. Ruth's eyes filled with tears.

"There! There she is! Can you see her? Can you?"

Eagerly, Pauli pressed her face against the window, but the coach had already passed the spot where Hannah stood. When the train stopped, Ruth waited until the other passengers had filtered by the compartment.

"You stay behind me," she said to the child. "We'll surprise her."

Pauli smirked, wrapping herself in Ruth's skirt as they walked through the coach to the exit. There Ruth stopped and scanned the platform for Hannah and the children. Seeing her, she waved her left arm enthusiastically.

"Hannah! Hannah!" she called over the din of the passengers getting off or climbing on.

The children saw her before Hannah did and pulled her along, yelling "Mommy! Mommy!" all the way. When they came to the coach, Hannah stopped, looking up at Ruth who had put on her most serious face. The children were about to race up the coach stairs, but Hannah had stopped so abruptly, it stopped the children as well, and they looked up into her devastated face. She let go of Penelope's hand and put her hand to her heart. She had just seen Ruth's bandaged arm, and she turned white. But then Ruth smiled and pulled Pauli out from behind her skirt. Hannah burst into tears and could, for just an instant, not move at all. But then she scooped up Pauli and covered her child with kisses.

Hannah had gone to the station every day after she and the children came home from work. Since she had no one to watch over them, she woke them at three in the morning and walked with them the four miles to work. She had organized a baby carriage at the relief center, and when the children were too tired, they curled up in the old carriage and she pushed them there.

She had to be at work at five in the morning, getting the small store that was attached to the bakery ready for customers, some of whom came as early as seven.

Penelope and Eva would go to the bakery proper at the back of the house because, that early in the morning, the most heavenly scents came from there. There was, for them, no scent as delicious as that of bread baking in an oven. They'd sit, quiet as mice, on a large, old millstone that, for some reason, had been laid down in the bakery. From there, they watched the baker who'd been up since three as well, kneading dough and pushing sheets filled with orderly rows of rolls and cake forms and round breads and long breads into a tall oven made of stone. Sometimes, when a roll did not turn out the way he thought it should, he gave it to the children, though he rarely spoke to them. But that did not matter to them who ate the rolls thankfully and slowly with the smallest of bites because they tasted like manna from heaven to them. But even if he had not given them anything, they still would have sat in the warmth and in the scent, convinced that Heaven was most likely just like this bakery.

When they came back to the attic room the night Ruth finally came home, Hannah put the key into the lock and said to Ruth, "You can't come in until I say so. And keep your eyes closed."

The children could hardly contain their excitement and kept jumping and yelling, because they had prepared a surprise for her. Hannah went inside and closed the door. A few minutes later, she opened it wide.

The old table wore a proper tablecloth and neatly placed cups and plates that didn't match. In the middle was a cake, a lit candle riding on top. Beside the cake was a vase with red roses. Ruth started crying as Hannah proudly surveyed the surprise while Eva and Penelope took Ruth by the hand and led her to the table. Hannah pointed at the cake.

"He let me have it for nothing. It's a week old, but it's still quite good."

"Oh, it's the most beautiful cake I've ever seen," Ruth sobbed. "And wherever did you get such roses?"

"Now these are not from me."

Significantly, she looked beyond Ruth who turned. Whitman had appeared in the door. Wordlessly, he reached for her and put his arms around her.

"But how did you know I was coming?" she sobbed.

"I took Hannah to the station on a hunch. I saw you arrive, but I wanted you to have this time to yourself, just you and Hannah and the children. And when you got on the bus, I drove straight here and parked the Jeep around the corner."

56

Of What Is Possible

Deeply moved at the scene I had just read, I looked up and at a sea of candles. There were but five or six, but the windowpanes reflected their light one to the other and so it seemed there was a sea of them. They burned quietly, their warmth spreading a tranquil hush over the room.

"So she did it," I said, more to the candles than to Penelope.

"Yes, she did it. And she couldn't have done it if he hadn't forged the visa."

"No, I suppose not," I said, shooting her a quick, proud smile, feeling miserable at the same time, because I would never be able to tell my father just how proud this forgery made me, would never hear his voice telling me the same story, in his words. I tried to imagine him, tried to recall his voice, but all I could remember were the words he had said so often about something kind he had done, 'It was nothing. What else was I gonna do?'

"Of course," Penelope said into my thoughts, "it may have been a far more exciting story if he had flown her to Berlin and gotten her and Pauli out. You can just see that scene in the movies with the Russians shooting at him as he lifted off in his plane into the wild blue yonder and whisked Ruth and the child to freedom and safety. Hollywood would like that. But this is not what happens in real life. Real acts of courage happen every day and no one even notices. I think just living, sometimes, is an act of courage. It reminds me of something that

George Eliot said at the end of *Middlemarch* about Dorothea. She said, *But the effect of her being on those around her was incalculably diffusive: for the growing good of the world is partly dependent on unhistoric acts; and that things are not so ill with you and me as they might have been, is half owing to the number who lived faithfully a hidden life, and rest in unvisited tombs.* When I first read this sentence, it would not have occurred to me to apply it to my mother. But when I found it again, years later, I memorized it, because it fits her perfectly. And if you substitute 'her' for 'his', it fits your father just as perfectly. And a thousand other unsung heroes."

"Yes," I said. Because she was right, of course. Both of them were unsung heroes, their deeds unlauded, and things were not so ill for both her and myself because of our parents. I was not aware until some moments later that I studied her trying to sort out my emotions. Only one of them I felt clearly: that I was grateful to her, so immensely grateful that she wrote the story down. But she was not looking at me, pondering something deeply, flipping through the stack of pages I had been handing her.

"I don't think," she said, "she knew the meaning of the word no. But it was more than that. War had already taken so much from her, and she was determined that, this time, it would not happen again. Martha would not get this child. She would not permit Martha to cheat Hannah out of something that was rightfully hers. Because Martha took full advantage of the confusion after the war to get what she wanted, without the least regard for Hannah or Pauli. Or anyone else for that matter. Besides, the world had gone crazy. As if all of civilization had gone mad. Families dead or scattered. Some of them did not find one another again until ten, fifteen years later. Fathers, husbands in prison camps. Some did not get out until years later, not knowing where their families had ended up. There are so many stories that no one has ever told. Children wandering the countryside, separated from their parents or orphaned. To get Pauli was just one small thing to her to set something right. Some members of the family said, years later, that it might have been better for Pauli to have grown up in a large house with all the luxuries Martha could afford her, but that's so easy to say if it isn't your child." She stopped, brushing the somber words aside with the flicker of a smile.

"You are a very unusual human being," I said which brought a moment of deadpan silence as she switched emotional tracks from her mother to me, not understanding what brought on the sudden change in subject matter. But I shook my head. I didn't know how to explain what I meant. I just had never met anyone who considered things so earnestly and sincerely. I think I was about to fall in love with Ms. Penelope Karstens though I'd known her only for a day. But it seemed to me I'd known her all my life. Falling in love was the last thing I thought I'd do when I first read my father's letter and agonized over writing to the daughter of my father's mistress.

She had put on a tape of Baroque music at some point as I sat reading. The music fit the mood of the candlelight perfectly. The rafters above now lay in the shadows, and it struck me that the whole of the room looked like one huge, cozy attic room.

"So this is the attic room," I said. "Grown up."

"How'd you guess?" She looked up at the broad skylight that was nearly dark. "How well I remember lying in bed in that attic room. I'd look up through that tiny skylight, exactly a foot by a foot and a half. The stars wandered in frames, and I'd lie awake and study them. I so wanted to see the whole of the sky."

"So what's it like sleeping with the stars nowadays?"

"Heaven!" she smiled.

"Do you always light candles?" I asked.

"Yes."

"I like it. It's nice." I turned my attention back to the manuscript and back to her. "Are you getting hungry?"

"A little, but I'd much rather you finish, then we can talk when we eat."

While I had been reading, she had kept refilling the coffee cups and, at some point, had put a second plate with cookies on the table beside my chair that I munched on without being in the least aware, except that they were delicious. Something with chocolate and nuts in them.

Dutifully, I returned to the remainder of the manuscript, handing her the page I had just read, and looked down at the next which was empty except for two words, 'chapter missing.' Startled, I stared at the words. Suddenly, I found them hilarious.

"What's this?" I asked, laughing, waving the page toward her. Superciliously, she stared at me, looking wholly innocent.

"It means just what it says. The chapter is missing."

"What does this mean?"

"It means that the…" She was about to repeat what she had said.

"All right, all right, I understand." I tried to look crestfallen and severe. "Ms. Karstens, you can't leave your readers hanging like that! How can I find out what happens next? First, you have me in tears with the mother and child reunion, and further reunions, and then, zero."

"I didn't know how to write it, so I left it out for now," she said unperturbed. "I mean, I have oodles of notes, but I don't know how to put it all together. So, why mess it up."

"I wouldn't call this story messed up."

She smirked. "Thanks. I think that's what I wanted to know. Anyway, since the chapter is missing, I'll just have to tell you what happened next."

"I don't know about that, since you said you weren't a storyteller," I joked.

"It's either this, or you won't find out what happened," she joked back.

"All right then, go ahead."

"Thank you. So. Let me see. I was going to say something like this: The days and weeks after Hannah's and Pauli's reunion were happy ones. Maybe because Ruth was happier. Maybe because life improved somehow. Ted hauled all sorts of food to the house, delicacies they never had: the softest bread, butter, Hershey's chocolate, juice. And sweets made of marshmallows, a treat that was entirely new to them. Which tells you just what a child's tummy is concerned with. He brought meat and fish in cans and so the dinner menus became healthier also. But that was irrelevant to the children. We couldn't wait for dinner to be over so that we could hit the box that had all the sweets...."

I did not realize until she paused that she had, unconsciously, switched from the third person point of view to the first person plural, 'we'. I had already identified her so closely with the story that the subtle change went unnoticed. I did not mention it, but she must have read my thoughts.

"It's been darn difficult to keep being objective in this story. I keep switching from me and we to her or him and them. I did that even when I was writing it. Maybe that's why I couldn't write the chapter, and I do want to keep myself out of it. But. Let me see how I could go on... As for Ruth and Ted, they went dancing often or had dinner at the club. Sometimes, they took Hannah, hoping that she would get to know someone. But Hannah was shy, and she preferred to stay behind and baby-sit. She felt much safer with the children. And yes, Ted bought Ruth clothes, slacks and blouses and sweaters and skirts, and whenever he did, she protested loudly. She didn't want him to bring her things because it made her feel like a kept woman. Then again, she wore everything proudly, because she loved good clothes and looked stunning in them. He simply never listened to her when she protested, because he saw no earthly reason why she should be destitute when he was in her life now."

She stopped again, thinking.

"Let's see. And they did things together that, as children, we couldn't even guess at. Even years later, she would never, ever, touch on the subject of sex, and so, in good conscience, I can't say whether or not they ever made love. And I didn't want to write about that because it was so private to her. But we loved his coming to the attic room, especially on the weekends because he'd always planned something—a picnic, or a drive in the country, or a hike once his leg got well. And he played the ukulele so sweetly. He used to take one of my mother's darning needles, threading a string through it, and, as he played, he let the darning needle dance over the strings or he'd pull them across the strings which made the sweetest sounds. And, of course, every time I hear a ukulele nowadays, it brings that room back to me."

I must have had a secret smile on my face, because she said, "Do you play the ukulele?"

"No. But he did. And when I was young and dumb, I thought it was the stupidest instrument ever invented. He looked so ridiculous, that tall man with that toy guitar. I felt embarrassed. Which goes to show you just how bright teenagers sometimes are. Of course, now I could kick myself to kingdom come. I mean, to me, my father couldn't do anything right. And, this minute, I'd give anything if I could play the ukulele. Because it would put that special smile on your face that you have when you talk about him."

"A shame," she said.

I must have looked a little forlorn because she asked, "What?"

I studied the candles. "I can still see him, leaning against a metal work table in the hanger, playing that ridiculous instrument, with everyone standing around singing and clapping. I'd go outside and the sound of that damn guitar would follow me, and right now, I'd give all I have if I could see him just like that right now. At some point, he must have given up playing, because he stopped bringing the ukulele to work with him. And the abominable truth is that I thought of this only now."

I turned back to the manuscript and remembered only then that she had been telling the story.

"Go on," I said. "I'm sorry about the diversion. If it was redemption I was after, I am getting it. Maybe some day I can talk about just what I feel right now. And it ain't pleasant."

And so she continued. There was nothing she could do to help me out. I had to trot along that sad road all by myself.

"Once," she said, "he took us to a movie on base, called *Gone With the Wind*, but we didn't understand a thing because the movie was in English, and we had picked up barely ten words of that language to show off to our friends. When the movie began, he began whispering translations, but he gave it up when the people behind us kept saying, 'Shh. Shh.' The one thing my unconscious remembered of the movie was the hauntingly beautiful music. Where the feeling memories of other people are sparked by scents or images, mine are sparked by music, sometimes only scraps of notes, a single bar even. I didn't see *Gone With the Wind* again until thirty years later, and when the music began playing, I burst into tears. I didn't know why because I didn't remember the movie at all, did not remember the story or the characters or the images. But the music had anchored itself into my unconscious that evening when I was six, and it came back to haunt me. It took many more years before I remembered that he had taken us to the theater and that I had seen the movie before. But the music is irrevocably connected in my mind with the days in the attic room. And then, of course, seeing the movie again so many years later, the devastation of Tara, the scenes of destruction during the Civil War, all of it sparked the memory of a feeling. That's pretty much what it was like after the war. So you can see that it would be difficult to write. I'm not saying that I will not write it. I have to, of course. Anyway, you can go back to reading. The next chapter should be all right."

57

A Long Lost Friend

About two months after her walk over the mountain, Ruth found Arno von Hesse waiting for her. She had gone to the relief center and had come back with two bags of clothes and shoes for the children and with food from CARE.

Sometimes, she lied to Ted, telling him that she had plenty of food and for him not to bring anything because she had, of course, no place to store things and refrigerators were unheard of. She was also extremely touchy on the subject of being a kept woman. All the while, she was deeply in love with him as he was with her, and so she kept going to the relief center to supplement the food she told him she didn't need and to get whatever used clothing she could get.

Turning the corner into her street that day, she put the bags down to rub her sore hands. Involuntarily, she looked up and saw a man leaning against the wall beside the entrance door to her apartment building. She recognized Arno immediately and waved and smiled. He waved back as she picked up the bags and rushed toward him, disbelief and relief written all over her face.

"Hello, beautiful!" he said.

They studied each other happily. Arno let go of one of his crutches and reached out to touch her hair.

"You look wonderful. And so alive. So wonderfully alive. I worried all this time." The longing in his eyes spoke volumes.

"How long before the train left?" she asked.

"Two weeks."

"Two weeks?"

"I missed your bread. They brought us watery soup every two days."

He smiled. His teeth were very white in his tanned face.

"How are things?" she asked.

"Fine, I suppose. She has plans. Big plans. Reconstruction and all that. Marshall Plan and all that. Money that can be borrowed. People will need things. Nice things, she said, after this war. A boutique, maybe." He laughed, a little forlorn, and hit his leg with one of his crutches. "And maybe I can go back to doctoring. Maybe psychiatry."

This struck him as funny, and he laughed out loud. "I don't need my legs for that. And a good many people need their head examined. Although this should had been done before the war…"

He pointed to the bags.

"I see that CARE is still part of the menu."

She blushed. "Yes and no." She began stuttering. "I had…I did…a man…"

Arno laughed at her embarrassment.

"An American?"

She nodded.

"He just walked in, if it's the same fellow. He said hello to me and offered me a cigarette. Anyway—nice man." He paused, studying her, then remembered why he had come. He handed her a paper bag that was tucked under his arm. She opened it and looked inside. The doll with its sleepy lashes smiled up at her.

"Oh, thank you so much. Pauli did not forget. Though she did wonder just when you would bring her. Oh, but what are we doing standing here. Come!" She reached for his arm. "Come upstairs. I so want you to meet Hannah and my children, and…"

But he shook his head.

"Some other time. Or rather, I don't want to. I want you all to myself for a long time. Just to talk. About old times. And to read to you." He studied her face a moment longer as if to chisel it into his memory. Then he turned and limped away. She looked after him, her hand ready to wave when he turned. But he disappeared around the corner without looking back.

58

A Proposal

Burdened with the bags, she climbed the stairs slowly and pensively, thinking that he was a very special man, thinking that she might never see him again, wondering if, ever again, he would be happy. He was a man who was born into melancholy for whom a half a glass of water was always half empty while to her it was always half full. From somewhere above her, she heard a whistle that made her smile. Almost instantly, Ted came jumping down the stairs, kissed her cheek and reached for the bags.

"Hello, dearest," he said. "Will you marry me?" Then he frowned. "CARE! CARE? Am I not taking good care of you? Don't I bring you everything I can think of? Why are you still going to that relief center?" He was exasperated.

"A man is no life insurance," she said. She dropped the bags. Suddenly she was tired, tired of her own inner demand of keeping a delicate balance between her independence and needing and wanting someone to take care of her, tired of having to worry about every little thing, tired of having to be cautious of his caring too much about her. "My mother always said that, and she's right."

Ted laughed and jumped up the stairs two at a time, carrying the bags. Ruth followed slowly. In front of the apartment door, he turned and grinned.

"All right! I won't ask you to marry me for a whole week if you promise to go dancing with me tonight. At the club. Dinner. The works. How's that?"

She frowned and feigned difficulty at making such a decision, then she smirked.

"Oh, all right! If you insist."

He had, in the meantime, returned to flying, and the little time he could come to see her was never enough for him. But whenever he did come, and he came as often as he could, he would ask her to marry him. She always said no. One day, he came unexpectedly and greatly surprised her. Immediately, she sensed that something had happened, and it had. He had gotten a telegram that his little boy had contracted polio.

They went down to the Rhine River, to the same place where they had sat after their first date. It was October, though it was warm, and they sat, arm in arm, on a bench, watching the river.

"So we have to make a decision," he said, "and the only thing we can do is to get married right away. I mean, it's gonna take weeks for the bureaucracy to grind its wheels what with all the paperwork. After all, for all they know, you are the enemy and they will investigate you backwards and forwards. But we can at least set all the wheels in motion."

Ruth shook her head.

"Does this mean you will not marry me?"

"It means I can't marry you."

"And why not?"

"Because you have to go and take care of your little boy. You have to share this with his mother."

"I see no reason why we can't all take care of him."

"He does not know me. He needs a full set of parents that are there for him. Only him."

"Lillian is extremely competent. I don't think she needs me there," he said.

But this only frustrated Ruth. "Oh, for God's sake. Men are so stupid. You can't worry about me now. You have to worry about him. If I go with you, you'd have to divide your time between me and Penelope and Eva and Alex, and you can't worry about that now. You have to worry about him. And, of course, she needs you there too. It's your child together. What has her being competent to do with her being scared to death? I would be out of my mind. Of course, she wants you there. She is scared. Every mother would be. She may have money, but that does not help her now. She needs you, because you are his father."

Whitman was frustrated beyond endurance.

"But I love you. Can't you see that? I love *you*. And why must this be so difficult?"

But she shook her head. "What if you love me only because you are here, in a strange country, and alone?"

"Don't try to talk me out of what I feel for you. I love you. You can stand on your head and…"

She got up. In a flash, she executed the most perfect handstand then fell to the grass. Whitman burst out laughing. She looked up at him.

"You are rather selfish, you know?"

"Me? Selfish?" That was news to him. After all, he had taken care of all of them for months without the least expectation of any kind of gratitude. She looked away from him because her eyes were full of tears.

"I have dreamed of going with you," she sobbed. "It's all I could think about. I thought of the house I might have. And going to a store, just like that, for food. And turquoise dresses for the girls. With little white petticoats…"

"Then do it. Do it. Come with me."

Across the river, the bombed city looked sad and grotesque. She shook her head violently. "No. I think you should go and take care of your little boy. That's the most important right now." She pointed toward the city. "And also this. This is my home. Poor and broken as it is, it is my home. How can I leave it?"

"Oh, for God's sake, Ruth. You can help your country more by coming with me and sending CARE packages back here. What good are you doing anyone here?"

But she kept shaking her head making him only more determined.

"Think of Penelope and Eva! Don't you think they would have a much better life there than here?"

"I don't want them to have a better life. I want them to have a hard life, a difficult life. It will teach them compassion and respect. For life."

"You can't mean that!"

All she could do then was to bury her face in her arms, her shoulders shaking with sobs. Whitman scooted off the bench into the grass beside her, holding her until the tears subsided. Resting his cheek against hers, they sat for a long time, watching the river.

He left for the States the next morning.

59

A Beautiful Story

I held the page in my hand for some time. I had a hard time getting the words out. "You mean they didn't marry because of me?"

"That was certainly one of the reasons."

"But it was the main reason?"

"Yes."

"Yes?"

"Of course."

"I don't believe it. I mean I do, but I can't believe that I was such an idiot who held it against him that he was in love with someone other than my mother. And all this time, the man had sacrificed himself for me."

"Alex, you didn't ask to get polio. I mean, that's absurd."

"Talk about a screwed up mess. Are you aware that I completely, totally, ruined my relationship with my father because of this?"

Maybe it was the violence of my words that made the candles flicker suddenly as if a hand had brushed over them, trying to snuff them out. She got up and closed the windows.

"I think a storm is coming," she said. "And I think that you are much too hard on yourself. You were only eleven. What does a child of eleven know?"

But her words were no consolation. I couldn't get the irony of it all out of my mind. As if some evil genie had twisted something totally innocent all out of proportion, determined to make a mess of things.

"Did they ever see each other again?"

"No. And it's never been clear to me why not. She always gave so many reasons, none of which were clear to me. Life in the States would have been paradise for us in comparison to all that desolation. I finally realized that she was afraid, afraid of prejudice. She could never forget Sheryl's treatment of her at the club. She thought she'd be totally isolated in the States. Except for him, of course."

"But that's absurd. Of course, there is prejudice in this country, I mean, obvious, but there are also those who know that the so-called little people don't have much political clout."

"I know that and you know that, but she didn't know that. The last thing she wanted to do was to go to a place where no one would ever talk to her, or to the children, or snub her because she was the enemy, whether she had ever hurt a fly or not." She smiled. "Don't think we didn't try to persuade her otherwise, years later, when we were a little older and began asking questions. But she would not change her mind. Besides, she married someone else."

"Married someone else?" I echoed dumbly. I had the feeble sense of her having betrayed my father.

Penelope leaned toward me as if she were about to explain something intently to a child. "But that's just the point. I tried to see her, no, I tried to write about her from her point of view, don't you see? Maybe you and I would have decided differently." There was the flicker of a smile in her eyes. "I mean, if I had met the man of my life, I'd go to the end of the world with him. But that's me. She didn't think that way, or even if she did, she lived in a time that you and I can only imagine. I mean, I lived then as well, but I was just a child. What did I know? So long as there was someone to love me and so long as I felt safe, I was all right. Life, at that time, was just too difficult alone. I mean, I can only imagine the emotional drain on her. Here she was with two small children and no husband and Hannah, who wasn't all too well, and Pauli. I mean, she wasn't raised to take care of all these people, having neither a career nor any money, nor any other resources. We didn't like the man she married, and he didn't like us. But he provided well for all of us, and he obviously loved her. In time, we learned to hate him." A small pause hung in the room then while she studied the storm that was about to break outside the window. Determinedly, she looked at me once again. "And it gets even more tragic. I might as well give it to you all at once."

She stood up and walked to the dining room table as if to get something, though I realized later that this seemingly aimless gesture was born out of her feeling too agitated to face me. She stood for a moment, looking out the west window where tall sunflowers were being whipped violently by the wind. But then she turned back to me, leaning against the table, casually crossing her arms as if that which she were about to tell me were nothing more than office gossip. "She died when I was twenty-seven. A year later, Aunt Hannah died. Two years later, Pauli died. And five years later, Eva. They all died suddenly and unexpectedly."

"Good God!"

It was all I could say. An uneasy calm rose from the candles into the silence of the room. Outside the window, the gray sky hung low, pregnant with rain as the wind tore at the roses climbing up the patio columns.

"What kind of hell did you live through?" I asked, finally, but she did not respond to that. Instead, she said, "And I want to understand why she had to go and get the child and walk all the way home with her, and for this child to barely become a woman before she died. It doesn't make sense to me. Does it to you?"

I shook my head. She came back to where she had left the manuscript on the couch and began pounding it gently into a proper stack on the coffee table.

"And now that you know the story, are you still interested in taking me out to dinner? I'm starved."

She was not that callous as to brush all she had told me aside as if it meant nothing. She turned, shooting me a tearful glance.

"I've been over this so many times, I can't stand it. The only thing I could do was to write it down. There isn't very much in this world that makes sense to me. Understandably. Except for writing things down, no matter how insignificant they may be to others. But by writing their story down, they will not be forgotten. Not their courage, not their misery, not their laughter." And through the tears wandered a very brief, impish smile. "I don't expect this story to prevent war. But then, you never know. Let's get out of here for awhile. I've lived with these people for so long, I've begun to hate them, and it's time I had a life of my own."

"What I really want to do is to hug you," I said. I didn't even know I was going to say that. But the feeling was so strong, something in me gave words to them before I knew it. Compassion and sorrow and wanting to console her and love for my father, the guilt I felt, all was mixed up in one hell of a powerful surge of emotion.

Her head cocked to one side, the whole of her face lit up with the warmth in her eyes. "There's a time and a season for everything," she joked. "If you want to freshen up a little, the bathroom is around the corner." She pointed to the right somewhere. "I'll go upstairs to change."

In the little bathroom, I washed my hands, staring into the mirror. There was something different about this guy with his graying hair and his lively, attentive blue eyes. Just what that was, I didn't know. And after all this, I thought, staring at this guy, I will have to tell her something so pedestrian. That he has left her something as pedestrian as money. Lots of it. And after what I had read, it seemed wholly insignificant.

60

A Veritable Feast, II

She took me to a lovely, old tavern in a small town nearby that had gone to sleep the moment the Civil War was over. The streets were empty and quiet, and the faded grandeur of Georgian, Greek Revival, and Victorian mansions shaded by high old trees kept a soulful company with lesser neighbors of the clapboard and tenement variety.

We said little on the way over. A kind of emotional paralysis had gotten hold of me, and it was good to just concentrate on the driving. Scenes of the story drifted in and out of my mind. They had left a curious echo behind, a kind of contemplative mixture of laughter and tears for the two young people who had snatched a smidgen of happiness from the tragedy of war. And at the fringes of their story hovered the profound remorse I felt for what I had done, or rather, what I failed to do. And then there was Penelope whom I could feel beside me and the fresh scent of her hair or her perfume that intoxicated me, and to whom I felt more deeply connected than to anyone else I had ever known though I had known her only for a few hours. It was as if we had shared a lifetime, and maybe, in a way, we had.

"I hope it doesn't hail," Penelope said into my thoughts. "One of these days, I'm going to come home to heaps of broken glass."

"Then I'll have to come and rescue you," I said.

"I'd like that."

Her smile hung in the car though I didn't turn to look at her, keeping my eyes on the road that was getting more dangerous by the minute. At some gusts of wind, I had a hard time keeping the car straight, and, driving beneath a parade of trees, slim, leafy branches came down on the windshield. The leaves clung flat and desperate to the glass and then were torn away again.

The pub was small, dark-beamed and cozy, decorated with nostalgic treasures and lit by candlelight.

"Perfect!" I said.

"I thought you might like it."

"So what shall we have?" I asked, studying the menu.

"I shall have…" she said.

I looked up. A tiny devil danced in her eyes and I knew exactly where she was headed, and so we ordered T-bone and baked potato and salad and green beans and corn.

"No green beans today," the waitress said. "Broccoli?" We frowned. "California mix? Steamed?" We raised our eyebrows, astonished at the mere suggestion and rejected that too.

"Peas?" she tried again. We shook our heads, dismayed, but then, reluctantly, accepted the suggestion. It came closest in color to the green beans.

"Butter and sour cream on the potatoes?"

"Of course," we said in unison. And then she left, and we smiled at each other like conspirators.

"Eva and I used to call him The Good American."

"The Good American?"

She laughed. "I guess we must have heard the story of the Good Samaritan, but that didn't make sense to us. We thought the person telling the story got it wrong and meant to say American."

"My dad would've gotten a kick out of this."

"But you said you had a letter? To my mother?"

"It came with the will. It's in the car. I brought the other letters too. I didn't read them, of course, since they were addressed to her. I didn't know that she…but maybe, sometime, we could read them together." That sounded awfully much like a come-on, but I didn't correct what I said. I wanted to see her again. I couldn't imagine not seeing her. I could already see myself driving once again up to her house when I remembered that she would be moving.

"I'd like that," she said, and for an instant I was confused. Did she mean my seeing her again? But then I remembered. She was referring to the letters.

"And there is something else," I said, "and far more important, actually." I corrected myself. "Maybe not far more, but important. He…"

The waitress came up to show me the bottle of wine I had ordered. I nodded. So long as it was dry, it didn't matter. She poured the wine and left.

"What?" Penelope asked.

"Let's leave it for later. It's possible that you will not eat a bite, just like your mother didn't, if I tell you now."

"She ate once he promised to give her something."

"I promise to give you the letter once you've eaten your dinner." I lifted my glass. "To our parents who brought us together. I think they had excellent taste."

"To our parents."

We sipped our wine and put it down. I felt I had to make a confession.

"Well, Ms. Karstens, I want to confess that I thought you were a mousy little creature with stringy hair and bad teeth…"

"You did?" she interjected, alarm in her dark eyes.

"…and there was a time in my life when I hated you," I continued undaunted. She frowned. "Instead, you turned out to be…well…exceptional, for lack of another word, and what I thought would be a shack with rusted cars all over the place turned out to be…well…I don't want to go home."

Her frown deepened. "What does this mean?"

"It means that I don't want to go home to Deadsville which is empty and dark. Truth is, I want to talk to you all night." Truth was, I couldn't see myself driving the two hours back to Washington, alone with my thoughts. Somewhere in the back of my mind weighed the shadow of my abominable behavior toward my father. But I didn't want to deal with this now. It would be with me until I found a way to forgive myself, and, that moment, I saw nothing even remotely like forgiveness for a long time to come.

"You can sleep on the couch I sat on," she said. "It pulls out into a bed."

"You don't mind?"

She shook her head. "I even have an extra toothbrush. People do wander in sometimes and stay."

The waitress brought a huge tray and began loading the table.

"There is no way in damnation I can finish all this," Penelope said.

"I can bring you a box," the waitress offered accommodatingly.

"Actually," I said, "we don't want that. We want a doggy bag," which momentarily stopped the waitress dead in her tracks. "We don't have that."

"We'll take the box," I said, graciously. Penelope shot me a quick, conspiratorial smile, and we began eating.

"There was a time," she said, "when I felt profoundly guilty for leaving anything on my plate. Her eyes were always watching. And I couldn't throw food away to save my life. I'd wait until it had mildew on it and was totally unfit for human consumption. Then I had an ironclad excuse to throw it out. For years and years, she looked over my shoulder."

Small talk was the order now, and I remembered that I had thought of taking her along sometime, to Rome or Paris, if she wanted to go. Wouldn't cost her a dime. I'd say she was my wife, at which she raised her eyebrows, a little uncertain of whether or not a trip to Europe was worth it if I was the prize. But her eyes did light up at the prospect of going overseas, and she admitted that she loved traveling. Sometimes, she said, she got homesick for Europe. She said money had been a little tight since her son went to college. He had a part time job and a scholarship. Still.

Which was, of course, a perfect opportunity for me to spring the pedestrian money on her. I pushed my plate aside, and it wasn't long before she did the same, and the efficient waitress whisked the plates away in a heartbeat.

"Coffee?" she asked. We nodded. "Sugar and cream?" I nodded. Penelope shook her head. "Just sugar," she said, and a second later, she had me laughing when she said, "One of these days, I'm going to walk into a restaurant, order a cup of coffee and calmly sprinkle salt into it."

"Salt?"

"Salt. I heard the Laplanders like it that way. And even if they don't, I want to see the expression on the faces of the other people watching me."

Laughing, I took her hand and shook it just a little. "You know, I like you."

"Thanks." The waitress put the coffee cups down, and I must have screwed up my face something fierce because Penelope asked, "What happened?"

"What happened is that my father left you some money. In fact, lots of money."

"Money?"

"Something like two hundred and fifty thousand dollars. In stocks and bonds."

I had always read that people's eyes got large as saucers at some unexpected surprise, but I had not seen it until then. She blushed and then she turned pale and put her hand to her lovely neck, wholly overcome as the news sank in.

"But why would he leave *me* money?"

"He didn't leave it only to you. He left it to you and Eva. But since…" I didn't finish the sentence. I couldn't say, but since Eva is dead.

"But why would he leave us money?"

"I don't know. He began buying stocks and bonds shortly after he came back to the States."

"But why?"

"Oh, for God's sake, woman," I laughed, "can't you just accept that he did it and take the money and have a great time? This was hard enough to say after all I've read and after all you've told me."

"Did he leave anything for you?"

"More than enough," I said, strangely moved at her fear of my being left out because of her.

She lit a cigarette and stared, for the longest time, at some spot behind me, which could only have been the elaborately carved wooden booth divider. Now and then, she shook her head.

"This is phenomenal," she said. "Phenomenal."

And then she did what I did not expect her to do though I should have because she was unpretentious and wholly unselfconscious. She smiled the happiest, broadest smile. In this culture of social masking, she didn't pretend to lie either to me or to herself. Where others, for fear they might appear greedy, would have hidden their joy over their good fortune, she admitted fully that it was absolutely wonderful.

"Do you know what this means?" she asked, eagerly leaning toward me, all the pleasure that wealth can afford in her eyes. I shook my head.

"This means that I can take a whole year off to write. And Cole can probably quit his part-time jobs. If he wants to."

The waitress put the check on the table and I paid with Penelope being elsewhere all the while, writing in her head already, I suppose.

"Ready?" I asked.

She looked at me with more gratitude than I had ever seen in anyone's eyes.

"Thank you," she said with great warmth.

"I had nothing to do with this. In fact, had I known about this when I was younger, I would've hated him even more. And you too."

"But there is a part in you that is your dad's, and I was saying it to him."

Briefly, I squeezed her hand, and we walked out into the lobby where we met a young couple that had just dashed in, soaked to the skin. Through the entrance door that was just closing we saw that the storm had broken and the rain came down in torrents.

"It's hailing," the young man said, stomping to shake the water off while the young woman stood shivering, hugging her arms. They disappeared into the tavern where, I hoped, a hot toddy would fix them up.

"Now what?" I said. My umbrella lay safe and dry in the backseat of the car which was parked a ways up the road. "Let's wait a few minutes to see if it lets up. If not, I make a dash for it. You wait here until I bring the car."

We waited, but it didn't let up, and I made a dash for it. By the time I got the car door open and myself inside, I was soaked. I picked her up with the umbrella, but the wind was so fierce, it nearly blew the darn thing out of my hand with the result that she was soaked by the time I got her into the car.

I had turned on the defroster, and she started shivering. I switched to heat which blew cold air. She would catch pneumonia if this thing didn't give us some heat soon. I reached into the backseat to get the Kleenex to help dry us off a little, and there was my jacket that I had forgotten I brought. I fished it forward and draped it around her shoulders.

"Thanks."

"My pleasure," I said, because it was. I wished I had a whole stack of towels on the backseat or at least a blanket to wrap her in. Maybe it was because I knew her story that she appeared fragile to me and I felt protective of her. Or maybe the small, caring gestures I had never extended to my father wanted expression now.

I pulled out. "How long were you married?" I asked. I don't know why the question suddenly occurred to me. Maybe because I remembered that I used to drape a coat over Alice more often than I cared to remember.

"Thirteen years," she said.

"What happened?"

"He loved women. More than was good for us. And you?"

"Twenty-seven."

"What happened?"

"What happened? Time and the weather?" I laughed. "No. She is, like my mother, a business woman." I thought this over. "You know, it never occurred to me until this moment that I married my mother all over again." This made me laugh out loud. "Hilarious! But I did. Alice kept a great house, full of antiques and art. She is an antique dealer. At first, it worked out well, because she flew with me to London and Rome and Paris and shopped to her heart's content. And I was young and ambitious, and I saw nothing wrong with celebrating success. She was great with dinner parties, and the house was always full of people. I think I grew tired of it, after awhile. About three years ago, coming back from yet another trip and the house was full of people, I just went upstairs and read for awhile and went to sleep. I don't think she ever forgave me. Not that I blame her, because I kept doing that. Here are all these people she wanted to show me off to. I can't blame her. If I didn't like the fast life, why didn't I tell her years ago?"

The storm had intensified, and we sought shelter under the overhang of a gas station where others huddled already, all of us and at the same time, no matter how cocky, fearing for our fragile lives that were no match to what the skies unleashed that moment. Hail and rain pounded the car like volleys of gravel.

We pulled in under the overhang, and the silence was instant though I couldn't help but think that this illusive, bright shelter would be gone in seconds if the wind picked up. The quick succession of deafening thunder all around us and the rush of water and hail that pelted the macadam made a mockery out of the once powerful floodlights that were of little use now except to turn the dense strings of rain into uncertain curtains of light.

"Only, sometimes, I just wanted her all to myself," I said. "To talk. Make love. Whatever. Spend time together. Sometimes, we tried that, but we had nothing much to say to each other. I'm an excellent pilot, and when I fly, I fly. I'm always aware that I do have two hundred odd people on board. I don't think it, but I'm aware of it, and there is little else I have the luxury to think about, and I don't. But is that all I am? I hope not. Some time ago, in my early forties, or maybe it began earlier, I became aware of missing something. I don't even know what that is. A connection to something. A deeper connection. To something. Whatever that is. I don't know."

As suddenly as the storm had come, it quit and one by one, the company of fragile humanity forgot their perilous existence and happily took off again.

Penelope had left a light on in the dayroom, and as we came up the hill, the lit glass wall was like a warm beacon that welcomed us home. A brisk wind came from the north as we left the car, chilling us both, and my wet shirt and pants clung clammy and cold to my skin, portending a massive cold, if not pneumonia.

The house had kept the warmth of the sun but it would not last. She went upstairs to change and called to me from the loft railing, throwing a gray sweat suit down to me.

"It's Cole's," she said. "He's about your size."

Not quite. Both legs and sleeves just a little short. I changed in the small bathroom, hanging my stuff over the shower rod to dry.

She had put on a sweat suit as well, though it was yellow and of a much softer texture. She laughed when she saw me.

"I thought, for sure, he was about your size," she said. I made a clown's face and pulled up the sleeves and the legs of the sweat suit to make my ridiculous appearance even more revolting.

"That's better," she laughed. "I'll just go and make coffee."

I studied the wood in the basket before the fireplace.

"I could make a fire," I offered.

"Perfect!" she said. I looked around for newspapers and matches until I realized that all was already tucked in the basket together with the kindling. The heavy wet air hung low in the chimney, but after awhile I got a good draft going, and the flames licked at the kindling and flared and caught the wood. I put on my wet shoes and went out to where I had seen the woodpile. The north wind blew the clouds ahead of him, and I could see the stars that were unusually bright, as if the storm had come in expressively to polish them. I got in a good supply of wood and remembered the letters on my last trip out.

When I came back, she had put pillows on the floor in front of the fire, and there she sat, waiting for me. She had lit some candles and sipped coffee, dreaming into the fire.

I handed her my father's last letter to Ruth.

"Don't read it until I've washed up," I said, my hands dirty from carrying the wood and sticky from sap.

"I won't."

I came back and settled down in front of the fire. I had not felt as content as this in a long time. She handed me my cup and took up the letter.

"For some reason," she said, "my heart is beating like crazy."

She opened the letter carefully and slowly as if she were afraid the letter opener would cut through the words and destroy them. She pulled out a single sheet. Merely taking the sheet out moved her so deeply, she began to cry. I reached for her hand, but she shook her head and unfolded the page.

"It's dated September," she said. "I guess that was two months or so before he died?"

I nodded, not looking at her but fiddling with the fire instead, because seeing her burst into tears tore something loose in me, and I had a hard time controlling my emotions.

"He didn't know then that she was dead," she said. "And that is truly sad."

Now the emotions welled up in me too. I stared at the fire to prevent her from seeing me, but she was not looking at me anyway.

Slowly, tearfully, she began reading the letter in the softest of voices, sniffling throughout.

"Dearest Ruth,

I have begun to get my affairs in order. I don't know why. Just a feeling. I want you to know that there hasn't been a day in all these forty odd years that I have not thought of you. A thousand times, I have wanted to come and see you. It would have been so easy, the planes have gotten so fast. But I knew it would complicate your life, and so I didn't. Maybe we will see one another again, if there is a place we all go to once we leave here.

I want you to know that I invested some money, for the girls, when I came back to the States. It wasn't much, you don't have to worry about that. But it's grown now to quite a bit of money. I have asked Alex, in my will, to find you and the girls and to tell them of the money himself and to give you this letter.

I know you will forgive me, but I have an ulterior motive. Alex, I think, has been very lonely lately. Not that I see him much. We have not been very close though I have tried. So this will not be easy for him, but I've had this dream that, one day, he would get to talk to Penelope. I can still see her, with her dimples and her sun freckles and that wild hair she always had. She was so intensely passionate and so quiet and contemplative and observant at the same time. I think they might be good friends. Of course, I have visions that she might be more than that, but this can't be because he is, right now, married to a country club sort. Very nice. But if you remember Sheryl, you know what I mean.

I hope and pray that you and the girls are well and that you are happy. Or, at least, relatively so, given that you are not with me. I've been well.

All my Love,
Ted"

She put the letter down and looked at me. Tears streamed down her face, and so we sat, in front of the fire, smiling at each other, teary-eyed, deeply connected by her mother and by my father, and by the gift of the story she had written down so that their lives would not be forgotten.

...

Since then, I have seen Ms. Penelope Karstens often. Sometimes I drive up to the Blue Ridge Mountains to spend the day with her. Sometimes, this one day turns into two days or even three. Sometimes, she comes to D.C. and we stroll through the city and have dessert in an outdoor café, either at the river or at Dupont Circle or in Alexandria. We share so much more than the past, and I think I finally found what I could not find twenty years before—a deep connection to someone.

Gradually, I have begun to forgive myself, but it is not easy. Guilt still raises its ugly little head now and then and I ache from it. But knowing my father, and knowing him better now because of Penelope, I like to believe that he has forgiven me. Or, as she said, "Being wise and kind, he would have understood." I have a hunch she's right.

Who knows where Penelope and I will go. We are both reluctant to tie the knot for fear that what we have now will disappear in the humdrum of married days. But I can't imagine not knowing her. Can't imagine that once she was not in my life. So, maybe one day, we will both be ready. We can wait. What we have now is enough and it is splendid. Maybe some day, we will have more.

***

Afterword

This book is dedicated to my mother, to my aunt Otti, to my cousin Leni, and to my sister Barbara. They all died much too young. The book is also dedicated to the Good American, wherever he is now. One can't write such a book , however, without also dedicating it to all the women who, after some insanity—whenever and wherever—manage, somehow and unflinchingly, to pick up the pieces and to go on.

About the Author

Ursula Maria Mandel lives and writes in a house on a hill with a view. She has previously published essays on Franz Kafka and on the fearless young life of polio victim Misti Washington.